CW01084237

FATHER SAM

FATHER SAM

STEVEN BOERGADINE

LUMINARE PRESS

WWW.LUMINAREPRESS.COM

Luminare Press
442 Charnelton St.
Eugene, OR 97401
www.luminarepress.com

LCCN: 2023917878
ISBN: 979-8-88679-414-4

Dedicated To a Compassionate Priest

I watched an old priest appear on the evening news, May 26, 1979. He stood near the steps of a Florida prison and spoke of a condemned man named John Spinkelink whom he watched die a torturous death in the electric chair after mentoring him for two years. He answered reporters who asked of John's last words, "The last thing that he said to me was that he loved me, and the last thing I said to him was that I loved him."

I had never been a Catholic, never became one, and am not one now. But that old priest? I will always remember him from that brief newscast. I kept him in my head until I wrote Father Sam over forty years later, about a priest who helped a prisoner named John.

THANK YOU

I'd like to thank the current and past incarnations of Harpies' Writer's Group of Cottage Grove, Oregon for their valuable feedback while I wrote Father Sam and a special mention to Harpies member, Dan Liberthson for his editorial suggestions throughout the entire manuscript, beginning to end.

Special thanks to Dr. Lizhe Wang who is a most steadfast friend and supporter of my writing journey.

Foodawa Culture & Media GmbH

Sponsor of "Father Sam" publishing

www.foodawa.de

lwang@foodawa.com

Tel: +49 6578 7616

Salmstrasse 62, 54528 Salmtal, Germany

A WORD FROM MY SPONSOR

It is our opinion that a load of talent and life experience makes Steve an excellent storyteller.

Foodawa Media sponsored the publication of, "Brother," his previous novel, and we are pleased to be on board with him again as he releases his new book, "Father Sam."

"Father Sam," is a heart pounding look at the incredible saga of a man who, as a young seminarian, drowning in self, washed out to a failed civilian life, was swept back to shore by an unrestrained calling to the seminary, became a man, powerfully independent of how and where he would serve the priesthood and then gave it all till the end.

Rvang

Dr. Lizhe Wang

Foreword

Steven Boergadine's *Father Sam* is an epic tale told compactly, starring a priest struggling to recover from a wild ride off the rails of conformity in his seminarian days and battling an incurable illness. A vivid, concisely drawn host of supporting characters, many of whom speak in well-rendered country dialect, add spice to the wonderful broth of the story. Rife with the moral quandaries inevitable in the life of a man trying to live ethically in a corrupt environment, *Father Sam* achieves depth and complexity while portraying memorable relationships. Foremost of these are the unlikely pairing of the seminarian and eventual priest with Sister Marietta, worldly-wise but impeccably virtuous and devoted, who supports Sam throughout his travails, and steadfast small-town Sheriff Marcus, who has Sam's back at every crisis. Then there's the alluring, poignantly damaged Gladys Spinks, who tempts the young seminarian into an act that will throw his future off kilter for decades to come.

Father Sam is indeed a rare novel, one that meshes literary flair with ingenious plotting and a raft of uniquely original characters—some good, some half bad, and others outright evil, but all superbly believable. Its portrayal of country and small-town life and personalities evoked for me the work of Faulkner and Flannery O'Connor. With elements of mystery and crime fiction backed by brilliant writing, the book grabbed me by the scruff immediately and hauled me along for the duration, never letting up. The suspense builds to a crescendo of irrevocable events and a finish that will leave even the most jaded reader tearing up. Prospective reader, I urge you to grab this book and carry it to the nearest cash register or select the Buy Now option if you're shopping on-line. I don't doubt you'll be grateful you did by the time you reach the end of this marvelous read.

Dan Liberthson, PhD

CHAPTER 1

Stormy Lives Collide

Roadside billboards don't serve much purpose on a Texas desert highway on a night like this. But a hitchhiker desperate for shelter when Mother Nature's in a bad mood will try anything.

On a violent winter night in 1984, folks are home. They're watching Johnny Carson sign off, tipped back in recliners, hearths flickering to the embers. Time to wash and brush, change to flannels and crawl under a pile of afghans and patchwork quilts.

But not for this thirty-three-year-old hitchhiker. He's soaked and shivering behind a lean-to he's fitted together from pealed-off remnants of one of those roadside billboards. The flat piece he broke off from the sign isn't holding back the elements much. Wild rain is blowing sideways—angry quills slung straight and fierce by tempestuous winds.

The hitchhiker needs help, and there's no one to give it. His lean-to blows away. As he gets to his feet, a fifty mile an hour two-by-four gashes his forehead and knocks him cold on the highway shoulder. His broken face turns the mud red.

Fifty-two-year-old escaped convict Cleveland Stockton will pull over soon. No choice now. The driver's-side wiper blade of the stolen '57 Mercury just lost its rubber. Screech, screech, screech. Metal against glass, zero visibility. It's driving him crazy. *Crazier* is a better way to put it.

Medically speaking, Stockton's near legally blind. Right now, he's moving five miles an hour at most, his face as close to the windshield as his size-fifty belly will allow. His heavy breathing is fogging up the glass and the defrost unit is on the blink.

Eye-weary from straining to see the road, Stockton decides to pull over. No replacement for the wiper blade, so he'll have to make do.

He squints through his thick-lensed glasses, looking for an overhead light to park under. None anywhere, so he pulls over. The skeleton of an old billboard groans its last and crashes. What a night. He gets out of the dilapidated Mercury to switch the passenger-side wiper blade to the driver's side. A bright idea given that his IQ is borderline deficient.

Curious about that fallen billboard, he gives it a look and makes out a human-formed lump lying near it. He switches the wiper, then fights the iced rain to go check out the lump.

It's the body of a young man. "You ain't alive, are ya, honey?" Stockton swipes a watch off the hitchhiker's wrist, snatches his backpack, and walks away.

A short gasp from the hitchhiker halts Stockton. He slogs back to the hitchhiker and lifts him with less effort than he did a barbell in the prison yard, carries him to the passenger side door and tosses him in.

The hitchhiker is out of the rain but not out of trouble.

CHAPTER 2

Homecoming Killer

A day-and-a-half later, the weather is perfect in the high country. Puffy, snow-white clouds decorate the blue sky.

Blood and mud have dried and caked on the hitch-hiker's face.

Stockton cruises along Old Mountain Highway. He pulls in at a single-pump gas station which doubles as a window-service hamburger stop.

A fella with the name "Buddy" stitched above his pocket flips burgers, pumps gas, and lives in a rusted, ten-foot Airstream parked out back.

Stockton leans against the window counter, finishing up his burger and coffee and eyeballing a tray of donuts that he wishes was his. Buddy is cleaning the grill when Stockton says, "Can ya put some gas in my car? And gimmee new wipers."

"Okey-dokey. Fill 'er up?".

Stockton grunts and nods the go-ahead.

Buddy lays the grill-brick beside a butcher knife. Grabs a couple wiper blades. Walks out to the Mercury, unscrews the cap from the gas tank, pulls the fuel hose over to it and sticks the nozzle in.

Fixing a wiper, Buddy sees the comatose hitchhiker

with his bloody head wrapped in a dirty T-shirt. "What the heck happened to this guy?"

Stockton is still hanging out with the donuts. "Changed a tire in the storm over there in Texas. Slipped in the mud and the tire iron got him one."

"Yah, heard about that big rain over there the other night. I can get ya a clean rag and hot water to clean up his face a bit."

Stockton grunts. "Thank ya."

The lock on the nozzle clicks. Buddy tops off the tank and screws the cap on. The windshield wipers are good, too.

"Where you got I might relieve myself?" Stockton inquires.

Buddy heads over to his trailer to get a clean rag and a basin of fresh, warm water. "Back here." Buddy points in the direction he's going.

Stockton figured that and follows. The handle of the butcher knife protrudes from his back pocket.

A few minutes later, Buddy is not around. The till is empty, and so is the donut tray.

Stockton guides the Mercury onto Old Mountain Highway. A long stretch of downhill lies ahead so he shifts to neutral and lets it coast to save gas. He's finally going home after escaping the joint a few weeks ago. He originally jumped on a boxcar and ended up who knows where but now he's got himself a map and wheels and a full tank of gas and headed to mountain country.

He rolls down his window, relishing the glee that only comes with warm wind whipping around, a full tank, and hitting the road to somewhere good. "My mamma don't raise no dummy." He gives the hitchhiker's thigh a gentle squeeze and speaks to him as if he were listening. "Will ya looky me, eatin' like I do. Where my figure gone to?" Stockton shoves a donut into his mouth.

The hitchhiker doesn't stir. He couldn't open his eyes even if he wasn't half-dead. Dried blood and mud have them glued shut.

That evening, Stockton is munching on the last of the baker's dozen and the hitchhiker is still out of it.

After rolling along all night, the Mercury turns onto Biggs Road. Stockton knows the Appalachians. It's where he's from.

A full day of traveling and another tank of gasoline, and the Mercury turns onto an unnamed dirt road. It's more like a glorified trail for off-road four-wheelers with roll cages. Into the dense forest now for a couple more hours of slow nighttime driving. Stockton's sugar-high keeps him awake.

He slows the Mercury and takes a shortcut through the dense, black forest.

He's got family up here. Bertha, his sister and their twelve-year-old-daughter, Fanny. Bertha never sent a photo of Fanny, but he hopes she'll call him Daddy.

The glow of dawn shows above the treetops, spilling light onto the road. Stockton stops the Merc. He gets out to see if the road sign is still there behind the tree branches. "Yep, it's there," he proclaims." A weathered sign is nailed to a tree: *blue gofer rode. 4 weelers iz best. CB works good. No fones aloud.*

The last stretch of driving is just ahead now. What a day this is. A lot of miles behind him. Home just up the hill. It's a good time to do his happy dance. He cha-cha's and chants, "Mamma don't raise no dummies, cha-cha. Mamma don't raise no dummies, cha-cha. Mamma don't raise no dummies, cha-cha."

He wishes he had his off-the-shoulder tassel gown. Big Bertha and he wear the same size. He'll borrow from her when he gets home.

The '57 Mercury isn't a four-wheeler, but he heads on anyway. Stockton winks at the human lump who is still unconscious beside him. "We be home soon, darlin'. I hope ya keep on breathin' for a bit. When ya see a sign blinkin' other side of the hill up there, we home then."

The hill is steep, but there's no morning dew to make it slick. Stockton shifts the Merc into first gear and floors it.

At last, Stockton sees the neon sign for the Cozy Inn Cabins. It's still blinking as he remembers, and the *b* still doesn't light up.

Stockton parks the Mercury on a sparsely graveled parking lot adjoining a cluster of ragged cabins. Mossy, rotting wood sidewalks connect each cabin. Dense forest stretches on all sides.

He unloads himself from the driver's seat, walks up a few steps to a wood porch and pounds on the office door. It looks like nobody is up yet. So, he pounds again.

The porch light snaps on, and the office door of the Cozy Inn Cabins cracks open. Manager Salvo is not happy to see Cleveland Stockton on his porch.

Stockton puts on his cordial face. "Mr. Salvo?"

"My God." That's about all Manager Salvo can say.

"I come home today," Stockton says.

Manager Salvo still hasn't opened the door much. "Cleveland Stockton?"

Stockton's still pretending to be a good guy. "Yes, sir. I come home now."

"Home? My ass, home. When'd you get out?" Manager Salvo pulls open the door, showing himself armed with a twelve-gauge shotgun. It's pointed at Stockton's knees.

Stockton backs away. "Why you got that pointed at me?"

"I ought to shoot your legs off. And a few other things with 'em." He lowers the shotgun. "What the hell you want up here?"

"My sister in her cabin, sir? I sure need to clean up myself and help my friend. He had a real bad accident over in Texas, sir."

Manager Salvo looks through the Mercury's window to see the hitchhiker. "Go down to the river. Wash yourselves there."

Stockton asks again, "Big Bertha in her cabin?"

"You deaf now along with everything else? What if she was here, anyhow? You think Big Bertha'd want to see you?"

Stockton gets a little pouty. "Well, she might."

"You escaped, Stockton? You got twenty years," Manager Salvo snaps at him.

"No, sir. I'm freed, and I'm out for good behavin'. You might try good behavin', too."

"Get your sick ass off my porch." Manager Salvo slams his door.

CHAPTER 3

The Priest, the Sheriff, and a Little White Lie

Father Sam's home is as modest in appearance as he is. Inside and out there's a wholesomeness that's undeniable. Just the way you'd want a log house to be and just the way you'd want the town's only man of the cloth to be. He's a little too good lookin' to be a priest, though. That's what Mabelline says. After all, he's only forty-six. But she knows better than to get her hopes up. She owns Mabelline's Café on Main Street just across from the jailhouse. She always cuts his piece of cherry pie a little fatter. He pretends not to notice, but he always asks for that cherry pie and he doesn't mind the wink that comes with it.

Just about everybody's got a friend in Father Sam. And many of them appreciate his handmade braided rugs. They look good about anywhere they're put down. He braids them out of wool scraps that townspeople drop in a box on his front porch. He sells his rugs cheap, but he'd rather trade them for canned, chunky cinnamon applesauce or a little firewood, but most any staple for daily living will do.

The Cherokee mothers bring their little ones by on Sunday mornings for Father Sam's free English class. They pull the worn-out wool coats, trousers, and blankets from that box and cut them into strips for him while they wait for their children to learn their ABCs.

Today, the morning sun brightens Father Sam's backyard, which stretches out to the edge of a forest of hickory, oak, and poplar trees.

Vegetable and flower gardens grow in freshly tilled patches near a heavily fenced-off enclosure that protects two beehives from black bears that love to steal his honey—that's where Father Sam is this morning.

A device puffs smoke into the air to keep the bees calm. Father Sam, wearing a beekeeper's hat and mesh veil, is checking on one of his queen bees.

Marcus Moberly is the sheriff here. An old, reformed bad boy. Sheriff Marcus is somewhere in his sixties, and right now, he's relaxing on Father Sam's big wooden back porch, sitting on the steps, drinking a cup of coffee he poured from his thermos, a sheriff's badge on his shirt, a CB radio next to him. Drinking coffee and shootin' the bull with Father Sam is Marcus's ritual most mornings. When the weather turns bad, it'll be Father Sam dropping by the jailhouse to sit by Sheriff Marcus's old Franklin wood stove. Same coffee, same pal, same bull.

Taking it easy, Molly, a redbone coonhound, snoozes in the shade of an old Apache wickiup, a small hut-like dwelling made of willow saplings and limbs. It stands close to the beehive enclosure.

Thunder from the shooting range of the House of Wonder started up about a half-hour ago. Sheriff Marcus isn't bothered by it. Even if he was bothered about the shootin', a persistent memory he never talks about keeps him looking the other way. The House of Wonder is Merle Swenson's place. *Mayor* Merle Swenson, that is.

That Victorian house they call The House of Wonder, standing mightily on that ridge and being the biggest building in all these parts, could sure use a fresh paint job, or at least a good steam cleaning. Dirty on the outside and dirty on the inside. The inside would take more than a power hose to clean it.

This is the town of McGuffin Ridge. It ought to be called Swensonville. The Mayor is a third-generation Swenson and inherited about everything, including that Victorian house on the hill and the Cozy Inn Cabins on the edge of town.

Father Sam isn't living in McGuffin Ridge to evangelize, assimilate indigenous people, build a church, or lead Bible lessons. Folks do ask him about the Bible pretty often, though.

Mainly, he's here to spend his days honoring his Cherokee grandmother by doing what she did up here in the Appalachians: serving everybody.

Deputy Sydney's voice barks from the CB. *Jailbird One, you hear that? Over.*

Sheriff Marcus picks up and speaks back to Deputy Sydney, "Jailbird One, here. That shootin' is none of our business. It's nothin' but the House of Wonder."

Deputy Sydney's voice comes back. *I know. Just practicin' my CB drill. I'm lockin' up. Be eaten' breakfast at Mabelline's. Out.*

Father Sam removes his beekeeper's hat, revealing a square-jawed, handsome face and a white collar.

Sheriff Marcus remarks about the noise coming from the House of Wonder. "Big dove shoot comin' up at the House of Wonder, yes sir."

Father Sam says, "Looking forward to Joe and Wilma's wedding. I'll be saying some words for them. What time is the shooting contest?"

"Usually just before sundown. It was last year. I'll go along with ya to the wedding and then get a seat for the shootin' contest just across the field."

Father Sam picks up a pail of compost from inside the enclosure and pulls a paintbrush out of it.

"You ready for a coffee?" Sheriff Marcus holds up the thermos.

"Yep," He dips the paint brush into the pail and begins slopping compost along the top edge of the fifteen-gauge chain-link fence.

"You inviting the black bears over for afternoon tea? You know they'll smell that and be here as soon as you turn your back."

Father Sam nods. "That's the plan."

It takes a second, but Marcus figures it out. "Ah-hah. How many volts ya got going through that wire?"

"Six thousand," Father Sam answers. "Now, if they'll come over and taste the appetizer, maybe they'll rethink their plans to harass my bees."

"Don't forget to turn the switch off when the kids come over."

Father Sam gives him a thanks-for-the-reminder look.

The shooting on the ridge continues. Sheriff Marcus prophesies the outcome of the annual dove shoot. "Practicin' ain't gonna help those boys, not while they're up against that little daughter of Bertha Stockton's. Gotta be born with what that twelve-year-old child has. What do ya call a kid like that? Seems like Fanny quit growing, and then she got good at shootin'. She's one of them savants, ain't she?"

"Hard to say, Marcus—a little flower in the human garden, I'd say."

"Yep, she's a little flower, all right. Dwarfed, on top of everything else."

"She's happy and productive. That's what matters. And gifted by God."

"Yep. For shootin', she damn sure is gifted. Seen it last year, the year before, the year before that."

Father Sam responds, "If the Mayor would reward her with some tutoring instead of those giant dolls year after year."

"Yep, she's got quite a collection, all right." Marcus thinks back. "Three of 'em, if I ain't mistaken. Yep, three years, three dolls."

"Reading and writing skills would do her a world of good, wouldn't you say? Mayor Swenson is your boss. Propose that idea to him. Tell him I'll be Fanny's tutor."

"Fanny's mama sure don't need to read or write," jokes Sheriff Marcus.

"You can be *her* tutor, old buddy."

Sheriff Marcus shoots back, "She'd end up tutoring me, if you know what I mean." He walks over to Father Sam continuing to gossip. "And that daddy of Fanny's sitting in the bighouse. Should've hung that big dog by his you-know-whats. Twenty years for what he did—that's all?"

Father Sam changes the subject. He puts down his paintbrush and lifts up a beehive-frame. "You know, Marcus, my new queen has been in there ten days now."

Sheriff Marcus places Father Sam's freshly poured cup of coffee on top of a fence post. "Uh-huh. She better be alive; she ain't alive, she ain't gonna lay no eggs, and if she ain't layin' eggs, there ain't no worker bees, and if there ain't no worker bees?"

Father Sam offers a punchline. "No honey for the corn bread."

"Now, Father, that there is a sin." Sheriff Marcus, chuckles.

Father Sam picks up the steaming cup, takes a drink of Sheriff Marcus's coffee, and asks him, straight-faced, "Speaking of sins, eating cherry pie for breakfast isn't considered a sin, is it?"

Sheriff Marcus answers with some theological logic, "Not if you and Mabelline would quit winking at each other."

Father Sam lifts up a second beehive and talks to it. "Why don't a couple hundred of you guys wake up and bite the good sheriff on his ankle?"

"Let's go get some of that pie," Sheriff Marcus says as he finishes his coffee.

They stroll back and sit down on the back steps while Sheriff Marcus screws the top back onto the thermos. A long minute of sitting. Just sitting. Father Sam's face suddenly pivots to the left as if something frightened him. Then, self-consciously he glances at Sheriff Marcus.

Sheriff Marcus quietly asks, "The horse been botherin' ya?"

Father Sam whistles for Molly. She gets up from her nap and joins them. Plops her face on Father Sam's lap and continues her nap. He gives her a scratch behind her ears. "Now and then, Marcus. I'm feelin' pretty good, though." It's a little white lie and they both know it.

CHAPTER 4

Too Much Sexy

Cleveland Stockton pulls into the weeds and parks the old Mercury. He carries the hitchhiker through the brush and makes his way to Big Bertha's cabin. The back way.

Inside, Big Bertha's twelve-year-old daughter, Fanny is playing with three rag dolls. They are the only pals she can relate to, the same dolls Sheriff Marcus mentioned to Father Sam. They're made especially for her by Mabelline, one of the sponsors of the annual shooting derby.

The dolls are about the same height as Fanny. On purpose. Fellow travelers on her autistic journey.

Heavy footsteps stop outside the door. Fanny panics. A fist bangs on the exterior, the handle rattles, the lock snaps. Stockton enters, carrying the hitchhiker. He shuts the door with a back kick.

It's hard to disappear in a one-room shanty that has no back door, but Fanny is gone.

"Bertha? You man home again now." Stockton drops the unconscious hitchhiker on the bed, face up.

Stockton is home. That's *his* opinion. He finds Bertha's bottle of whiskey, takes a long swig, then tips the bottle to the hitchhiker's lips. Whiskey runs down the hitchhiker's placid chin.

"You a so messy boy." Stockton tips the bottle again, dribbling whiskey on the hitchhiker's forehead this time. He stirs the hitchhiker's brow with his index finger, dissolving the crusted blood and mud with the whiskey. A nice, cherry-red rouge for his own flabby cheeks. He purses his lips and slathers more on his kisser while he's at it, then, puckers up and blows a kiss to the out-cold hitchhiker, "Too much sexy?"

Prancing to the vanity, he finds Bertha's eyeliner. He removes his thick glasses, gets close to the mirror, and finishes putting his face on. Cleveland Stockton is feeling special. His belly folds onto the vanity and pushes his glasses over the edge.

Four sets of eyes watch the freak show. Fanny and her three doll-pals are as still as stone. They stare at the monster who crashed their private world.

It's time for Stockton's happy dance. But he's gonna dress for it this time. He cha-chas to Big Bertha's closet and changes into her off-the-shoulder tassel gown. He feels more and more alluring.

Suddenly, he feels four sets of eyes on him. His demented mind and poor vision tell him that four gentlemen are admiring his curves. And they didn't buy tickets. He twirls and teases and blows them kisses. The lucky gents are going to get a free song and dance right now.

He cha-chas towards the blurry admirers, singing his refrain, "Mama don't raise no dummies, cha-cha. Mama don't raise no dummies, cha-cha." He manages a stumble-bum pirouette, holding up the bottom of his gown with one hand to create a feast for the leering eyes. Time for audience interaction. "How you think, gentlemens? Too much sexy?"

He moves close to Fanny and the three dolls. He reaches for the first doll and touches its nose. "Ahh, how sweet it is." He's convinced they are fascinated by him. Fanny is *doll* number three. Fortunately, the closer Stockton gets, the worse his eyesight becomes. He cha-chas to doll number two. A playful pinch on the cheek. Fanny's next. Lucky for her, he turns away, tosses a coy look over his shoulder, and shakes his booty. He turns to face them. He puts his hands on his hips and gives all four sets of leering eyeballs a scolding.

"Shame on all you rich bad boys. I know what's your game." He wags his index finger. "You not foolin' me. I be passin' the hat later, boys."

Stockton cha-chas to the bed where his clothes are heaped, finds his trousers and pulls off the belt. He drops the trousers back on the bed. A pistol slips halfway out of a pocket. Doll number three shifts her eyes to the gun for a millisecond.

Stockton's the queen of burlesque now. He waves the belt in a circular pattern above his head and dances, twerking with abandon, too enthralled with himself to notice he's crushing his glasses. "Too much sexy, cha-cha. Too much sexy, cha-cha." And then, "I know what y'all come for, gentlemens. Mamma don't raise no dummy." He grabs the hitchhiker's ankles, drags him to the end of the bed and turns him face down.

Fanny's face mirrors the agony of what the comatose hitchhiker is enduring. To her, the hitchhiker is a doll friend who was carried into the room, thrown on the bed, and now is being attacked by the bad, stinky monster. Fanny makes sure her three friends shut their eyes before shutting her own tight as can be. The sick sound and smell of human violation pollutes the room.

Steven Boergadine

Stockton carries the bleeding hitchhiker into the bathroom. His lewd cha-cha continues. "Too much sexy, cha-cha. Too much sexy, cha-cha." He's just getting started.

Stockton steps into the tub. Holding the hitchhiker with one arm, he reaches for the shower handle. "Where that baby face?" Stockton holds the hitchhiker so his face will catch the shower's cold downpour. It loosens the blood and mud and whiskey, draining it from the hitchhiker's pulpy face.

The hitchhiker's swollen eyes twitch. Stockton has been eager for a sign of life in the hitchhiker's face. "Look at you. Just a winkin' at me. Oh, darlin'." Stockton slips and falls. His head bangs against the edge of the porcelain tub, stunning him.

The cold water continues to rain on the hitchhiker's face as he lands on Stockton's bloated girth. Survival instinct stirs in the hitchhiker. He drags himself from the tub like a wounded soldier, instinctively clawing his way out of enemy territory, helpless, unarmed.

The hitchhiker doesn't know he has an ally. A sniper. A can't-miss sniper. Fanny's frozen face softens at the sight of the hitchhiker's attempted escape from the bathroom. She slips away from her three dolls and kneels down at the side of the bed.

Cheap metal shower rings jerk free from the curtain rod as Stockton pulls himself up from the tub and wraps himself in the shower curtain. "Darlin', where you at, honey?" A few seconds go by. Then Stockton appears in the doorway wearing his one-piece saree. Feeling stunning as ever, he asks his cold-cocked captive, "Is my makeup a mess?"

Fanny's tiny hand creeps toward Stockton's gun from the hidden side of the bed. She finds the handle and pulls it slowly toward her, remaining out of view of Stockton's unspectacled, diverted eyes.

Stockton poses over the hitchhiker as the escape attempt ends. The hitchhiker is motionless. A human-formed lump.

Fanny stands. "Too much sexy," she says and aims—a straight line trajectory.

Surprised, Stockton stumbles backwards. A wall stops him. His head is immobilized against the wall just to the left of a gold-plated Chi-Rho monogram hanging from a nail.

She fires twice. Black holes appear where his eyes were. Dead on his feet, he falls onto the hitchhiker's legs.

Bloodstains mark the wall where the back of Stockton's head had stabilized. Not a drop touched the gold-plated symbol of Christ.

Steven Boergadine

CHAPTER 5

Bloody Good Morning for a Photo Op

P aparazzi Mickey doesn't live with Big Bertha although he is sweet on her. He's got a cabin a couple doors up from hers. He snaps awake. Bad dream or gunshots? He's not sure what woke him up. He peeps through a window. It looks safe. He opens his door and sees Manager Salvo come running. It doesn't look safe now. He shuts his door, throws on some clothes, grabs his camera, and cracks open the door again to watch Manager Salvo take his chances.

Inside Big Bertha's cabin, the blood of the two men is everywhere. Fanny lets the pistol drop to the floor. She starts to open the door so she can run away. But outside, Manager Salvo knocks first. She scrambles back to her doll family.

Paparazzi Mickey stays in his own doorway. "I swear I heard shootin', Salvo. I'd be careful now."

"Shut up, Mickey," snaps Manager Salvo. He knocks harder. "What the hell is going on in there?" He carefully opens the door. So far, no more commotion. He pokes his head inside. "Oh, shit almighty." The sight of two dead, bloody bodies sends him running to his office.

Paparazzi Mickey slams his door and parts the curtain to watch Manager Salvo run. Something is in there that needs to be photographed. Curiosity has him. He fixates on the heap of money he can make by selling controversial photographs to gossip magazines. He waits a minute till he figures nothing dangerous is gonna come running out of Big Bertha's cabin. He props his door open with a shoe just in case he'll need to get back inside real fast, then stealthily creeps to Big Bertha's cabin with his camera hanging around his neck. The door is ajar, so he nudges it with his foot as he holds his camera at the ready. The door slightly opens. "Bertha, honey, you dead or something? Thought you wasn't comin' home last night." He pushes the door further open with his foot and peeps inside.

One look and a smell of the inside of Big Bertha's cabin is more than Paparazzi Mickey can take. "Ah, Jesus almighty God." He does a one-eighty and heads for fresh air.

Fanny doesn't know what to think. Too many heads popping in and out. She's sticking with her dolls.

In his office, Manager Salvo is on his CB. Nobody is picking up his signal. He panics and switches channels. "Anybody out there? Dammit anyway. Are you out there? Anybody?"

FATHER SAM AND SHERIFF MARCUS ARE GETTING UP from the backporch to head to Mabelline's.

"Molly, keep an eye on those two bears over yonder." Father Sam gives Molly a see-ya-later scratch on the head.

Sheriff Marcus's CB goes off. *Cozy One, calling SOS. SOS. Over.* He and Father Sam wait for more. Father Sam doesn't know the voice and asks, "Who is it?"

"Salvo, on the edge of town. He runs the Cozy Inn Cabins," replies Sheriff Marcus.

They listen as another voice picks up on the CB. *Yeah, yeah, Cozy One, I hear ya. What's up?*

Sheriff Marcus recognizes that voice, too. "That's Bobo the barkeep at the House of Wonder."

Manager Salvo talks fast. *Bobo, that you?*

It's me, yeah. You're up with the jaybirds, Cozy One. What'chu all wound up about?

Ah, shit, man. Bobo. It's a damn emergency over here.

Bobo tries to cool Manager Salvo down. *Affirmative, Cozy One, slow down now.*

Father Sam and Sheriff Marcus keep listening to determine if they should hold off on the cherry pie and go lend a hand to Manager Salvo.

I got two guys dead here, man. Shot, I think. I saw a gun. In Big Bertha's cabin.

Bobo gets serious. *Put a zipper on it, buddy. I'll tell Mayor Swenson. Over.*

Father Sam and Sheriff Marcus run for Sheriff Marcus's Jeep.

CHAPTER 6

The Photos

Paparazzi Mickey ties a scarf over his nose and enters Big Bertha's cabin. At once he sees Fanny. It shakes him. "Ah shit! Dammit, what you doin' here, doll girl?" Fanny is braced against her dolls.

"Good Lord, girl, did you see all this happen?"

She can't answer. The only words she's ever said were the ones a few minutes ago when she shot the stinky monster. There's no telling how she managed to say what she said. The autistic experience is a lonely mystery to most.

"Stay put, Fanny honey, one little second." Paparazzi Mickey backs up to get a shot of Fanny, the dolls, and the two bloody bodies all in the same frame. The camera clicks and flashes. Cleveland Stockton, the hitchhiker, Fanny, and the three dolls, are memorialized, all in one photograph.

Interaction with Paparazzi Mickey, a familiar face, thaws Fanny's nerves. She scampers out the door and glides onto a footpath through the woods to the House of Wonder. Fanny's always welcome there.

"Be that way, doll girl." Paparazzi Mickey continues shooting, making jokes over the bodies. "Y'all, don't move now."

These photos are gonna be valuable to a whole lot of tabloids, he figures. He nudges the hitchhiker's bloody hand closer to the gun and shoots a close-up.

For his next shot, he levels his camera close to Stockton's face, then recognizes him. "Oh, Jesus! That's Fanny's daddy. Oh damn. Oh my."

He scrambles for the door and collides with Bouncer Bill, who is entering with his six-gun drawn. He wears that six-gun on one hip and a hunting knife on the other, and a wad of snoose in his cheek. "Ah shit! Dammit, Mickey! You wantin' to get your ass shot off? What are you doing in here?"

"This is some heebie-jeebie shit, Bounce. That's Cleveland Stockton right there. And some young peckerwood layin' there with him. Both dead as can be."

"Go on outa here." Bouncer Bill tries to brush off Paparazzi Mickey.

Paparazzi Mickey is on Bouncer Bill like a young pup. "This here's news-worthy, Bounce."

Bouncer Bill grabs Paparazzi Mickey by the scruff of his neck and pulls him outside. "Out. C'mon."

"Give me one pose, Bounce. Listen to this: *Bill the Bouncer solves cathouse murder in McGuffin Ridge.* I like it, I like it. How 'bout you? Print that right under your picture. They'll know you all around the country."

Bouncer Bill spits out his used wad of snoose, ignores Paparazzi Mickey and heads for the cabin's office.

"I'll need a fast ride later, Bounce." He watches Bouncer Bill go inside the office, then sneaks back into Big Bertha's cabin to shoot close-ups. He figures Mayor Swenson will arrive any minute. He'd best be quick and careful with this golden opportunity. Certain folks might accuse him of claim jumping.

CHAPTER 7

Dead as a Mackerel

The dictatorial proprietor, Mayor Swenson, opens the Cozy Inn Cabins' office door without a knock and barges in.

Bouncer Bill and Manager Salvo shrink back.

Mayor Swenson verbally abuses the two yes-men. "Since when you rentin' my lodgings out to every damned tomcat that comes around here?"

Manager Salvo squeaks, "Wasn't like that, Mr. Swenson."

Mayor Swenson doesn't want to hear what it wasn't. "You shut up when I'm talkin.'"

The sound of fast rolling tires skidding to a stop in gravel gets Mayor Swenson's attention. He looks through the window to see that Father Sam and Sheriff Marcus have just parked next to his long, black, dirty Cadillac.

Paparazzi Mickey hears Sheriff Marcus's Jeep pull in, too. He pokes his head out the door of Big Bertha's cabin to see who's coming.

Father Sam and Sheriff Marcus see him. "Whatcha got goin' on, Mickey?" yells Sheriff Marcus.

Mayor Swenson ramps up his rage as he hears the interaction between Paparazzi Mickey and Sheriff Marcus. "Now we got the do-nothin' Sheriff and that half-breed preacher here. Bounce, is this my establishment?"

"Yes, sir."

"Is this my town?"

"It is."

"Is this my damned mountain?"

"It's your mountain, Mayor."

Mayor Swenson takes off his hat and thrashes Manager Salvo repeatedly. "How about the New-York-goddammed-Times, Salvo? They coming, too? Jesus!"

Manager Salvo makes a cursory attempt to defend himself. "I chased him off once. But he busted in after."

"Mr. Swenson?" Bouncer Bill tries to intervene.

Mayor Swenson turns on Bouncer Bill. "Go tell that Sheriff, Mayor Swenson is taking care of his business, in his establishment, on his mountain, in his city, just fine!"

Bouncer Bill finally makes himself heard, figuring it's important to Mayor Swenson. "One of them dead guys is that shit-heel brother of Big Bertha."

Manager Salvo adds, "I was trying to tell you."

Mayor Swenson doesn't pay much attention to Bouncer Bill or Manager Salvo. "Go on now. I want them outa here." Then it registers. "What?"

Bouncer Bill answers, "Yeah, Stockton—Cleveland Stockton."

"Yeah, I told him to get off the steps when he came by askin' about Big Bertha," adds Manager Salvo.

"Stockton?" Mayor Swenson is befuddled.

"Yep," says Bouncer Bill.

"Yep," says Manager Salvo.

"Cleveland Stockton? He's doin' twenty years for raping Big Bertha, his own damn sister."

Bouncer Bill is insistent. "Nope. He's …"

"In her cabin," Manager Salvo adds.

"Dead as a mackerel," Bouncer Bill punctuates it.

The profundity of the situation settles in.

"I'll be go-to-hell." Mayor Swenson gestures towards Father Sam and Sheriff Marcus. "They know Stockton's one of 'em?"

"Not from me," says Manager Salvo.

"What was it? Murder-suicide?"

Bouncer Bill and Manager Salvo shrug.

Mayor Swenson starts the thinking process. "We don't want no state law up here looking for that sick maggot. First place they'll look is here. Don't need 'em nosin' around in my business."

Mayor Swenson heads out the door. He has parting words to Bouncer Bill. "Go get 'em buried in the woods, Bounce. Go on. And send them two nosey clowns back down to Main Street, where they belong. I'll be up at the house."

Mayor Swenson mutters to himself as he tromps across the gravel to his dirty Caddy. "Ain't that some shit? Big Bertha's brother, killed in her own damn room."

CHAPTER 8

Oh My God, He's Alive.

I n Big Bertha's cabin, Sheriff Marcus drapes a towel over the hitchhiker's bloody nudity while Father Sam stands looking at the leather wall hanging that has the Chi-Rho symbol embossed into it. Two splashes of blood decorate the wall beside it.

Father Sam looks down at the crimson, swollen face of the young man.

Paparazzi Mickey is still shooting photos when Bouncer Bill makes a heavy-footed entrance.

"Stockton's eyes both shot right through," blurts out Paparazzi Mickey. "That's some straight shootin', right there". He quick-draws imaginary pistols from both hips. "Bang, bang."

"Dammit, Mickey, show some respect." Sheriff Marcus looks closely at Stockton's face. "Stockton? I'll be doggone. That's him, sure as heck. Never-mind what I said about respect. Holy moly, his eyeballs shot straight through, like he had surgery on 'em. I've never seen anything like that."

Bouncer Bill pushes Paparazzi Mickey toward the door and gives him a kick in the butt, then follows him outside. "Mayor Swenson's not gonna like you talkin' so dammed much, Mickey."

"Stop kickin' me around, Bounce."

"It's my job to kick you around if you need it," fires back Bouncer Bill.

Paparazzi Mickey pulls a photo from his camera bag and holds it up to Bouncer Bill's face. "This your job, too? Who's that right there? Who is that in a compromisin' position with Mayor Swenson's ol' lady?"

Bouncer Bill snatches and pockets the photo.

"Take it. I got more. A pile more," blares out Paparazzi Mickey.

"I'll see you later. Don't you go nowhere," Bouncer Bill says as he turns away to enter Big Bertha's cabin.

Paparazzi Mickey has no fear now. "I see agitation in ya, Bounce. I'll be around."

Inside the cabin, Sheriff Marcus and Father Sam are standing over the two bodies when Bouncer Bill walks in. "I'll be handlin' this thing for Mayor Swenson. Y'all go on back to town and forget about it," Bouncer Bill commands.

Sheriff Marcus likes the idea. "Dandy by me, Bounce. C'mon, Father, let's …"

"Oh my God. He's alive," gasps Father Sam as he kneels beside the hitchhiker and checks his pulse.

They all gather around the hitchhiker. Father Sam barks out orders, "Find Doc Willard."

Bouncer Bill barks back, "This ain't yer problem, Preacher."

Father Sam commands Bouncer Bill, "Right now, this is Doc Willard's problem, Bill. You need to help us get him to the Sheriff's car."

Sheriff Marcus is on his CB. "Jailbird Two, you out there? Over."

"This boy's in a serious state of shock," yells Father Sam.

Steven Boergadine

The CB crackles. *This is Jailbird Two. Over.*

"You seen Stork Chaser anywhere?" Sheriff Marcus speaks into the CB.

"*Yep, losin' at fours, whores, and one-eyed jacks.*" Deputy Sydney's response crackles back through the CB.

"Where?" yells Sheriff Marcus.

Mabelline's back room, Deputy Sydney says.

Father Sam pushes the rescue mission. "He's dying. Help us get him to the car, Bill!"

Bouncer Bill gives in. Looks like the hitchhiker's gonna die anyway.

The three men reach down and pick up the hitchhiker. As they race him to the Jeep, Sheriff Marcus yells into his CB, "Get Doc to set up for some life-threatenin' trauma. Fast as he can."

They place the hitchhiker onto the back seat of the Jeep as carefully as the dire situation will allow. Sheriff Marcus and Father Sam jump in and speed off.

Bouncer Bill walks back toward Paparazzi Mickey. "Put that damned camera down and talk to me."

Sheriff Marcus drives as fast as he can while he communicates the hitchhiker's desperate state.

Father Sam is watching over the hitchhiker. "He's turning blue. Pulse is slow."

Sheriff Marcus yells into his CB above the engine noise. "Tell Doc we got a young man losin' blood, turnin' blue, and his pulse is slow, too. You gettin' ready for us?"

Deputy Sydney's hyper response comes through the CB. *Doc's in a jail cell makin' it ready. Mabelline's helpin' out. Gettin' clean towels, hot water, and chicken soup. Doc's got his black bag open now. Settin' up medical tools, sterilizin', the whole shebang.*

The Jeep arrives at McGuffin Ridge's Main Street. A jailhouse, a general store, and Mabelline's Café come into view. Sheriff Marcus brakes to a stop at the jailhouse. Mabelline holds the jailhouse door open as Doc Willard, Deputy Sydney, Father Sam, and Sheriff Marcus carry the hitchhiker inside.

The Ups and Downs
of Paparazzi Mickey

Paparazzi Mickey doesn't have any trouble selling those hotter-than-hot photographs in the big city. *The People's Tabloid* picks out the good ones and pays him off. That leaves Paparazzi Mickey with a few left-over negatives.

A Mexican employee of *The People's Tabloid* says he'll buy the rejects to sell to a tabloid across the border if he can have them for a good price. No problem with that offer either. Paparazzi Mickey feels good about selling every last negative he has, including the rejects.

His windfall makes him feel like he fits in around the metropolis. But that feeling wears off after a while. Struttin' around with a pocket full of dough gets a little old. He looks everywhere for a place a mountain boy can eat up. Halfway decent corn bread and shuck beans with bacon and the rest of it not to be found.

On top of everything else, he gets to feeling lonely for Big Bertha, so Paparazzi Mickey looks for a pawn shop that he'd been to a long time ago.

That was a few years back when he tried to sell cockfighting photos to a magazine. Turned out he couldn't sell those photos. Back then, tantalizingly gory photos of animals weren't newsworthy, but bloody shots of an escaped, incestuous, rapist, killed by his lover are fine and dandy.

He remembers how downhearted he felt about the prospect of returning home empty-handed. He avoided that downheartedness by springing for a little hand-tooled leather wall hanging for Big Bertha. He even had a personal note engraved on the back of it. The pawnbroker said the image on the leather wall hanging was a religious symbol. Paparazzi Mickey thought that'd be nice. It would look real special hanging on Big Bertha's wall. That was all a few years back.

Things are different now. This time, Paparazzi Mickey's trip to the big city is a big success, so he's going to go the extra mile for Big Bertha. A wedding ring will do it just fine. He gets a good deal from that same pawnbroker before he heads for home. He's pretty sure Big Bertha doesn't know about that breath test that'd reveal it's not a real diamond.

An express Greyhound takes him as far as it can, then a local to the suburbs and then some hitchhiking and walking gets him to the motor pool where passenger vans are dispatched to transport coal miners up the main highway where, one by one, they'll get dropped off at junctions where a friend or family will pick them up.

Near one of those junctions, Bouncer Bill sits in his idling four-wheel-drive Land Rover, waiting for the passenger van to drop off pain-in-the-ass Paparazzi Mickey. Giving him that long, bumpy ride to and from the major highway was a fitting deal to make, Bouncer Bill figured, to keep Mayor Swenson from seeing those damned photos of his wife and him. He'd like to just stop in the woods and shoot Paparazzi Mickey in the head, but Paparazzi Mickey's big family are darned good trackers. They'd get all the relatives and dogs and some of their Cherokee friends, and then they'd form search parties. Sooner or later, they'd find the body and, sure as hell, some clue would pop up and lead back to Bouncer Bill. So he figured it'll be best to just give Paparazzi Mickey a damned ride when he needs it. Heck, maybe he'll even get a tip out of it.

On the way back to McGuffin Ridge, Bouncer Bill tells Paparazzi Mickey that Señor Javier and his crew will fly in tonight on the way back to South America.

He stops running off at the mouth just in time to not tell Paparazzi Mickey that Señor Javier is swapping a plane load of drugs for a plane load of guns that were flown in yesterday. One slip of the tongue about that subject and Paparazzi Mickey would be wanting to go out to the secret airfield and take pictures of those guns and drugs. Bouncer Bill knows he'd be the one to end up in a shallow grave if he let mention of that get out.

He diverts the theme of the chitchat. "This time around, there's gonna be some blood sportin' and a party to give 'em all a chance to wind down."

Paparazzi Mickey is all ears. "Cockfightin' at the House of Wonder, Bounce? Lordy, lordy ain't it my lucky day though," he exclaims. He quits talking but goes on thinking about it. *I got me a Mexico contact now that'll buy anything I bring 'em. Got me a wedding ring. Got me a Big Bertha. Got me a ride to the junction when I need it. My future is lookin' promisin'. Daddy'll be proud of me.*

Bouncer Bill replies, "Señor Javier is deadly serious about challenging Mayor Swenson's prizefighting game-cock, so there's gonna be high stakes peso's and dollars changing hands."

Paparazzi Mickey is glad as can be that he didn't waste another day in the big city.

CHAPTER 10

Low Down House of Wonder

A rainy night on that back road to McGuffin Ridge slows Bouncer Bill down some, but there's still time to catch most of the activities inside the House of Wonder. Namely, the cockfights.

He parks his Land Rover close to the door of the House of Wonder. "I'll pick up my suitcase later, Bounce," says Paparazzi Mickey as he slings his camera bag over his shoulder and opens the entrance door. Bouncer Bill follows him in, and they head through the crowded main room. Wall-to-wall poker games are maxed with players and gawkers watching over the players' shoulders. A bar area serves up moonshine and drugs and a lady to take you upstairs if you have the money. A local hillbilly band in the next room is fiddling and drumming and banging on the old mahogany upright. The sound system ain't high class, but it's loud. And that's good enough for drinking and dancing.

Paparazzi Mickey wants a drink. "Here you go, Bounce." He hands Bouncer Bill a couple fives. "You go on. I'm gonna get Bobo to fix me up here." He orders a whiskey and pulls his camera out of the bag to get ready.

Bouncer Bill makes his way to the door that leads to the basement where the cockfighting pit is located. The action is heating up as he descends the stairs to the high stakes blood sport.

Mayor Swenson and Señor Javier are front and center, up close to the railing that surrounds the deep pit where the fighting takes place.

Big Bertha is holding the bets like she always does. She sees Bouncer Bill and looks around to see if Paparazzi Mickey came in with him. She doesn't look too happy.

Mayor Swenson calls out to Bouncer Bill, "Get the pole and net ready to go, Bounce. Did you bring tricky Mickey back?"

Just as Bouncer Bill is about to answer Mayor Swenson, a flash of light quiets the room. It's Paparazzi Mickey at the top of the stairs, aiming his camera at the crowd below him.

Big Bertha scowls at Paparazzi Mickey.

Mayor Swenson livens up the suddenly silent room. "You go on ahead and get some action shots for us now, Tricky."

"You know my camera's aim is true, Mayor." Paparazzi Mickey takes a few steps down and stops to maintain a shooting perspective from the stairway.

"His aim is true, Big," Mayor Swenson playfully hollers to Big Bertha, who is still scowling in Paparazzi Mickey's direction.

"All you boys from south of the border just keep the back of your heads to Tricky Mickey if ya don't want your faces to be photographed." Big Bertha belts out a translation to the Spanish speakers in the crowd and then gives Paparazzi Mickey another scowl.

Paparazzi Mickey is used to that scowl. She's mad about something. He doesn't give it too much thought. He's busy thinking about a good camera angle from the stairway down to the fight arena. He'll cheer up his Big Bertha later with that wedding ring.

About then a trap door in the fighting pit slides up and Blackjack, a fighting cock, prances into the pit. He's got razor-sharp knives strapped to his legs.

Mayor Swenson raises a glass of corn whiskey. "Amigos, there stands my Blackjack, the only redheaded Blue Miner in existence. Three-to-one on Blackjack winning this thing inside a minute."

There are no takers but Bouncer Bill stands ready with a net on a long pole just in case modifications are necessary.

Mayor Swenson gives Bouncer Bill a go-ahead nod. He climbs down a rickety ladder into the pit. One rung breaks. He slips, but makes it down to extend the net over Blackjack and force a hood through the net and over the champion gamecock's head.

"Blackjack's good as blind now, señors. Any comers?"

Señor Javier puts out a wad of bills and nods to his man working the trap door pulley. The door slides up.

Señor Javier's Yellow Leg Hatch moves into the pit. The fight is on—not much to it. Blackjack wins inside a minute.

Señor Javier is broken-hearted.

Without a note of consolation in his voice, Mayor Swenson rubs it in, "Blackjack cannot lose to no Yellow Leg Hatch. You shoulda known that. But I'll take your moolah just the same."

Big Bertha puts the winnings in front of Mayor Swenson. He scrapes in the cash and puts a bill in her chubby palm. "Bertha, baby. How are ya, darlin'?"

She doesn't respond to Mayor Swenson's jovial question. She's not in a jovial state of mind right about now.

CHAPTER 11

Paparazzi Mickey Hits Bottom

Señor Javier and his men begin to exit up the stairs to the gambling room.

Mayor Swenson bloviates, "Javier, everything's on the house for you and your señors. Ya hear?"

Señor Javier nods as he and his men file out, with Paparazzi Mickey following.

"Where you goin', Tricky?"

"Just goin'," answers Paparazzi Mickey. He stops to talk respectfully to Mayor Swenson and at the same time he notices a couple of the bruisers edging over toward him. It's becoming clear to him that Mayor Swenson intends to pursue the agenda he's been warming up to.

"Mighty nice duds you are wearin', Tricky. Got Big Bertha lookin'. Did ya get me some good shots of Blackjack killin' Javier's bird?"

Mickey nods back to him. "Yeah, I did."

"Big, honey, ain't your boy a gilded lily?"

Big Bertha looks blankly at Paparazzi Mickey.

Mayor Swenson continues, "I guess Big's speechless. I guess she heard you got fine money for those photos of *her* brother in *her* cabin."

Paparazzi Mickey starts to plead his case, "Bertha, I bought you a …"

The two bruisers grab Paparazzi Mickey, hold him, and rifle his pockets. One of them pulls out a wad of bills. "Hey, that's mine," he yells.

"You sure about that, Tricky?" Mayor Swenson's threatening tone is getting more certain now. "Give me that money," he orders his bruiser. The bruiser slaps it in his boss's hand. Mayor Swenson flips through the bills. "This is a shitload of cash for you, Tricky. You got any more?"

Conceding to the escalating seriousness of the moment, Paparazzi Mickey says, "That's everything I got."

That's not enough for Mayor Swenson. "Where're the negatives?"

"I sold everything bulk, Mr. Swenson."

"Sold to who, Tricky?"

"I ain't tellin' ya."

Mayor Swenson signals. "Throw him down there in that chicken shit where he belongs."

The bruisers toss Paparazzi Mickey into the pit. He lands hard.

Paparazzi Mickey agonizes from the pain of the crash landing. "Ah shit, man! You broke somethin'. Ah, God dang it! Call my daddy, Bertha." He's finding it hard to talk.

Mayor Swenson isn't letting up. "Who paid you all this money?"

"A magazine."

"Name it."

"*The People's Tabloid.*" Paparazzi Mickey can hardly speak now.

Mayor Swenson tells his bruisers, "I need a couple of ya to go down below and pull Tricky out through Blackjack's trap door."

Paparazzi Mickey begs his woman. "I broke somethin',

Bertha. I need somebody to get Doc Willard for me, okay? I don't want those boys to pull me outta here. They'll break me worse." He struggles to reach into his coat pocket and dig out a little jewelry box. He opens it. He pulls out the fake wedding ring. He holds it up so she can get a clear look at it.

Her scowl melts.

He keeps up the sweet talk. "I bought this here diamond ring for you, babe."

Big Bertha moves to the edge of the pit where the ladder is.

Paparazzi Mickey is fading. "Get Bobo to contact Doc Willard. I don't have any feelin' left in my legs."

Big Bertha stares at that wedding ring long enough to get glassy-eyed.

He holds the ring up as he lies back flat to relieve the pressure.

Big Bertha is feeling something for her man and that diamond now. She gets situated on the top of the ladder and starts to descend.

"Don't come down here, babe. Go tell Bobo to find the doc."

Big Bertha isn't listening to a word her man is saying now. The ladder shakes and creaks as she plants one foot after the other till her foot reaches for the rung that Bouncer Bill busted off. When her foot can't find a place to support her massive weight, she loses her balance and falls backwards. *Crack!* Big Bertha lands on Paparazzi Mickey's face, breaking his neck. He dies right then and there. She rolls off him, looks at his wide-open eyes, and shuts them with her hand.

Mayor Swenson stands at the edge of the pit looking down. "You go ahead and keep that ring for yourself, Big. He owed ya." He looks over to Bouncer Bill at the door. "Bounce, go get somebody to fix that ladder so y'all can help Bertha get up outta there."

THE NEXT MORNING IS A TURNING POINT IN MAYOR Swenson's attempts to stop the presses. A turning point that turns impossible. He is in his private office talking on the only phone in McGuffin Ridge. He has the rights for McGuffin Ridge telephone operations as self-appointed Mayor and owner of the land on which McGuffin Ridge sits, and he doesn't like phones. They don't contribute to the exclusivity he needs in his domain. So they're against the law—his law.

He's on a call with someone at *The People's Tabloid*. "You the news editor over there, Mr. Burk? My name is Mickey Stollard," he lies.

After a brief how-do-you-do, Mr. Burk believes Mayor Swenson is Paparazzi Mickey.

"I hate to tell you this, Mr. Burk, but my assistant who I charged with the responsibility to get signed releases from the owner of the Cozy Inn Cabins and the other releases from relatives of the dead, well, he fell back on his duties, sir. I mean to say, I just discovered those releases were made good by his own forging skills, and he is causing me a heap of legal problems, so …"

Mr. Burk cuts off Mayor Swenson. "Well, Mr. Stollard, the presses are rolling, and the signed releases are the signed releases. Nothing can be done now. I'm looking at the contract here, and it appears you were paid a fair amount. You best take your concerns to an attorney. Good luck with it."

Mayor Swenson slams the phone down.

CHAPTER 12

He's John Doe from Mexico

The morning sun is shining on Father Sam's back yard. The outdoor English class is almost set up. Father Sam takes a break to go stir something up in his kitchen.

Sheriff Marcus is not feeling his sunny self, as he wanders into Father Sam's back yard and plops down on the wooden backporch steps. The warm wood feels good on his back-side and that first coffee will make things even better.

Father Sam comes out the back door and pushes a hot cup into Sheriff Marcus's hand. "I heard you hacking and wheezing from across the road, Marcus. Drink this."

Father Sam places red and blue children's benches in front of a chalk board as he continues setting up for the kid's outdoor class.

Sheriff Marcus sniffs at the contents of the hot cup. It's not coffee, that's for sure.

Father Sam notes Marcus's look of disdain. "Drink it, my friend."

Sheriff Marcus puts the cup beside him on the porch and pulls a copy of *The Peoples Tabloid* from his back pocket. "Mickey, that weaselly photographer. Remember him messin' around with the murder scene? He got himself some tantalizing pictures, alright. He sold 'em to this here magazine." He holds it up for Father Sam to see. "He sure did put McGuffin Ridge on the map, I'll tell you that."

Father Sam doesn't bother looking at the magazine. He's about finished setting up the backyard for the English class. "How's your prisoner doing? Did you come up with a name for him? Where he's from? Anything?"

"Doc did some stitchin' on him before he left for the Smokies. Grandchild's baptism."

Father Sam approves of that. "Sure."

"Before he left, Doc said let the fella sleep. Mabelline's been bringin' soup over and spoon-feedin' him. He wakes up long enough for that. Then he keeps on sleepin'. I looked through his belongings. His name's John. No American money in his knapsack. A wallet with a few pesos, some pictures of a couple Mexican gals, and odds and ends with Spanish words printed on 'em."

"Marcus, those wild violets growing behind your garage?"

"Yeah? What about 'em?"

"Pick a bunch for me, you mind?"

"For Mabelline? Now, Father."

"Nope. I'm going to dry them, grind them, and you can feed them to your prisoner—John. It will help purify his blood."

"Might a known." Sheriff Marcus finally takes a drink from his cup. He wrinkles his face. "Damn. Excuse my French but what am I drinkin' here, daffodils or some darned thing?"

"*Una de gato*, Marcus. It's good for you."

"Unya what?"

"It's called 'cat's claw.' Drink it."

"Cat's claws?"

"Bark from a tree," Father Sam adds.

"Sure. Nothin' like a hot mug of bark from a tree."

Dr. Joe Blackfox, a thirty-year old Cherokee research scientist enters with tribal children in tow.

Molly gets up from the sunny spot near the wickiup and waggles toward the kids.

Father Sam shakes hands with Dr. Blackfox, manages a greeting in the Cherokee language, then flips back to English. "Hi, Joe. How are you? Children, you may play with Molly."

Dr. Blackfox's English is as good as his Cherokee. "Very well said, Father." He acknowledges Sheriff Marcus. "Morning, Sheriff."

Sheriff Marcus stands and is about to leave. "Howdy-do, Dr. Blackfox. I'll just be excusin' myself now, gentlemen. Better get on back to the jailhouse. Prisoner is restless this morning. Don't want Sydney to get shook up about it."

"Wait." Father Sam quicksteps to an old, wobbly-legged, chestnut table near his back door and picks out two full canning jars. "Homemade Fuji apple butter. One for Mabelline. One for yourself." He places them on the porch railing.

Sheriff Marcus empties his cup and walks it back to the wobbly table. "Well, thank ya kindly, Father. Let me send Sydney over to screw some braces on the legs of this little table for ya later today."

Sheriff Marcus's CB sounds off. *Jailbird One, come in, come in!*

He nods to the two men and heads off, preoccupied with Deputy Sydney's frantic call. He engages his CB. "Yeah, Jailbird Two. I'm here. Over."

Deputy Sydney goes on. *Prisoner is gettin' a little testy. Over.*

Dr. Blackfox has observed the concern shown for the new prisoner. "It seems the prisoner has regained his health."

Father Sam agrees. "Seems so, yes, if he's getting a little testy, as Sydney puts it. I think that's a good sign. It's been almost two weeks of recuperation. But his injuries were quite serious."

"I'm flying out to my clinic next week, if you need anything."

"Thank you, Joe. I'll check with Marcus and Mabelline. They've been pretty hands-on helping with the prisoner's road to recovery while the doctor is out of town."

"I'll leave the children with you and Molly. If you need assistance, the mothers are cutting wool on your front porch." Dr. Blackfox starts off, then stops. "Father, you know Wilma and I are planning our wedding?"

"Wouldn't miss it," says Father Sam.

"It'd be an honor to have your blessing during the ceremony."

"Well, Joe, the honor would be mine."

"And, you know we have a ritual. Bride and groom drink from a wedding vessel. We'd be appreciative if you were to create a special beverage for us. For the ceremony."

"I sure will, Joe."

They exchange big smiles as Dr. Blackfox leaves Father Sam to tend to his teaching duties.

CHAPTER 13

Skeleton In the Closet

Father Sam finishes storing the benches and black board on his back porch. He picks up the two jars of apple butter that Sheriff Marcus left on the railing, tucks a rolled-up braided throw rug under his arm, whistles for Molly, and together they mosey over to the jailhouse.

The jailhouse doubles as Sheriff Marcus's quarters. Several of Father Sam's braided rugs already lie on the floor. It's a homey little jailhouse most of the time.

Sheriff Marcus is brewing coffee.

Deputy Sydney has a mop and bucket and is about to open a heavy door at the back wall that leads to the cellblock where there are four jail cells.

There's a rap on the door. Sheriff Marcus opens it, and in walks Father Sam. Molly lies down outside. Sheriff Marcus puts a pan of water out for Molly and then shuts the jailhouse door.

"Morning." Father Sam hands Sheriff Marcus the two jars of apple butter. "You forgot these."

He sees Deputy Sydney and waves a howdy-do at him, then lays out the handmade wool rug. "It looks good in front of the door. What do you think?"

"I like it," says Sheriff Marcus. "What's my tab up to now?"

"A cord of hardwood," says Father Sam.

"All right," Sheriff Marcus answers.

Father Sam adds a late fee. "And some kindlin.'"

As Deputy Sydney opens the door and enters the cell-block with the mop and bucket, the yelling of the enraged occupant spews from jail cell number one.

John Doe's getting healthy enough to show he's indignant and ignorant of what led up to his landing in jail. "What is this, man? I ain't done nothin' to nobody! Why am I in jail?"

Deputy Sydney shuts the door behind him, muffling the noise.

"Still don't have a last name for him," Sheriff Marcus says as he picks up John's wallet. "Some pesos and a picture here. Somethin' written on the back."

Sheriff Marcus removes a photo from the wallet. "You know some Spanish." He gives it to Father Sam.

Father Sam looks it over. "It's his wife. Her name is Anita. And his daughter."

Sheriff Marcus mutters, "And her señor in the cala-boose? I'll tell you what." He pulls a faded, aged piece of thick paper from the wallet and puts it on the table in front of Father Sam. "This ain't much to see. Looks like a coupon. In Spanish, too." Sheriff Marcus turns away to pour coffee.

It's not a coupon. It's an old circus pass. Father Sam picks it up and silently reads the print. *El Circo Familia pequeño del Cuernavaca.*

Sheriff Marcus turns to Father Sam. "You want a cup of ..." He's shocked to see a look on his friend's face that he has never seen before.

Father Sam stares at the circus pass. His face twitches, his eyes glaze over. His hands shake, and he pulls them away from the circus pass as if it were drenched in ricin. Suddenly, he can't breathe. He tries to stand but can't move now.

"What? My God, man, you hearin' that horse again or what?"

Father Sam manages to stand on shaking legs with Sheriff Marcus's help. He stumbles to the counter. Pours a shot of Sheriff Marcus's corn whiskey.

Witnessing Father Sam nipping on moonshine is another first for Sheriff Marcus. He takes the bottle and stashes it in a cupboard. All he can do is watch his friend go to pieces, but he sure hates to see him drink that rotgut. But the drink seems to quiet the anxiety attack. The sight of that circus pass brought a bad spell of something onto his old buddy.

Father Sam gains control of himself. "Oh God." That's all he can say right now as he lurches for the front door.

Sheriff Marcus doesn't think it's a good idea for him to leave just yet. "Where ya goin'? Sydney'll go get biscuits and stew for us. You stay put till I get some food in your belly."

Sam stops at the door. "Oh God."

"I got the 'oh God' part, Father. What's goin' on?"

"Johnny," Father Sam whispers.

Deputy Sydney opens the cellblock door. Brings the mop bucket out.

"Go on over to Mabelline's and bring us some stew and biscuits," orders Sheriff Marcus.

"You got 'er." Deputy Sydney tips his hat and starts for the door.

"And take Molly on home before you do. I got a feelin' this is gonna take awhile."

"Sure thing, Sheriff." Deputy Sydney shuts the door behind him.

It's time for Sheriff Marcus to take charge of his pal. "Sit down."

"One more drink," whispers Father Sam.

"I ain't pourin' it." Sheriff Marcus's jaw tightens at the thought of it.

Father Sam gets the bottle from the cupboard and pours. He slugs it down and then goes straight for the cellblock door, opens it, and goes to jail cell number one.

Sheriff Marcus is stupified at Father Sam's sudden behavior, but this he's got to see.

Father Sam walks close to jail cell number one. John sees him coming. He puts his face between two bars, waiting for the priest to say something.

"John?" asks Father Sam.

"I am busted up, I'm sewed up and I'm locked up. You here to tell me why?" John snarls.

Father Sam studies John's eyes. "Do you know Cleveland Stockton?"

"Who? No, I don't know anybody. I don't know where the hell I am."

"He was murdered."

"So? What's that to me, man? Why is a priest talkin' to me?"

Father Sam studies John as if he were an apparition.

Fearing Father Sam might lapse into another seizure, Sheriff Marcus pulls at his elbow. They turn and walk away from jail cell number one, open the heavy door, and leave John to marinate in his anger.

Father Sam pours himself another drink. "Just wanted to look."

"Well, you looked," spouts Sheriff Marcus.

"His last name is Spinks." Father Sam pours another drink. Slides it to Sheriff Marcus. "You'll need this." Then he pours another for himself. With a feint slur in his words, he asks, "Marcus, can I make a confession?"

"A confession? That's a little out of keepin'. I guess you can, though."

"I need your ear, my friend. That's all."

Sheriff Marcus leans back and gives Father Sam an open ear. At least his buddy will stay put till Sydney gets back with the stew and biscuits.

"Twenty-four years ago, Marcus, in a little town on the Texas border. Something happened there that I ran away from. Something shameful. It has caught up with me." Father Sam gives a furtive nod toward the door of the cell block.

Sheriff Marcus hopes this isn't going where it sounds like it's going.

CHAPTER 14

Caught Looking

I t's the first time Sheriff Marcus has ever cast a wary eye toward his pal. *What's Father Sam running from that's so damn bad that a couple shots of corn whiskey has got him tellin' on himself?*

Father Sam begins unpacking his conscience.

IT'S 1960. THE CALLING OF THE PRIESTHOOD IS STRONG in Sam, but so are other callings. Every good-looking, red-blooded, twenty-one-year-old young man knows about that. Sam is just Sam, a seminarian, a wannabe priest.

Sam lives on the outskirts of a distressed border town and does his duties serving the church. He is also an all-around assistant to a fine, spiritual woman named Marietta—Sister Marietta. She is a nun, all right, but a different kind of nun. A down-to-earth kind of nun. She is Sam's best friend as well as his mentor.

Sister Marietta and Sam are the sole keepers of what once was a Catholic mission. It's still a white stucco building with a red-barrel tile roof, but serves a practical purpose as a social agency now. Out front, on two legs stuck firmly in the ground, there's a sign that expresses

Steven Boergadine

a clear liturgical purpose: *ST. PAUL'S MINISTRY FOR HUMAN ASSISTANCE.*

Near the sign is an Apache-style wickiup.

A hard-dirt parking area sprawls across the front of St. Paul's Mission, and a federal food and clothing distribution center sits to the left.

Gowdyville Road meanders past the front of the mission. If you were to drive down the road, you wouldn't see much along the way, just a few shacks on dirt lots here and there.

Sam is at his desk, typing a letter to his mother. He looks like he'd be more comfortable shoeing a horse or riding one. He's wearing jeans, Tony Lamas, and a denim shirt.

Next to his Royal manual typewriter is an old, hand-made book with Cherokee lettering on its deer-skin cover.

Sam stops typing and opens the old book again. The feeling in his heart needs to be refreshed. What to say to his mom? It's a blessed occasion for him, writing this letter.

The antique book always opens to the same place—the worn photo of a Cherokee medicine woman who holds a little boy close to her. The Cherokee medicine woman is Sam's grandmother on his mother's side. The little boy is Sam.

A bottle of prescription drugs and a mug of coffee are sitting beside the old book.

Sam reads what he's typed so far. "Dear Mom. I'm sorry to hear of the passing of Grandmother. Thank you for her medicine book. She was surely a blessing to all the people she cured in the Appalachians. I'll learn Cherokee and read it someday. Maybe I'll find a remedy for migraines because I sure have a doozy right now."

After the unconscious act of massaging his temples and washing down a prescription pill with coffee, he decides his letter is flippant. He pulls it from the carriage, scrunches it, and tosses it into his wastebasket.

He leaves the letter writing for now. Near the coffee and pills there's a half-dozen tickets to a Mexican traveling circus that were sent over by a rancher who bought them at a charity auction. Sam picks up three tickets and stashes them in his pocket, gets up, and walks into the waiting room. He finds, waiting quietly, sixty-year-old Fernel, a local farmer, and a young mother named Mrs. Rodriguez with her seven-year-old twin daughters.

It's a plain room with a few chairs and a painting of Chief Joseph hanging on the wall. It's always slightly tilted to one side. Seems impossible to keep it straight up and down for some reason.

Sam addresses everyone, "Good morning, folks. Hasn't Sister Marietta arrived yet?" He knows she hasn't, but asking breaks the ice.

Sam sits down beside Mrs. Rodriguez to maintain a personable air and speaks to her in Spanish, "Are you here to sign up for the Federal surplus food program, Señora?"

She lets him know that she can speak English and in a proud voice, says, "I need my little ones to receive the vaccination today, Señor."

Fernel overhears Mrs. Rodriguez and pipes up, "That goes for me too, son."

Sam gets to his feet. "Medical assistance has changed to Thursdays. Sister Marietta can talk to you both about that. She'll be coming through that door any minute."

Sam places a day-old cardboard bakery box on the coffee table. "While we are waiting for our favorite nun to arrive, how about partaking of the fifth deadly sin? Be my guest."

Steven Boergadine

The two little girls lean over to the brown pastry box to pick a favorite as Sam reaches to the ear of one of them. He does a slight of hand, pretending to pull a circus pass from her ear. "What do we have here?" He reads the inscription on the circus pass to Mrs. Rodriguez, "*El Circo Familia pequeño de Cuernavaca.* There's a traveling Mexican circus in town. I can give you each a free ticket. It closes tonight, Señora."

The kids plead with Mama. She says yes and Sam puts the three tickets in her hand.

Then he turns to Fernel. "How ya doin', Fernel?"

Fernel beams. "You remember me?"

"Sure. You don't have any use for a couple of circus passes, do ya? I can check your ears."

Fernel chuckles. "No, sir. My boy's got all growed up."

Sam adjusts the portrait of Chief Joseph as he chats. "You still live on Horn Road?"

"Yep, I do, son."

"You ever find any flint out on your place? Arrowheads, tools?"

"My kids looked real hard. Years ago. Bird points was about all they found, though."

Sam shows interest. "Yeah? I've been digging around here. Haven't found much." Sam hears a horse nickering. It happens now and then, usually when he has a migraine. He massages his temples. "Did you hear a horse just now?" He knows the answer.

Fernel gives a puzzled expression. "No, sir."

With a please-excuse-me nod, Sam goes for the door. He looks around from the front steps. As he figured, no horse in sight.

Massaging his aching temples, he's suddenly distracted from his migraine by a sexy, earthy, irresistible, inebriated older woman—older than him, anyway. She's carrying groceries to her car. Sam intones under his breath, "Gladys Spinks. The devil. With breasts." Something about Gladys Spinks always gets to him. He stares unashamedly at her curvaceous silhouette.

Suddenly, he hears the voice of God. A female God. "The lust of his eyes comes not from the Father but from the world, Brother Westburn."

It's his best friend and surrogate mom, forty-year-old Sister Marietta. Today, she's in her nun's habit. She strolls toward Sam. Sister Marietta has accepted that Sam is still a young bull and it's going to take awhile. She has no severe judgement of Sam at times like this, nothing but a big smile and a wry sense of humor.

Sam turns on the charm, "Ahh, she's a poor drunk thing stumbling through my original sin."

Sister Marietta can be a little coy. "I'd say she's holding up pretty good for thirty-nine. Good morning, young man."

Sam responds, "Why do I suspect you've been with Monsignor Alvarez?"

"Because I'm not dressed like you? By the way, the monsignor is very pleased with your work in outreach."

"I'm pleased that he's pleased," says Sam.

"He feels your commitment to the seminary system has been remarkable."

"God has easy access to us in a seminary," says Sam.

"Of course." Sister Marietta chuckles. "The seminary is His House."

Sam lightens up their exchange. "So much the easier to yield the heart to His Will, in His House … except when Gladys Spinks walks by."

"It is a slow and passionate journey, Sam."

"The p-word. Quick, the rosaries."

She opens her hand and rosaries dangle down. "They're never far away, Sam."

"You are such a nun. Your faithful await you inside."

She quickens her step. "Oh, Goodness. I really need to get out of this habit."

Sam kids around. "I'd unzip you, but people would talk."

"Stop dreaming." She hikes up her habit enough to reveal the old cowboy boots she generally wears to work. "What do you think?"

"I think you should go square dancing."

A postal delivery van pulls in.

"There's Hector," says Sister Marietta.

Out in the parking lot, Gladys stumbles and spills her bag of groceries. "Fuck!"

Sister Marietta hears Gladys's profanity. She smiles. "I'll get the mail. You give Mrs. Spinks a hand." She hurries off to meet Hector.

Sam watches Gladys bend over to pick up the spilled groceries. Her abundant cleavage transfixes him mercilessly. She looks up and catches him looking. An inescapable moment of self-consciousness follows. He approaches Gladys.

When Gladys Spinks talks, not a word leaves her lips that isn't drenched with seduction. That's the way Sam hears it.

"Hi, Sam."

"Hi, Gladys."

"Did I curse in the Lord's presence, Sam?"

"I hope He was taking a break, Gladys."

"Were you lookin' at my … groceries?"

"Let me grab 'em." With both feet in his mouth now, Sam mindlessly steps forward to pick up the spilled goods and is about to smash a small box of blue birthday candles with his cowboy boot.

"Don't! Johnny's birthday candles. I need nine good ones."

He steps gingerly to the side of the box of candles. "Oops, okay, sorry. Johnny's birthday?" Then he remembers the tickets for tonight's little Mexican circus—a timely birthday present from St. Paul's Mission. He reaches into his pocket. Not there. He gave them to the Rodriquez family. There are a couple more on his desk, though.

Sam picks up her strewn groceries and notices a box of devil's food cake mix. He won't say what comes to mind.

Gladys picks up a carton of eggs, then the carton slips out of her hand. "Oh, you fuckin' eggs." She berates herself for cussing. "Uh-oh. Shut up, Gladys."

Sam picks up the egg carton and a small box of candy. "One egg broke. The candy is okay."

"Those are Johnny's favorite."

"Red licorice? Well, I'll remember that, Gladys."

Gladys pulls a flask from her car and offers it to Sam. "Can I tempt ya?"

"You already did." There's a twinkle in his eye that shouldn't be there.

Gladys sees the twinkle and takes a nip. "I'm wearin' ya down?"

"Nah. I have a bulletproof soul," says Sam.

"I wish I had one of those. You wanna loan me yours?"

"You shouldn't say that, Gladys."

She seems almost sober for a moment as she captivates Sam's serious side. "You're a good one, Sam." She puts her hand on his cheek softly. The warmth from her touch travels right down Sam's spine. She continues, "Johnny needs some influence on his soul. Can you be that influence now and then?"

That expression of motherhood from Gladys removes all the young lust that had gathered in Sam's heart during the entire morning. But his migraine is back. "Anytime," he says.

Gladys pushes, "You promise?"

Gladys's face takes on a look that Sam hadn't appreciated before now. Vulnerable and wounded and virtuous.

He's lost for a minute. "I promise."

"What's that?" She points to the wickiup.

"A wickiup. I made it."

"Healthy man stuff. Can Johnny drop by and learn about it?"

"Sure."

"What's it for?"

"Sort of a memorial. My grandma died. She was a medicine woman. Cherokee."

"Well, Grandma'd like that."

"It's Apache. Hope she don't mind."

Gladys gets in her car and starts the engine.

"Stay on the road, Gladys."

She pulls onto Gowdyville Road as Sam walks around the property, picking up litter.

IN THE JAILHOUSE CONFESSIONAL, SHERIFF MARCUS pipes up. "So ya had some fire in your belly when you were a young fella, huh?" He pours another shot of hootch.

"I calmed down when she showed her mom side," says Father Sam glibly.

CHAPTER 15

Not The Dead Sea Scrolls

"I went to shameful lengths to acquire my share of carnal knowledge, Marcus."

Sheriff Marcus isn't having it. "A passion for life as a young man ain't a surprise to me, Father. There ain't nothin' shameful about it, either."

"You might be surprised yet," says Father Sam.

SAM STANDS ON THE SPARSELY GRAVELED CRACKED earth in front of St. Paul's Mission and watches Gladys's old car move slowly through the visible heat waves rising from the blazing surface of Gowdyville Road.

Jonah the Cow ambles toward Sam. The fence must be broken. "Jonah, get back. Go on." Jonah turns around and ambles back to where she came from.

Sam drops litter in an old refuse barrel that sits on the edge of mission property. He reaches deep into the barrel, lifts the false bottom and picks up a recent covert delivery—a magazine with a half-dressed girl on the cover—she's in full color and glossy. He rolls it up and sticks it in the hip pocket of his jeans.

After he pushes Jonah through the gate, back into the pasture, he walks over to a shed where essentials for maintenance are stored. There are bales of hay, sacks of grain, tools, a chain saw, hardware, and a tack area for stable gear. He stashes the girlie magazine inside a toolbox that has a padlock on it.

He starts loading materials for fence repair into his 1954 Ford pickup. A fifty-gallon metal drum sits in his pickup bed with a water hose leading into it. He'll refresh Jonah's trough while he's out there.

Sam hears the wood screen door bang shut at the back porch of the mission and sees Sister Marietta head his way. She's back to wearing blue jeans, a plaid flannel shirt, and those cowboy boots. He calls out to her, "Hit that water, will ya?"

Sister Marietta turns the spigot off and then trots to his pick- up.

"Hop on," says Sam. She does, as Sam gives the lock on his toolbox a no-look, double-check tug. He climbs behind the wheel, starts it up, slowly maneuvers along the bumpy pasture, and stops at the slightly open gate.

Sister Marietta hops off the running board and pulls a letter from her shirt pocket. It was delivered earlier by Hector the postman. She hands it to Sam. "From the Evangelization Board," she says.

Sam's hands are wet and he's got work to do, so he lays it on the tailgate of his pickup.

Sister Marietta means for him to give the letter the attention it deserves. "Sam?"

He sees she's not kidding around, so he dries his hands on his pants and opens the letter.

"Let me hear you read it," she says.

He gives it a quick going-over. "We all agree that the seminarians serving the Holy Church have a responsibility to evangelize to unchurched residents of our parish community. Proclaiming the glad tidings of Jesus Christ is the hallmark of our spiritual lives."

Seems to him like a form letter. "Okay, great, I couldn't have said it better myself." He stuffs the letter in his shirt pocket and gets back to work.

She gets serious. "Read the rest of it for me, Sam."

Sam unfolds the letter and picks up where he left off. "It is hereby declared that after careful review, the Evangelization Board feels that the responsibility to maintain church-funded social services currently extended to the James Spinks family shall be terminated immediately." Sam stops reading. Now he knows why Sister Marietta is so serious.

Dropping the letter on the pickup bed, Sam gets back to work. He sticks a short hose into the top of the fifty-gallon drum and siphons water into Jonah's trough.

Sister Marietta decides to let Sam know more than she should about what's behind the letter. "I want you to know why this is a serious matter. Gladys's husband has a partner at the brewery. They're making bathtub gin and selling it under the table."

Sam's feeling a little sarcastic. "And the Evangelization Board's onto it, God bless 'em."

She fires back. "No, the FBI is, God bless 'em."

Sam's not taking it seriously. "The Federal Bureau of Investigation? For brewing bathtub gin in the Texas desert? How'd that become a federal issue?"

Sister Marietta lays out the dirty facts and then some. "The Yaqui elders in the Sonoran Desert have an epidemic of cirrhosis in their teenagers. It's James Spinks's dirty booze. Sonoran Desert is Mexico. Mexico makes it a federal crime. Thus, FBI."

"And Gladys? What's *her* crime? Taste testing?"

"C'mon, Sam. She's not Betty Crocker. You saw her today."

"Sorry." Sam means it. He knows he's being a little too bratty to his mentor.

Sister Marietta can see Sam has cooled off, so she continues, "There's more, but it's too sensitive to discuss for now. The agent in charge of the investigation is concerned about the boy. And to what degree Gladys is involved. All unknown for now. I'm not going to second guess the FBI."

Sam takes it in and gets back to work.

Sister Marietta's not finished. "You have a scheduled orientation with the family tomorrow morning for church assistance. Cancel that. Between you and me and the fence post, tonight the Feds are going to make a house call."

"A raid? They'll get devil's food cake," Sam quips. "It's the kid's birthday."

"You'll have to scratch that family off your list, Sam."

That's a hard order to take for Sam. "The kid, Johnny, the nine-year-old birthday boy. Is he on that list? He needs a role model. Wouldn't you agree?"

"I'm sorry. The board wants complete severance. You are being ordered to stop thinking about that family, Sam."

"Ordered to stop thinking? Monsignor Alvarez, J. Edgar Hoover, and the Evangelization Board all order me to stop thinking?"

She guesses a change of subject is needed. "My gosh, it's getting chilly." She turns to walk toward the mission. "This ol' cowgirl needs to retreat to a nice, quiet abbey. See you Monday morning."

"Have a hilarious time, Sister."

"Oh, Monday morning. How could I forget? The monsignor is coming to visit us. Can you dress up?" She trots off.

Sitting next to Sheriff Marcus's Franklin stove, Father Sam drains his glass. Slams it down on the tabletop. "I thought I was in control, Marcus."

Sheriff Marcus emits a wise chuckle. "At twenty-two, you ain't in control of nothin', Father."

CHAPTER 16

Sam Falls Through the Cracks

Father Sam dips deep into corn whiskey guilt. "Ain't in control of nothin'? You're right, I lost control of my soul." His religiosity gets a little sidetracked. "My sins are like scarlet, they shall never be as white as snow. Do you follow me, old buddy?"

Sheriff Marcus is a patient listener, but there are limits. "If you're gonna start rewriting the good book, I'm gonna have to move my chair a little farther away."

Young seminarian-wannabe Sam gets back to the task of fixing the fence that keeps Jonah as well as Sam's old mare from wandering onto Gowdyville Road. His head throbs and he grimaces. He hears the nickering of a horse right behind him. He turns quickly to see if it's his mare—it's not. She's on the far side of the pasture, nose to the ground, sniffing for grass. He walks around to the passenger side of his pickup, opens the door, and reaches into the glove box. A couple prescription pills are left in a bottle. He shakes them into his hand, puts the empty bottle back in the glove box, and walks to the fifty-gallon drum to pull the water hose out of Jonah's trough. He puts the hose up to his mouth and washes down the pills. Then he sits on the running board, holds up the hose, and lets the cold water pour over his throbbing head.

After about five minutes of drenching his migraine, he walks over to the broken gate. Jonah had pushed it open with her head. He sees it needs a new hinge and latch. The old rusted one's been threatening to give out for months. It's finally done in.

He'll need to go to the hardware store. Sam cinches the gate in place with some rope, then pulls his pickup over to the mission entrance and dashes inside to get another bottle of pills. He checks his desk drawer. None there. He sees the last two circus tickets for tonight. The voice of his conscience is on high alert.

Don't think about dropping by the Spinks' home with those tickets, nothin' there for you but the devil's food.

His ego speaks up.

Go get Gladys and Johnny out of the house before the Feds ruin his birthday, if you're any kind of a man.

Common sense makes sense to him.

Mind your own business, go to the hardware store, stop rationalizing, and fix the darn fence.

A touch of denial offers a little guidance.

Maybe you'll see some kids while you're at the hardware store.

He slips the circus tickets into his pocket.

His conscience, his ego, his common sense, his denial—be gone. It's fate that makes the decision.

Driving down Gowdyville Road, he sees Gladys's car crashed into a ditch. Lord knows it could be bad. He stops and runs to her car. There she is, knocked out—or passed out. There's no blood.

He's relieved. She just fell asleep and drove off the road. Good thing the ditch was there to bring her car to a safe stop. It's gonna take a tow truck to get it out, though.

Sam quickly goes to his pickup and brings back a rag soaked with cold water from the fifty-gallon drum. "Hey, Gladys. Wake up." Sam dabs her face.

She opens her eyes and looks straight into his. It's an instant, primal connection. Sam's brain floods with thoughts unfamiliar to him except when he looks at certain magazines.

He helps her climb out of her car and transfers her groceries to the bed of his pickup. He's glad he decided to make that trip to the hardware store. Maybe he's meant to be a knight in shining armor for her and her boy. He shifts into third gear and heads for her place. The hardware store can wait. He needs to convince her to take Johnny to the circus.

Gladys is recovered now and still feeling the sauce. "Oh, God, I'm a basket case." She sizes him up. "Did you come from Heaven?"

He thinks hard about that. "Maybe. Yeah, in a way I guess."

"You're a real gentleman, aren't ya?"

"Yeah, sometimes. I was gonna come by later."

"You were?"

"Yup."

"That's good."

"I've got a surprise."

"Oh. For Johnny? Or me?" Gladys slides close to him and lays her hand on his thigh. "Is the Lord your shepherd all the time?"

Gladys' touch bothers him. "Most all the time," he says.

"I've been feelin' your eyes, Sam."

Sam knows she's referring to earlier today.

Gladys points out the window as they speed by the forest. "You got trees like those where you come from?"

"Madrone? Sure." he says.

"We call 'em somethin' else," Gladys says.

"What do you call madrone?" John asks.

"Naked Indians. That's what we call 'em around here. Ain't they nice? You're not a Texas boy, are ya?"

"No."

"You a California boy?"

"I'm not a boy."

"You're a man from somewhere nice, aren't ya?"

"Oregon."

"Oh yeah, I heard about Oregon. You're one of them lumberjack men. Any madrone grow in Oregon?"

"Yeah."

"What do y'all call your madrone?"

"Madrone."

Gladys has a little laugh.

Sam guides the conversation to a warm and fuzzy place. "It's good for wood stoves in winter. 'Cause it's hardwood."

She moves her face close to his ear and whispers, "Hard-wood. Burns all night, don't it?"

Sam's willpower gives up. He swerves his pickup onto a forest road. He doesn't see the sign. *PRIVATE LOGGING ROAD*. He speeds just out of sight of Gowdyville Road and parks.

Sam and Gladys disappear below window level.

Three woodsmen are taking a break nearby. They hear Sam's pickup come to a stop. They take a look, thinking it's their foreman or a forest ranger. When they realize what's going on, they decide to have fun. All three of the woods-men sneak up close to Sam's pickup and pull the ropes on their chain saws. The burst of three chain saws shatter Sam and Gladys's woodsy reverie. Gladys screams. Sam starts up the pickup and peels out.

IN THE JAILHOUSE, FATHER SAM IS DRUNK AND SITTING with his head in his hands, staring at his feet.

"I'd of done the same thing," claims Sheriff Marcus.

"What? Scare a couple of people out of their wits like that?"

"No, the other part, the drivin' hell-bent-for-the-toolies and parkin' with Gladys."

CHAPTER 17

The Devil Is Your Own Damned Self

F ather Sam stares into his past, sipping on the whiskey. Sheriff Marcus gets impatient. "You gonna tell me what the devil happened?"

"Glad you brought that up, Marcus."

"Brought what up?"

"The devil."

"Devil? The devil is your own damn self, if you ask me."

"Here's to my own damn self then." Father Sam pours another for Sheriff Marcus and for himself and continues reflecting.

SAM BARRELS ALONG GOWDYVILLE ROAD. GLADYS couldn't be sitting any closer to him.

"You can slow down, honey. They ain't followin'," she teases.

Sam slows his pickup.

Gladys is not letting up. "I like being craved over by you."

Sam drives past shacks with tar paper siding and leaky rooftops patched with plastic tarps held down by old tire drums. He parks near Gladys's house.

Steven Boergadine

Gladys gives Sam a wanting look. "Nobody's here."

Sam needs to convince her to take Johnny to the circus, but he knows better than to tell her why he wants to get her and Johnny out of the house by tonight. He thinks about it as he brings in her groceries. He's about to reach into his pocket for the circus tickets and make his pitch, but she pulls him toward a bedroom. "Live dangerous," she whispers.

Sam resists. She lets go.

"They ain't around, Honey." Gladys finds a bottle of scotch and swigs. "C'mon." She puts the bottle in his hands. Sam's free-will quits on him again. He doesn't even wipe off the bottle top. He tips it up for a long swig as she steers him into the bedroom. His first drink of alcohol ever.

Five minutes alone and there's no turning back for either one of them. Their absorbing moments are suddenly interrupted by a sound more startling than the shriek of chain saws—the sound of playing cards flapping against bicycle spokes. The sound stops outside the front door. Sam is shocked back to reality—twice in the same day.

Gladys is undisturbed. "It's Johnny's bike. He won't come in here. It's my private place."

Sam cups his hand over her mouth as he hears Johnny enter the house.

The bedroom door is cracked open wide enough for Sam to peek through it with one eye. He watches as Johnny spots the groceries spread out on the table. Johnny rummages through them, finds the box of red licorice, and sticks it in his back pocket.

Gladys bites his hand. He lets out a subtle yelp.

Johnny looks toward the cracked open door. His eyes lock onto Sam's. It is the longest moment of Sam's life.

He waits for the boy to fling the door open and see him entangled with his mother.

But, Johnny runs through the kitchen and down the basement stairs.

That's Sam's chance to jump up and get dressed and head for the door. He is about to leave when Gladys blocks him. Sam whispers to his persistent lover, "Gladys, you have to get Johnny out of here." Sam pulls two circus passes from his shirt pocket. "Take your boy to the circus tonight. Don't stay here. You're in danger." He presses the circus passes into her hand.

Gladys isn't listening. "I got to ya, baby. You know it. Finish what you started." Her whiskey'd, breathy proclamation almost changes his mind about leaving.

He pulls away and tries one last time to warn her. "Get out of the house. Take Johnny to the circus. I'm sorry. Forgive me." He feels a churning in his stomach. Gladys hangs on to him. Sam turns, pulls himself away again, and gets to his pickup. Before he can open the door, he stops, hangs on the handle, bends down, and throws up. That long swig of scotch didn't sit well in his virgin tummy.

"Sick boy," Gladys yells from her doorway. Gladys is furious. She slams the front door, grabs the bottle of scotch, drains it, then hurls the empty at the kitchen wall near the entry to the basement. It shatters loudly. She screams bloody hell at the succession of men that have violated her life. "Yeah, I forgive all of you bastards."

Would that Sam were not on that crimson list—but he is.

Gladys moves slowly through the kitchen toward the stairs that lead to the basement. "Johnny?" She stands at the top of the stairs. "Jim?" The two tickets are still clutched in the hand of her non-throwing arm.

THE SOUND OF DEPUTY SYDNEY ENTERING THE JAIL-house interrupts Father Sam's R-rated confession. "Excuse me, gents." He places stew and biscuits on the table. "There you be." He quickly heads back out. "Left mine half-eaten at the counter. I'll go finish now while it's hot. Good evening to ya."

Sheriff Marcus yells after him, "Cuttin' wood tomorrow, Sydney. Bring your chain saw."

Father Sam isn't drinking now. Just sitting. Soul searching.

Sheriff Marcus fills up a bowl with the hot stew and slides it to Father Sam. "Can you eat and confess at the same time?"

CHAPTER 18

Ain't Chasing the Devil Away Today

Father Sam slides the stew and biscuits back to Sheriff Marcus and says no to coffee. If he's gonna talk about the hard stuff, then he's gonna have to drink the hard stuff.

"I ran, didn't I?" Father Sam pours another whiskey.

"I woulda got outta there, too, with that raid about to happen," answers Sheriff Marcus.

"I didn't stop running."

STILL OUTSIDE GLADYS'S HOUSE, SAM WIPES THE VOMIT from his chin with the arm of his shirt and climbs into his pickup. He doesn't look back as he shifts into first gear and floors the accelerator. He speeds by a feed store where two black Dodge Coronets are parked. Government cars. Stern-faced G-men have gathered to wait for the rest of their posse. Soon they'll strategize, then they'll raid the Spinks's place.

The war within rages on. Sam's conscience tells him his unrestrained misbehavior with Gladys was disobedient and self-serving.

Yeah, Sister Marietta warned me. Heck, she ordered me to quit the Spinks case altogether.

But, didn't Sam do right by stopping and helping her?

Jesus would have done the same. The leper, the blind, the dumb, the downtrodden. How could I not help Gladys lying unconscious in her wrecked car?

How about the bewitching attraction between Sam and Gladys?

How could I help myself? Her hand on my thigh. That madrone-burns-all-night dirty talk. She tempted me.

The rationalization wheel keeps spinning in Sam's tormented mind.

It was my choice to drive off the highway onto the private logging road. It was my choice to push her down on my pickup's seat. Sure, she pressed all my buttons. But I reacted by making the wrong choices.

He ponders the woodsmen's role.

The chainsaw prank must have been God's intervention. The woodsmen were guardian angels.

Sam's brain swirls like a courtroom drama. Was I seduced or the seducer? Which came first, the beam or the mote?

The dichotic war-within leads Sam to the logical conclusion:

The devil made me do it. The devil made me do it. The devil made me do it. The devil made me do it. The devil …

Sam hears a horse nicker. He doesn't look around, he knows better. He reaches into his glove compartment and grabs the prescription bottle. He shakes it. No pills, and drug stores are closed. Maybe aspirin will help. Or a whole damned bottle of aspirin.

Life is crap right now. What happened? Yesterday he was a twenty-one-year-old do-gooder. What happened? A refrain serenades his brain.

The devil made me do it. The devil made me do it.

It's the only way to look at it.

Sam sees the Bullfrog Tavern. He has passed by it quite a few times, but this'll be a first, to go inside a tavern. No law against it. He turns twenty-two next month, and still hasn't seen the inside of a tavern. It must be his day for first times.

Sam finds a place to park in the gravel lot and makes his way through the door and into a brim-full beer joint cranked up with hundred decimal Texas swing music … it's happy hour at the Bullfrog Tavern.

The old-timer bartender approaches and barks over the noise, "Yeah?"

That must be the bartender's way of asking him what he wants to order.

"Aspirin?" Sam barks back.

"That's it?"

There's expectation in that question, so Sam feels obliged to order something to wash down the aspirin. "A beer."

"A glass?" asks the bartender.

"I guess so," says Sam.

The song on the juke box ends.

A young cowboy couple enters the tavern—Hank and Elma. Hank stops in the doorway and looks back out the door. "Hot damn, Elma. Will ya look at that?" Hank's watching three black Dodge Coronets pass by on the street outside. "Shit, man. Where's the funeral?"

The bartender scolds the young cowboy, "Quit lettin' the flies in, Hank."

Hank shuts the door and talks to Elma. "Honey, what-cha wanna drink?" He recognizes Sam, who is still sitting on a bar stool near him. "Hey, you're the fella from the mission, ain't ya? Whatcha doin' in here?"

Sam doesn't lie. "Killing a headache. How are ya?"

Hank looks around for his lady. "Elma, what do ya want?" She's already dropping loose change in the juke box. Hank tells the bartender, "Hell, make it three whiskeys. And give one of 'em to the Good Samaritan to go with that beer." Sam doesn't turn it down. "I, uh, thanks, uh, Hank." The beer and aspirin are already in front of him.

Hank invites Sam to join him and Elma for shuffleboard when he feels like it.

A couple aspirin and the beer don't do much for Sam's headache, so he chases them with the whiskey that Hank bought him. Then another beer. Then some more aspirin. Then another whiskey. Soon he's mindlessly dancing to honky-tonk music along with Hank and Elma and the rest of the bar crowd. His headache is long gone for now. But his spiritual ache isn't going anywhere.

At about two-fifteen a.m., the bartender yells, "Last call."

Hank and Elma leave for home. Sam doesn't. He drinks and dances till closing time.

A random cowboy gives him a couple brightly colored pills and says, "Have a good trip, preacher boy." Sam puts them in his shirt pocket.

The last of the crowd leaves the Bullfrog Tavern. Sam wanders out with them, finds his pickup and climbs inside. The long-necked bottle of beer in the rear pocket of his blue jeans doesn't break, but it sure makes it hard to sit comfortably. He pulls it out and drops it on the floorboard, then lays his head against the driver's-side window.

Next morning, Sam is sleeping deep, his head still against the glass. Bombs explode in his brain. He jerks awake—no bombs, just the cleaning lady tapping a fingernail on the outside of the window his head was lying against.

She orders him to go home. Then she drags her cardboard box around the parking area, picking up empties and scraping up broken glass.

Sam starts his pickup and creeps down the road. He finds a drug store, shows the storekeeper his empty prescription bottle, and gets a refill. He dumps too many in his mouth and washes them down with the long-necked bottle of warm beer that's rolling around his floorboard. He remembers the brightly colored pills the cowboy gave him and pulls them out of his shirt pocket and downs them. Why not? His life is crap. The worst headache he's ever had.

I guess this is what they call a hangover.

Sam has the devil all figured out now. He washes a couple more pills down with the rest of the warm beer. He decides to not fight with the devil today. Instead, he's gonna invite the old boy to his wickiup. He's gonna have it out with him.

FATHER SAM LEANS BACK IN HIS CHAIR AGAINST SHERIFF Marcus's countertop. "The devil whooped me pretty bad that day, Marcus."

"I like a good fight. What happened?"

CHAPTER 19

Man with Many Women

The drinking isn't slowing down. Hard to tell who's drunkest. "Listen." Father Sam cups his ear as he animates that sound of a staple gun. "Tack, tack, tack, tack, tack." He punches the space around him with slow, deliberate gestures. "Tack, tack, tack, tack. What's that sound, Marcus?"

Sheriff Marcus observes Father Sam's foolishness. "I don't care. A clock."

"Tick, tock, tick, tock. That's a clock. Tack, tack, tack, Marcus. What is it?"

"Gimmee that bottle." Sheriff Marcus grabs the bottle and pours himself a shot. "I don't give a damn if it's tick, tock or tack, tack. It's a clock."

Father Sam clues him in. "No. Not a clock. It's the sound of the devil, mister." He takes back the bottle and pours himself another.

Sheriff Marcus is fed up. "Uh-huh. I'm waitin' to hear the sound of that ass whoopin' you got from your devil, before that whiskey bottle runs out on ya."

From inside the wickiup comes Sam's chanting and the persistent sound of a staple gun. *Tack, tack, tack, tack.*

Outside of the wickiup, Sam's unsaddled mare is tethered to a freshly erected post.

The sound of the staple gun stops. The devil has made his mark.

Sam steps out of the wickiup puffing proud on a fat Havana. He's wearing a loincloth, cowboy boots, no socks, no pants, and no shirt. He has beads around his neck—eight-pound fishing line strung through baby carrots and radishes. Slung over his shoulder is a rake handle with a bowstring of that cheap fishing line and a feed-sack quiver filled with short, crooked branches. Only his madness is authentic.

Sam holds the Havana in his teeth, mounts his horse bareback and maneuvers it to a position behind the wickiup. He holds his bow in his left hand and waits for *the enemy*.

A black Lincoln Continental pulls onto the mission grounds. Sam spurs his horse toward the Lincoln.

Monsignor Alvarez is behind the wheel. Sister Marietta is with him. They watch a schizo-eyed, half-naked man with a cigar clenched between his teeth gallop his horse to the front of the Lincoln and block it. The half-naked man draws a short, crooked branch from his quiver, notches it, pulls back his bow string and lets the no-go arrow go—slightly clipping his mare's left ear and dropping a few inches in front of her.

Monsignor Alverez is shocked. "What is he … isn't that Brother Westburn, Sister?"

Sister Marietta is stunned and tongue-tied. She gathers her wits and asks Monsignor Alvarez to remain patient as she eases out of the car. She cautiously approaches her young protégé and studies his face. "Sam, for heaven's sake, you're smoking." She steps towards him and whispers. "What is wrong with you?"

Steven Boergadine

Sam dismounts and hands the reins to an imaginary groom.

The reins drop to the ground. The mare wanders off and stops beside Jonah the cow, who has rambled through the open gate. Together, they watch the humans.

Sam backs up toward the wickiup and stops, plants his rake handle like a walking stick and holding himself erect, clutches his cigar like a Bowie knife. Ready to fight.

Sister Marietta sees his eyes are not right. Nothing is right about this. "What is it, Sam?"

He stands fast in front of the wickiup's entrance. "You no enter."

Monsignor Alvarez gets out of the Lincoln and softly treads toward them. "What's the idea, Brother Sam?"

Head raised in a regal pose, Sam squints and speaks with command to both cavalry soldiers he sees standing before him. "My people," Sam says.

Monsignor Alvarez and Sister Marietta look at each other. She says, under her breath, "Stress."

"Let me take care of this, Sister." He tries to connect with Sam. "God bless your people. Tell me more."

"Soldiers take my people."

Monsignor Alvarez asks, "What is your name?"

Sam answers, "Man With Many Women."

Monsignor Alvarez goes along with it. "Very well, Man With Many Women."

"Women hungry," Sam says.

Sister Marietta wants to end this. She whispers, "I'll phone for an ambulance."

"No, no. We'll try a little intervention here. Where are your women? We'll send venison." He looks to Sister Marietta for advice. "Venison is buffalo meat, is it not?"

"Not," replies Sister Marietta as she studies Sam's body language.

Sam moves to further block the wickiup entrance. "You no enter."

"His women are in there, I think, Monsignor."

"I thought the soldiers took them."

"No, I don't think the soldiers took the women," she guesses.

Sam becomes unsteady. His face grows pale, his eyelids go to half-mast, and he faints backwards into the wickiup.

Sister Marietta rushes inside to help him and shrieks, "Ohh!" Monsignor Alvarez bursts into the wickiup.

The inside of the wickiup, from top to bottom, all the way around, is covered with cut-out photos of naked women, stapled to the walls—glossy magazine photos he'd been saving from the months of deliveries to the false-bottomed trash barrel.

Sister Marietta and Monsignor Alvarez stand side by side, looking, not a sound from either of them as they take it all in.

Finally, Sister Marietta offers her dry assessment. "His women, I would guess, Monsignor."

Lost in the wallpaper, Monsignor Alvarez finally responds to Sister Marietta. "Yes. Perhaps you should call emergency now, Sister."

IN THE JAILHOUSE, SHERIFF MARCUS SAYS, "DAMN GOOD thing you had that nun around."

"She was my best friend, my mentor, my mother, my

guardian angel, my Saint Borremeo." Father Sam guzzles the last of his glass.

"Your what? Never mind. How'd you explain yourself to her."

"Selected amnesia."

CHAPTER 20

Just Plain Sam

heriff Marcus makes a philosophical observation. "You listen to me, Father. That young man sittin' in my jail cell is lucky to be alive. Hell, I was ready to vamoose that bloody cabin when Bouncer Bill told us to get outta there. But you saved his life, just like that nun saved yours. So, that makes you his Saint somethin' or another. What're ya' gonna do about that?"

"I'll mortify myself. Forty Psalms worth of mortification, please." He stretches his wavering arms, opens his trembling hands. His face long with self-pity.

Sheriff Marcus gives him a no-pity-stare-down.

Father Sam lowers his hands. "Nothing? Then, I'll run. How 'bout that, Marcus? Run, Sam, run."

"Get on with your confessin' and start makin' some sense. What'd you do after that nun saved you from yourself?"

MANY DAYS AFTER HIS MELTDOWN, AND MANY MILES away from St. Paul's Mission, strapped down in an infirmary bed, Man With Many Women opens his eyes. He's just plain Sam now. "What happened?"

Sister Marietta is looking down at him. She's been there a long time. She asks the attending nurse to give her the gastric suction results.

Sam blinks till Sister Marietta's motherly face comes into focus.

After the nurse presents the paperwork, Sister Marietta reads the data. "What happened? Hmm. Whiskey and beer happened, aspirin and miscellaneous pharmaceuticals happened, hallucinogens and Lord knows what else happened."

Sam becomes very quiet. His eyes don't want to stay open.

Sister Marietta wants to know if Sam has all his marbles. She dabs his head with a wet cloth. "Talk to me, dear."

"I saw the Feds ..." He summons the good sense to hold his tongue. The episode that started in the woods with Gladys was humiliating. The raunchy finish at the Spinks' home was worse. Johnny seeing him through the crack of the bedroom door—there's not a more dreadful memory to wake up to—and then driving away as fast as his pickup could go. "Oh God." He puts both hands over his face. Self-loathing devours him. His Catholic calling is on the wane.

Sister Marietta reads this in his face and shines some light on that subject. "Sam, Sam. We fall, we get up, we fall again, and we get up again. It's how we sacrifice our will to His. Little by little, my son."

Sam hears the message, but he rejects it by finding the only place that feels safe right now—sleep. She gently pats his forehead with the damp cloth, says a little prayer, then walks to the light switch by the door, flicks it off, and leaves.

She didn't tell him he's been in a coma for two weeks.

Sam undergoes physical therapy in the infirmary for a few more weeks. After he leaves the infirmary, he leaves the seminary.

Driving his pickup from Texas to the West Coast gives him time to plan an escape from his *calling*. He hasn't made wise decisions lately. Looks like it's gonna stay that way. He wants to become the opposite of who he is. He wants to become a San Francisco hippy.

It's the 1960s and Sam is fully investing in his twenty-something, free-spirited, dandy self. It's a time of liberation for many of his generation. Till now, Sam has always been different. For him, liberation has always been about answering his calling—to seek the mysterious confirmation that his religion brings to his inner being. But change is growth, they say, so he turns his back on his personal mystical mystery and joins his drug-fueled, newfound peers.

Young people are rebelling against war, against parents, against bras and against organized religion. He does his best to join in as a bell-bottom-jeans-wearing, turquoise-jewelry-wearing, ponytail-wearing, anti-establishment kind of guy, but when it comes to the *turn on, tune in, drop out* counterculture philosophy, he can't betray his core. Kaleidoscopic journeys to nirvana using chemical shortcuts grow old for Sam. They smack of brain recreation and that's about all. The baby boomer era drags by, giving way to Generation X as he continues to try on the social mores of the times. Neither shoe is a very comfortable fit for Sam.

Now the criminal element has begun to taint the happy-hippy scene—it's time to go home. He cranks up his old pickup and gets out of San Francisco. He figures he did a lot of growing up in those few years while he shared a cheap apartment with three girls above a head shop near Golden Gate Park.

Steven Boergadine

IN THE JAILHOUSE, FATHER SAM IS BLUBBERING, "I DIDN'T say goodbye to Sister Marietta—my best friend. I didn't say goodbye. I ran off to San Francisco, I didn't write. I didn't thank her, Marcus. I ran."

"Yep, you ran alright. Now, don't you start cryin' like a drunk fool. We all run when we're young. And runnin' away sometimes takes us where we need to go. You didn't tell her because you was afraid she'd talk you into stayin'."

Father Sam gives Sheriff Marcus a snide look. "So I was being virtuous, is that it?"

Sheriff Marcus fires back. "I didn't say that. Were ya?"

"You and your sin-covering eye," Father Sam mutters.

CHAPTER 21

Uncle Sam Doesn't Want You

"So, you think you got all grown-up in San Francisco. All those love-ins didn't suit ya?"

"Love-ins? There was no love after Gladys. I don't know what she did to me, Marcus."

"She stole your cherry, is what she did to ya. You never got over it."

Father Sam takes offense at Sheriff Marcus's crudeness. "You think so? Does my propensity for Mabelline's cherry pie factor into your Freudian, psychoanalytical baloney?"

"Have a drink. Get to the punchline."

SAM DRIVES HIS PICKUP TO THE I-5 AND THEN POINTS it north. The timber industry is always hiring in Oregon. It's easy to get a job working in the woods or in a sawmill there. Especially in his hometown.

Sam chooses the sawmill. Entry level labor. He'll *pull on the green chain.* Green because the logs are not kiln-dried yet. Giant circular saws hew the logs into boards that drop onto slow-moving chains. Sam's on a crew that pulls those boards off the chains and stacks them on the ground—on wood pallets so the straddle carriers can pick up those stacks and move them to the kilns to be dried.

Sam wears a hard hat, oversized heavy-leather mitts, and a thick leather apron to protect himself while he man-handles eighteen-foot two-by-sixes and two-by-eights, eight hours a day. He likes the change. A working man now.

His pal, Kofoid, yells over the screeching of the saws, "Break time, homey."

Sam grabs his black metal lunchbox, and they head to the break room for fifteen minutes of smoke-em-if-you-got-em.

Sam and Kofoid sit down on a metal bench at a metal table. Sam hears the horse again. It's been showing up more often. He grimaces as the headache attack strikes.

Kofoid has seen it before. "Bummer. You okay, man?"

Sam's pained eyes say he's not okay. He opens a bottle of prescription pills.

"How 'bout the Doghouse Tavern later? Shoot some pool. Couple beers, some peppermint schnapps. Broads love schnapps, man. And they'll love you, if ya let 'em."

Sam nods. It's something to do.

Kofoid elucidates some birds-and-bees wisdom. "Schnapps tastes so sweet, chicks forget it's booze. They get shit-faced, and you get laid."

Sam isn't listening. He's chasing demons with pills and chasing pills with coffee.

Kofoid gets nosey. "Those any good?"

A FEW MORE YEARS GO BY. SAM IS STILL WORKING AT THE sawmill. One day he enters the lobby of the town's only post office and happens to see another Sam—a human sized poster of Uncle Sam, decked out in a red, white, and blue tux and top hat. *Uncle Sam Wants You,* the poster reads.

Sam drives to Portland, where he has an appointment at the US Army induction center. He stands in a line with other young men, ready to sign up. The Vietnam War is raging. Sam's a conscientious objector, so he'll ask for field-medic training.

Most of the time, Sam looks like he just left a Haight-Ashbury love-in. His hair is long, and he wears a headband. Turquoise and other precious stones hang around his neck and wrists. He left his bell-bottoms in San Francisco.

A screener approaches the recruits, flips through paper-work. "Westburn, Sam?"

Sam raises his hand.

"You have a long history of drug use, Mr. Westburn."

"Prescription drugs. Migraines, sir. I have doctor's paperwork."

"No, sir. The Army can't use you, Westburn. Sorry."

Sam leaves the induction center. He stops for a moment on the cement steps that lead down to the sidewalk because a big pain attack is coming on strong. He holds fast onto a handrail. The horse nickers, then a head pain like none before. He crumples over. A fellow reject sees he's in trouble and helps break his fall. Someone calls for an ambulance.

At a Portland hospital, lab tests and brain scans reveal a tumor. A few days later, Sam is wheeled into the OR. An anesthesiologist prepares him for a craniotomy—explor-atory brain tumor surgery. Within seconds, he is sedated to unconsciousness.

During his first day in the ICU, Sam's brain begins to sample the immediate surroundings but it's not time for his cognitive functions to restore just yet. As his brain retreats to its canopy of darkness, an inner world of bright light appears. He recognizes his Cherokee grandmother as she reaches out to him—he goes to her. She closes her arms around him and then grasps him by the shoulders and looks into his eyes. She tells him he will be happy and have enough time on earth to fulfill his spiritual calling, that he will be of service to many. But of the many, it is one person who will bring him to his full potential as an angel on earth. His calling is strong, she says. He must obey its prompting. Sam wants to know about the horse, the nickering, the headaches. She tells him the horse is there to remind him that real life has not yet begun, that the brain tumor confirms the imperfection of his temporary physical life. All physical kingdoms: animal, vegetable, mineral, human, begin and end and must be allowed their cycle, she warns him. One day, he will see the horse, a magnificent Appaloosa. Real life will follow. She kisses him on the forehead and fades from view. The inner world of light dissolves and Sam remains in recovery for another day.

Sam wakes in the ICU. He is not sure about what just transpired, but he'll keep an open mind.

Six months later, he's had enough rest and relaxation. His medication is more effective now that he's been diagnosed. He has an inoperable, slow-growing, malignant tumor. For now the symptoms are manageable with the proper drugs, but the long-term prognosis is not good. It's time to move on. He's been studying Cherokee traditions, language, history; he's been looking at numerous western belief systems and world religious doctrines. He sees no need to abandon his Catholic roots, but he wants to navigate a unique, mystical priestly path. Unorthodox, but it's his choice. He'll reach out to an old friend for guidance.

Sheriff Marcus says, "Well, that thing in your head kept you out of the war."

"Kept me out of Vietnam. Didn't keep me out of the war."

CHAPTER 22

Old Friend

"Marcus?"

"Yeah?"

"Anything left in that bottle?"

Sheriff Marcus slides it across the tabletop.

Father Sam holds it up to the light to check the level. He gives Sheriff Marcus an inquiring look.

"Empty it," says, Sheriff Marcus.

"I'm getting to the hard part, Marcus." Father Sam tips the bottle upside down and lets the last drop drain into his glass.

THE WEATHERED REDWOOD SIGN THAT READS ST. PAUL'S MINISTRY FOR HUMAN ASSISTANCE is leaning a little to one side and could use a fresh coat of paint, but some graffiti needs to be sanded off first.

Sister Marietta is in the lobby, dusting off the painting of Chief Joseph, when she hears the office phone ring. She leaves Chief Joseph tilted and goes to answer. "Sister Marietta. May I help you?" She has prayed for this phone call for many years. "Sam? Where on Earth are you?"

Sam is at a phone booth not very far away. Sister Marietta runs out near the dilapidated sign and watches for him to come driving down Gowdyville Road. When Sam's old pickup pulls in, she cries with happiness—it goes both ways.

After dinner, they stroll out to the aged wickiup. "The house that Sam built," says Sister Marietta.

Sam looks inside the wickiup, just to be looking.

"I changed the wallpaper," she tries to humor Sam. He doesn't get it, so Sister Marietta tells him of the encounter that she and Monsignor Alvarez had with *Man With Many Women*.

After some silence, they return to the mission office.

Sam inquires carefully, "What ever happened to … uh …"

After a difficult pause, Sister Marietta knows where this is going. "The Spinks family?"

Sam looks to her for more.

She knows this is going to hurt him. "Oh, dear, I wasn't sure if you knew."

He shrugs and shakes his head.

"While you were comatose, Gladys was charged with murdering her husband."

"What?"

"It was reduced to manslaughter."

"Did she do it?"

"She plea-bargained. The Feds found her inebriated, covered with his blood, sobbing near a photo-set in the basement of the Spinks home. The photo-set was a mock-up of the holy manger, if you can believe it. Dirty business. She had slashed him thoroughly." Sister Marietta stops talking. She goes to a cupboard and digs out two newspapers. She hands Sam one of them. "It didn't get national attention, but here's the local story."

At the bottom of the front page, Sam reads "The Feds raided the Spinks home. James Spinks found dead. Evidence showed child-smut activity. Paperwork traced to bootlegging business. Gladys Spinks sentenced to prison."

Sam is shaken. "What about the boy?"

"Johnny was never found."

"I'm sorry. Is Gladys in state or federal or … where is she?

"She's free now, Sam."

"Oh. That's good," he replies.

Sister Marietta hands Sam the second newspaper. Another front-page story in the local, written a few months after the previous story. Sam looks at the headline. SPINKS FAMILY MEMBER DIES BY SUICIDE IN PRISON. His face goes pale.

"Gladys couldn't bear that Johnny disappeared. I visited her. She was more beautiful than ever, Sam. Living a better life inside than outside—that's how she put it. She put on a happy face for me, Sam. But for her nine-year old son, to just vanish? She couldn't live with that."

Sam gets up and looks out a window toward the old wickiup, the distant trash barrel, the gate of the fence that was never fixed, lonely Gowdyville Road passing by. He sees Jonah is gone. His old mare is gone. The pasture is overgrown.

"Here." She hands him a Bible. "Isaiah 41:10 is helpful. Why not stay in your wickiup tonight? Alone time. You always liked that. It's a warm and beautiful night. I'll get some blankets for you."

In the wickiup, the glow of a lantern gives Sam enough light as he sits on a pile of Mexican serapes laid across his sleeping bag. Clutching Sister Marietta's rosaries, he chants, prays, meditates, reads Isaiah 41:10.

The next morning, more catching up over coffee as they both nibble on the fifth deadly sin—day-old donuts.

"The surgery didn't fix the problem. But it identified it." Sam parts his hair and shows Sister Marietta a scar. "That's where they went in. They told me it's not going away. The headaches still come. The horse? It's called an auditory hallucination. But to me, it seems to have a nameless identity, beyond the reasoning of science. But science and soul kind of co-exist, I've concluded over my short life."

Sister Marietta's eyes search his. Something is being left unsaid. "Sam?" It's hard for her to ask. "Are you …?"

After last night's revelation about the Spinks family, Sam wants to take it easy on the subject of death. "We're all terminal, Sister," he gently assures his mentor.

Her searching eyes get glassy. She grabs him in a bear hug and holds on till he starts talking.

"Remember the book I inherited?" Sam figures it's a good time to lobby for Sister Marietta's sympathy vote.

She pulls herself together, finds a tissue, and blows her nose. "From your grandmother? The book with the deerskin cover."

"Yep. I know more about my grandmother now. She was half Cherokee. Her mother married a Scottish trader. They established a trading post and helped set up a mission in the Appalachian Mountains. I feel my grandmother's presence at times. I'm told she was blessed with some kind of mystical healing power. She grew up around that mission, got married there, and lived her life in those mountains."

"It's great to see you so positive," Sister Marietta ribs him, "but you're up to something." She waits for him to make his case.

Sam knows he has a winning smile. Ladies at the Doghouse Tavern told him so during his years of pagan recess. The peppermint schnapps approach is out of the question, so he'll have to inebriate his beloved mentor with the winning smile. "I want to be ordained, and then I want to minister in the Appalachians. Grandmother left my family her house—a log house, up there. That's where I'll live someday. I don't care much about steeples and stained glass. Just want to redeem myself for as long as I've got. I want to wear the collar. I'll put in the time here to finish my duties."

"Oh, Sam, you silly goof. I'm speechless. Welcome back to the fold."

"I'll get a shovel and go firm up the sign. Maybe go to the hardware store and buy some paint and sealer and a latch for the gate. Mind if I get us a cow and a horse?"

FATHER SAM FINISHES OFF THE WHISKEY. SHERIFF Marcus is hunched over a steaming mug of coffee. Father Sam is too drunk to go on confessing. "Do you think God wanted me to go back to the mission, to the seminarian cause, my friend?"

"Yep. Believe so," answers Sheriff Marcus.

"I went back to my perfect seminarian world and blocked the sinful memories. Don't you think so?"

"What memories you talkin' about? You frolicking around with Gladys? Those memories? The hippy chicks, the Doghouse Tavern? Booze, drugs? That was just you growing up. Life ain't a perfect bridge lined with gold where we trot along till we see Saint Peter wavin' the checkered flag. It's an old weather-beaten, swingin'-in-the-wind, wood bridge, Father. Loose, rickety slats, weak cables. The bad weather testing its strength every damn day. We slip through the cracks, don't we? Life ain't never gonna be exactly what all them higher-ups in your religion tell ya it should be. They know better—and you can bet those higher-ups have slipped off that swingin' bridge more times than you. A lot of 'em just quit, too. You didn't quit."

"You're just repeating Sister Marietta, my friend."

"Maybe you need to hear it more than once. That thing inside your head causing you so damn much agony must be makin' you hardheaded along with everything else it's doin' to ya."

"I should have helped her get out of that house. And Johnny, too." Father Sam makes a woozy gesture toward the cell block. "God sent him here to punish me."

"Now, let me get this right. You're sayin' that after twenty-some-odd years God is just now getting around to punishing you?"

"There's a long line of us," responds Father Sam.

Sheriff Marcus has a little laugh. "You ain't in *that* line, Father."

"Where was my pastoral love for God's creatures, Marcus?"

"You got plenty of it now. That's what matters."

Father Sam isn't convinced. "Do I?" He puts on his coat. "Thank you, Monsignor Marcus, but I don't agree." He opens the door and stumbles onto moonlit Main Street.

Sheriff Marcus yells at Father Sam as the door shuts, "You think punishment is the best God can do for ya?"

CHAPTER 23

The Big City D.A.

Assistant District Prosecuting Attorney, Fenton Jones still has the suave, natural-tanned, bright-smiling, island-boy appearance he had in his twenties. He is now approaching his fiftieth and still hell bent to make something of himself.

DA Fenton Jones was born in the US. His parents were hard-working Jamaican immigrants who wanted to raise their son to be like them—just plain honest. They knew no other way to be. But as placental mammals sometimes do, Fenton came out of the chute backwards—just plain dishonest. He knows no other way to be.

Justice for all is irrelevant right now. It's political season. For a trigger-happy, vote-hungry assistant DA, that means hunting season—hunting for the easiest route to the public eye. Justice can wait. DA Fenton Jones needs votes.

He's pontificating from behind a microphone on a stage in an outdoor public square. Lots of room for news reporters and cameras and townspeople and supporters holding up banners, if there were any. He spouts his canned speech to the sparse crowd of right-wing evangels. "My friends. For every rapist, murderer, and sex-offender we put in prison, two are set free. Life in prison doesn't mean life in prison any more. Life in prison means a couple years of time and then open the doors and parole 'em for good behavior. Now, we've got a citizens group campaigning to abolish capital punishment here in our God-loving state. Well, my good friends, I'm here to tell you that, not only will I, if elected, keep our capital punishment system intact, but I will improve it by shutting the doors of quick paroles on these sex offenders, and I will open the doors of death row ever wider to contain them all."

An eye-for-an-eye and a high moral aim are important in these parts. DA Fenton Jones knows folks around here grew up believing that at any minute the rapture can whisk them away to paradise. So he's fixing to capture their votes before they disappear.

After the empty-town-square rally, DA Fenton Jones enters his low-rent campaign center, where loyal Miss Matilda, his secretary, awaits him and waits on him.

Miss Matilda moved south and attended a fine southern finishing school when she came of age. She grew up a stick-figured kid whose parents were aspiring actors in Hollywood. For them life consisted of play-acting in tiresome scene study and improv workshops that led to an occasional under-five appearance on an afternoon soap opera and then lying on the beach and staying stoned. So, she figured, she'd go south where she could learn some high-class behavior. Miss Matilda needed to get far away from her mama, who told her to get smart after she started filling out. Getting smart meant getting good at the low-class casting couch game. But Miss Matilda got away from the West Coast and her pot-smoking, sun-tanned parents. Now she's a southern lady, and the casting couch game is not so low-class here.

The first words Miss Matilda hears when her boss, DA Fenton Jones, bursts into the office are, "Those Bible-thumpers aren't interested in my words, Matty. I need something they can shoot off their guns about."

Miss Matilda has *I've got a surprise* written all over her face.

DA Fenton Jones reads her face. "What? Tell me you have good news from my finance director?"

Miss Matilda tells DA Fenton Jones that there's no news on the fund raising front, but—she pauses teasingly, which gets DA Fenton Jones's rapt attention.

Just then, the phone on her desk buzzes, and she answers it. "One moment please." She mutes the line. "It's your cousin Hubert calling from Jamaica. Third time today he has called. He has explosive news."

DA Fenton Jones gets interested very fast. "Explosive?"

With a let's-get-a-mint-julep-after-work wink, Miss Matilda silently, if not a little sensually, mouths the word back at him. "*Ex-plo-sive.*"

He tells her to stay on the line, stay in the mood, and take notes, then sprints into his office and shuts the door as she un-mutes the line and tells Cousin Hubert, "One moment, sir."

DA Fenton Jones picks up. "Hey, cuz, miss you, my man. How's life undercover?"

Cousin Hubert is a DEA mole. He's planted in a Jamaican gang that has recently made a guns-for-drugs trade arrangement with the Mayor of one of those hide-away mountain villages. The village is McGuffin Ridge. Cousin Hubert lays it on DA Fenton Jones. "His name is Merle Swenson. The locals know him as Mayor Swenson—he's a self-appointed mayor."

"Okay. What part of that is explosive for me, Hubie?"

"The DEA has a man on the ground—that would be me—picking up strategic intelligence. Every move that mayor makes is being logged. We're not going to act on the intelligence yet. So you've got some time to make a case."

DA Fenton Jones knows there's more, but all he's hearing right now is routine DEA analysis. "What kind of case?"

Cousin Hubert means the DEA isn't ready to make arrests or raid the place—just laying an evidentiary foundation. "Now, what I'm gonna tell you is sensitive. Don't go up there and mess up my case, bro. I know you need this. Take it and run with it, but don't mess up the DEA's work."

"I got it, Cuz." He doesn't. "Run with what?"

Cousin Hubert then offers *something those Bible-thumpers can shoot off their guns about*—the incidental discovery of the lascivious John Doe matter. It's just what DA Fenton Jones needs.

The DEA's tracking of a small-time mayor's relationship with Jamaican gun dealers and South American leftist guerilla rebels isn't igniting a game plan in his mind, but DA Fenton Jones is listening desperately. He senses something is coming.

And then Cousin Hubert finally breaks down the John Doe, Cleveland Stockton drama.

"Say what? Murdered in his sister's home?" DA Fenton Jones perks up.

"That's right—sister. The mother of his daughter. You hear what I'm saying, bro?" implores Cousin Hubert.

DA Fenton Jones is trying to wrap his brain around this story. "The mother of his daughter." This is getting good. "His sister is the mother of his daughter. Jesus, what else?"

"Stockton was an escaped con."

The game plan is igniting now. DA Fenton Jones digs for more. "Escaped? What was his crime?"

"Raping his sister."

"Damn. Who's that John Doe character that was found with him, unconscious—the shooter? Did they escape from prison together?"

"There's no report that they escaped together," says Cousin Hubert. "He's probably the boyfriend."

"Ah, her boyfriend."

"His," Cousin Hubert clarifies.

"His? Well, diggity, doggity, damn, Hubie. What else?"

Cousin Hubert informs him about *The People's Tabloid* coverage.

"But, look, bro, a photo-impact was all they got. You know, splash up some bloody photographs and that's it. They didn't have a story. The tabloid added some teasers, but no real story."

"I need to get the real story then," says DA Fenton Jones.

"The photographer's missing. But his photos were damned sick, Fenton. There's real high-count political mileage for you in this case. A real story. Not a gossip piece. Get yourself a copy of that edition of *The People's Tabloid*. Look at the photos."

DA Fenton Jones finishes his back-channel chit-chat with Cousin Hubert and buzzes Miss Matilda's desk. "Matty, can you come into my office, please?"

"I'm holding for the Tabloid, sir. I'll be right there once I've finished with them."

"Thata girl," says DA Fenton Jones. He packs up his attaché. A light knock on his door and Miss Matilda enters.

"Where is this mountain village? My jurisdiction?"

Miss Matilda has been taking notes and doing research on the fly. "McGuffin Ridge. It was annexed to Pominski County in the sixties."

"What, up there with the Indians? I need it to be in my jurisdiction. Is it or not?"

"Not," she says. "Let's see what we can do. Circuit Judge Schmidt has charge of any preliminary hearing activities deemed necessary in that region. I get on well with Judge Schmidt."

"I'm sure you do." DA Fenton Jones hasn't forgotten her let's-get-a-mint-julep-after-work wink. "Shall we go talk about our next move?"

Next moves are Miss Matilda's specialty, but for now she spouts an all-business attitude. "*The People's Tabloid* has a copy of the edition in question. They will messenger it to the office. We can subpoena the negatives if we need them in the future."

CHAPTER 24

Mayor Swenson Vs Miss Matilda

A few days later, Mayor Swenson's greatest fear has come to get him—a vote-hungry, low-ranked DA, looking to have him for lunch. The wolf at his doorstep right now is only the DA's office girl, and she's bad enough.

Pacing back and forth as far as the phone line will stretch, Mayor Swenson tries to hold up under the grilling of Miss Matilda. "Yes, ma'am. We've been waitin' on his recuperation."

Miss Matilda makes Mayor Swenson's red-headed Blue Miner seem like a clipped-winged parakeet.

She forewarns Mayor Swenson that DA Fenton Jones's constituents have caught wind of the mountain town drama. Cleveland Stockton's murder, she declares, needs to be prosecuted by her boss. She's collecting the available details. And she wants them yesterday.

Mayor Swenson informs her, "Hold on now, we know his name is John. Looks like he's in his thirties. Got no last name that we can find on him."

She is not happy to hear that. "Why is that, Mayor Swenson?"

"Well, ma'am, he is still too weak to question. We'll get more details when he comes to his senses. Right now, he is just John Doe."

What Mayor Swenson is wishing for right about then is that John won't make it out of his coma. If that damned priest hadn't have pushed Bouncer Bill around in Big Bertha's cabin, Mayor Swenson would have already made arrangements for John Doe to become *John Who?*

Now, he hopes it takes more than what Doc Willard's black bag has in it and Mabelline's chicken soup to raise up that young man from near death. Hopefully, the news will break from the jailhouse that a casket and a reservation on *Boot Hill* have been ordered for John. He doesn't know that John Doe has already been identified as John Spinks by Father Sam.

Meanwhile, Miss Matilda pushes. "What do you know about him?"

"Ma'am, that trash magazine might be the only way of knowing anything at all about Mr. John Doe."

"Where did *The People's Tabloid* get their photographs and information?"

"Investigation of that matter is underway. I have a man at the scene of the …"

"Where's the photographer? We need his deposition."

"That'd be one of our citizens by the name of Mickey Stollard, we call him Paparazzi Mickey. He took them photos and then he sold 'em, and then he lit outa here to parts unknown, money jingling in his drawers."

"Mayor Swenson, we have reports that you were the last person to see him late at night, and the next morning he was gone. *The People's Tabloid* states that this Mickey Stollard called from your private phone line the last night he was there. Where did he go?"

"Maybe he called somebody, if you say so. My phone is available to any loyal patron of my establishment here."

"Where did he go after he called the tabloid?"

"I'd say he went home to his cabin, which is near the scene of the crime."

"The scene of the crime is a run-down flop house owned by you."

"Dog-gone it, ma'am. You tryin' to pin this thing on me?"

"Mayor, if we wanted to pin this on you, we wouldn't be trying. We'd be doing." Miss Matilda hangs up.

CHAPTER 25

Fanny Oakley

The weeks roll by and soon the annual dove shoot on Mayor Swenson's property is on everyone's calendar. It's held this time every year on the same property that the House of Wonder sits on. A lot of folks refer to the House of Wonder as the *House of a Damn Shame*, but once a year they look the other way.

Mountain people and the Cherokee tribe have evolved together to make the dove shoot more than a celebrated sharpshooter showdown. It now has a homegrown, county fair spirit about it, and they've grown themselves a headliner: Fanny Stockton.

Fanny is a big draw in McGuffin Ridge, but not because she's an oddball curiosity. Locals and everybody for miles around look at Fanny as the near-and-dear, kick-ass mountain girl she is. Of course, it doesn't cross Fanny's mind that she's famous or that she's a kick-ass mountain girl. She lives completely and biologically *in-the-now*. She doesn't know who Annie Oakley was and doesn't know that she is considered her modern-day incarnation in this neck of the woods. Fanny isn't known for talking or listening, just shooting. No one knows if she can voice an opinion on any subject.

If you're the gambling type, you'd do well to bet on Fanny winning her fourth annual competition in a row. And you can bet there are some hot-shot competitors, though they've got nothing but respect for Fanny. The gun slingers around here can knock down a rabbit that's going full speed while zigging, zagging and hopping. But they can't do what that dwarfed twelve-year-old savant can do. They're going to try, anyway—in that county fair spirit.

Just across the field from where the dove shoot will be held, a colorful gazebo has been propped up to be the canvas wedding chapel where Dr. Joe Blackfox and Miss Wilma Duncan will pledge their vows to each other. It'll be a low-key, mostly traditional Cherokee wedding ceremony, not an ostentatious affair, by any means. Dr. Blackfox could afford a high-brow bash if he wanted it, but today is a day for the people to come together and be on common ground with one another. Their wedding ceremony is a welcome part of the carnival drumbeat that will pulsate till about dusk.

Dr. Blackfox and Wilma wear blue shawls as they enter the gazebo, where Father Sam and Sheriff Marcus sit amongst tribal elders, musicians, and guests. The whisper of a spirit flute circulates inside the gazebo like a sweet breeze. The heartbeat of Mother Earth satisfies the soul as it issues from a drummer's steady hand. There's a small bonfire to symbolize attributes given by the creator.

The bride and groom stand before a Cherokee minister. He asks them to present small bestowals to each other from their hand-held baskets. Dr. Blackfox and Wilma describe the feelings in their respective hearts as they present these symbolic gifts to each other.

Together, they will partake of a special beverage from a Cherokee wedding vase— a drink that Dr. Blackfox, knowing Father Sam's penchant for mixing up meaningful organic concoctions, had asked him to brew-up as a fitting libation for this very day.

As for Father Sam, ever since he spilled his guts in that confession tantrum, Sheriff Marcus can barely get him out, not even for cherry pie at Mabelline's.

Sheriff Marcus hopes attending the wedding will bring some color to Father Sam's face. That Father Sam has brought a *honeymoon tea* for the ceremony is a sign that his old buddy is re-emerging. Drinking that first cup of coffee by himself every morning is getting old for Sheriff Marcus. He risks a little jab at Father Sam's funny bone. "That raspberry tea you brought for the happy wedding couple will sure take away the happy if it tastes anything like that Cat's Claw tea you made me drink."

Father Sam takes in the humor and gives Sheriff Marcus a smile. "It's a little more than raspberry tea, Marcus. It's a fertility tea."

Sheriff Marcus dismisses the idea. "Hell, I had fertility tea running in my veins when I was their age."

"Well, I guess I did, too, didn't I?" Another little grin from Father Sam and things are looking up.

After the Cherokee songs end, the minister nods to Father Sam, who then offers a few words of friendship and blessing. He is not ministering, just speaking from his own Cherokee heart. "And now, I offer my blessing to the union of Joe Blackfox and Wilma Duncan. I humbly join the tribal elders as witnesses today. Just as Kanati and Selu came together in the ancient day to be the example of Cherokee union between man and woman, so, too, do Joe and Wilma unite as one."

Dr. Blackfox and Wilma shed their individual blue shawls as if they're shedding their old lives. The Cherokee minister then wraps one large white shawl around them both to symbolize that they are one in spirit.

A cloudless, marbled, blue sky highlights the day. Outside the gazebo, freshly scrubbed children with tummies full of sweets and hearts full of carnival energy are racing from table to table sniping walnut pound cake or apple stack cake or hoe cake or any other treat that is sweet and can be shoplifted at a full gallop. The family pooch scampering with the kids gets its share, too.

The background charm of the daytime fun and games and eating and drinking is made all the merrier by anticipation of Fanny Stockton's appearance, which is on everyone's mind.

Father Sam and Sheriff Marcus are sitting under a weeping willow, polishing off their lunch.

"It's good to see you out enjoying life again, Father. Has that horse been botherin' you much?"

"Now and then." With a lilt in his voice, he says, "Let's hope it won't drive me to drink, Marcus."

Sheriff Marcus gets up. "Ahh, you'll be alright. Well, the lovebirds have said I do, and I'm done with lunch, and you're eatin' my helping of Mabelline's cherry pie, so I guess I'll walk on over to the shootin' contest and get a good seat."

"She cut these particularly small for the picnic, didn't she?" Father Sam says.

"Yes, sir, Father, she sure did. You take care of yourself. Glad to hear that horse ain't pestering you lately."

"Come on by for coffee, Marcus. It's been a while."

Sheriff Marcus likes that idea and pats his old friend on the shoulder, then finds a trash barrel to toss his paper plate and plastic fork into and starts to walk away. But he stops, returns to Father Sam and sits down again. "I think you ought to know somethin'."

Father Sam stops eating and gives his buddy serious attention. "You think I ought to know what?"

"Bouncer Bill came by the jail to inform me that my prisoner is subject to some kind of investigative hearing by a circuit judge and bringing along a district attorney to boot. Looks like they'll decide if he's gonna be arraigned for murder or manslaughter or just get left alone, I guess."

Father Sam loses his taste for the cherry pie. It was certain things would eventually get serious regarding John's culpability in Cleveland Stockton's murder investigation, but it still hurts to hear about it the first time. "Oh my, that sounds serious. We knew the day would come. What are John's options for legal representation?"

"He oughta not be charged with a damn thing, if you ask me."

"What's that mean, Marcus? I'm heartbroken over this, but certainly John's involvement needs to be legally resolved."

"Mayor Swenson might have some knowledge about big city elbowing into our business, I don't know. I'm real sure he's the one that the DA notified, since it was Bouncer Bill that came callin' to inform me about it."

"Why would John not be charged with a crime? Who knows what went on in that room? He had a gun in his hand and a dead man beside him. John was beat up badly. Justifiable homicide? Self-defense?"

"Let me tell you something real chilling and I wish it didn't have to come up." Sheriff Marcus gets brutally frank. "Cleveland Stockton raped John Spinks. I know you didn't know that. I figured it out at the time we saw 'em laid out on that floor, knowin' the background on Stockton and seeing what I saw before I covered John up. But then Doc Willard pretty much told me it's what he determined, too, after he put the stitches in John."

Father Sam is speechless for a long moment and then he whispers almost prayerfully, "Lord, Lord, Lord, with what debauchery humans accost one another." Father Sam is dumbfounded. "How can it be proven though, in a court of law?"

"I wish I knew, Father. I wish I knew. Doc Willard can offer his deposition. Other than that, you and me, Salvo, Bounce, Mickey, if he turns up—we can tell the judge what we saw in that room after it all happened. That's about it. It's gonna be John's circumstantial evidence against the court's circumstantial evidence. There's no eyewitness. I don't like the odds too much."

From across the field, a series of rifle shots sound off.

"They're getting warmed up over there. I'll be seeing you later then." Sheriff Marcus heads toward the shooting range to watch Fanny Stockton rule the day.

CHAPTER 26

The Discovery

After five or six elimination rounds, an emcee lines up the last three sharpshooting contestants—two grown men and Fanny. "Let's have our three finalists right over here."

Sheriff Marcus sits in the six-tier bleachers. They are barely able to hold all the fans from McGuffin Ridge and beyond.

A table is set with two bronze statues and a doll about the same height as Fanny Stockton. Mabelline always fixes up the dolls with open-and-close eyes that she orders from a sewing club catalogue. Just a push of her finger on the back of their necks makes them go to sleep.

The emcee holds a mic up to his mouth and belts out the intros. "Let's hear it for 'em. Freddy Patterson, Earl Egbert and Fanny Stockton."

The crowd yells and claps as Freddy Patterson and Earl Egbert walk to the front of the crowd. Big Bertha gently prods Fanny to join her competitors. The crowd erupts for the little star as she moves forward.

"Fanny, when you gonna grow, dear? You're 'bout half the size of a minute, you know that, honey?" The emcee is a fan, too.

The three finalists step up to their marks, side by side, rifles ready.

"You boys both shootin' with 410s? I guess you have a chance. What you got, Fanny? Twenty-two caliber rimfire, looks like."

A whistle sounds from the tower that regulates the action.

"Alright. Ready, Freddy? You're first. Don't be the worst."

Freddy shows a toothy grin as both he and the audience appreciate the emcee's corny humor. He raises his 410 as five discs shoot upward and outward, then fires in succession, hitting two. The crowd cheers in a good-natured way as the emcee keeps the formalities going.

"Alright. That's two out of five for Freddy Patterson. Seen you do better, buddy. Earl, let's see what ya got."

The discs shoot upward. Earl fires, hitting two.

"And Earl got his two. Fanny, you made these boys nervous, honey."

Fanny pays no attention to the affections of the crowd or the small talk of the emcee.

The whistle sounds, and the discs burst into the sky. Stoic Fanny raises her rifle and shatters all five discs.

The emcee yells, "She did it! She damn sure did it again!" The crowd stands and applauds, cheers, and chatters.

It's been a real fine day.

Mayor Swenson gets busy collecting his money from the losers that bet against Fanny. With a fist full of cash, he calls Fanny over to the awards table. "You are just something else, darlin'. Come get your new friend now."

The emcee pipes up on his mic, "Handmade, as usual, by Mabelline Maxwell over on Main Street. Stop in at Mabelline's on your way home if your bellies aren't poppin' your buttons by now."

Fanny collects the doll. Big Bertha picks up Fanny's prize money.

Sheriff Marcus is sitting real still as the crowd departs. He's the last person sitting in the bleachers. Something is bothering him. Then—a flash of memory. He gets up and hotfoots it home.

It doesn't take long for him to get to his jailhouse. He bursts through the door as Deputy Sydney is busy washing dishes. "Go on over to Father Sam's place and bring him here now, Sydney." He tosses Deputy Sydney the keys to the Jeep. "Take the Jeep. Get goin'."

"Yes, sir, Sheriff." Deputy Sydney heads out the door.

Sheriff Marcus spreads out a tattered Spanish language magazine. It features several of Paparazzi Mickey's photos—the rejects he sold for next-to-nothing to a Mexican employee of the US publication of *The People's Tabloid*.

Sheriff Marcus has a magnifying glass in his hand. He's looking as close as he can at a single photograph featured in the Spanish magazine.

The jailhouse door opens and in come Deputy Sydney and Father Sam.

Father Sam notices Sheriff Marcus's pent up energy. "My, my, Marcus, what's so urgent?"

"I saw the shootin' match." There's a look in Sheriff Marcus's eyes that is not normally there.

"Okay. You saw the shooting match. I heard she won again. What else?"

"Oh yeah, she won, all right—and you know the prize they gave her is another one of Mabelline's dolls. That's four years. Four straight years of winnin'. And four years of winnin' adds up to four dolls."

Father Sam nods, acknowledging the obvious, and waits for Sheriff Marcus to make his point.

"That's when it hit me," adds Sheriff Marcus.

"Well, I must say, you're acting like you've been hit by something. What hit you, Marcus?"

Sheriff Marcus invites Father Sam to the table where the magazine is laid out. He taps on the open page with the magnifying glass. "This here is a Spanish language tabloid. A Mexican drifter left it in Mabelline's magazine rack. It's got some photos of the Cleveland Stockton murder scene that weren't in the US tabloid. Notice anything different?"

Father Sam feels the hyper-attentiveness of his buddy. He scowls at the grotesque photos of the murder scene in Big Bertha's cabin. The victims lying in blood. The four dolls in the background. "I didn't look at the other one, but no matter, what am I looking at here?"

Sheriff Marcus educates him. "See that picture right there? They didn't use that one in the US version. Bad lighting, background is shadowy. Looks like Mickey's focus was on the two dead bodies in front there."

"So, what's your point?"

Sheriff Marcus taps the picture with the magnifying glass. "Behind the two bloody bodies, do you see what I see?"

"I see Fanny's Dolls."

"How many?"

"Four. Four dolls."

"You sure?"

"Well, yes. One, two, three, four." Father Sam points to each shadowed image.

Deputy Sydney hangs up his dish towel and takes another peek from behind.

"Fanny won the shootin' match today. She didn't have four dolls until today."

"Well, I see four in the picture," says Father Sam.

Sheriff Marcus hands Father Sam the magnifying glass. "Take another look and use that."

Father Sam scans the images up close with the magnifying glass.

Over his shoulder, Deputy Sydney bends to see what Father Sam is seeing.

"Oh my." The words barely make it out of Father Sam's mouth.

Deputy Sydney sees what Father Sam sees. "Ohhh, lordy," he mutters.

Still trying to make sense of it, Father Sam remarks, "If she was there by chance, poor child, what she must have witnessed."

Sheriff Marcus blurts out the obvious. "She damn sure is a witness. If she was there when that photo was taken of her, then she witnessed Cleveland Stockton's entire freak show. And I tell you what else, Father, she mighta been the one that pulled the trigger."

Father Sam is shocked by Sheriff Marcus's speculation.

Sheriff Marcus sees Father Sam is about to raise doubt. "Now hold on, Father. Let me talk it through. Doc Willard said something before he left town. It's adding up now. He said that young man had been unconscious several days—comatose he said. That killin' took place the same day we found him barely breathin' in Big Bertha's cabin. Doc said the wound on his head was an old wound. Probably the reason he was comatose. Those other wounds, 'scuse me for mentioning, down behind John, were fresh wounds."

"That's a lot of speculation, Marcus."

"There's nowhere to hide in that room. Skinny little Fanny looks scared stiff in that picture. She watched that whole nightmare in some kind of shock. Stockton's clothes were layin' on the bed. His gun, too, I bet. He wouldn't take it to the shower. He had a shower curtain wrapped around him. He was soakin' wet. Fanny got his gun. Fanny don't miss. Those two shots were perfect. Two bull's eyes. She can shoot bull's eyes all day long."

"Fanny killed her own father," considers Father Sam with ninety-nine percent certainty.

Sheriff Marcus is blunt. "He wasn't no father."

Father Sam can't deny the logic of Sheriff Marcus's speculation. But they must be sure. "What can we do, Marcus?"

"We gotta find Fanny. We'll start with Salvo at the Cozy Inn. Maybe he saw somethin' fishy." He grabs the magazine, folds it up, and sticks it in his pocket and heads for the door.

Father Sam's right behind him—a hundred percent now.

Deputy Sydney views the discovery of Fanny's photo in the Mexican tabloid as real good news for their prisoner. He's taken a liking to John over time, and he's not gonna be shy about sharing the good news. He walks over to Mabelline's to grab today's special—that's a cup of coffee and a bowl of chili with cheese and onions. As he sits at the counter and tells Mabelline all about it, DA Fenton Jones's cousin, DEA Agent Hubert is hearing all about it, too, as he sits a few seats away eating a bowl of chili with cheese and onions.

CHAPTER 27

Dead End

Sheriff Marcus cranks up the Jeep, and as they take off for the Cozy Inn Cabins to chat with Manager Salvo, he says, "Can't say I ever heard her talk. Not a peep. Like they say in the ol' cowboy movies—her guns do the talkin' for her."

Father Sam speculates, "We must presume that Fanny and her mother have relocated. Mr. Salvo should know where they went."

"We'll knock on Mickey's door while we're here since he's the one who took the picture." Sheriff Marcus pulls into the Cozy Inn Cabins parking area, and they walk along the moss slickened, rotten wood walkway to the cabins.

They see Big Bertha's cabin door wide open and a cleaning crew scrubbing top to bottom inside. The cabin has been emptied. No furniture, no clothes, no dolls, no Chi-Rho hanging on the wall.

They turn around to walk to Paparazzi Mickey's door, and Manager Salvo is standing in the way. "What do you want here?" says Manager Salvo.

Father Sam politely asks, "May we inquire where Bertha Stockton and her daughter Fanny have moved?"

"Don't know what to tell ya exactly. I hear Fanny had to do some shootin' somewhere. That's all I know."

"That's news to us. Thank ya for that," says Sheriff Marcus as he jumps into the conversation. He tries to keep from being confrontational. "Yep, she getting to be a real guest of honor around the country. Fairs, stock car races and whatnot. Do you know which town they took off to?"

"No idea, Sheriff. They don't report to me. Just gone shootin' is all I heard," replies sassy Manager Salvo.

"Did they move to another cabin, sir?" Father Sam's natural courtesy keeps Manager Salvo's attitude light.

"No, Father, they got their belongings stored at the House of Wonder. My guess is that they'll keep rooms over there for the time being. It's up to the Mayor."

Sheriff Marcus cuts in, "And Mickey, what about him. He around anywhere you know of?"

"Nope. He owes rent, though. Better show up soon or his daddy'll have to come pick up his belongings."

"If we see him, we'll be sure to remind him for you," ingratiates Father Sam.

"Now if you'll excuse me, gentlemen." Manager Salvo nods and proceeds to Big Bertha's cabin to check the workers.

Sheriff Marcus calls after Manager Salvo. "Whatcha know about Fanny being inside of Bertha's cabin the mornin' of the killin'?"

That is one question too many. Manager Salvo stops and turns around. "Yeah, Sheriff, she was in there playin' house with her damn dolls the whole time. What the hell kinda question is that?" He walks away.

Sheriff Marcus and Father Sam's charm-offensive abruptly fails and they climb into Sheriff Marcus's Jeep.

"I thought I was bein' nice about it," ventures Sheriff Marcus.

"You did fine. Now we know Bertha took Fanny off to a shooting engagement."

"But where?" Sheriff Marcus plots the next move. "What do you say we go to the House of Wonder and nose around? Maybe we can get an idea of the wheres and whens from the bartender."

Father Sam surmises they'll need to use a careful approach to interviewing Fanny. "When we find her, I propose we ask only yes and no questions."

"Yep, Father, you ask 'em, and if she's able to understand what you're askin' her, she can nod her head one way or the other. I'll witness when she means yes, or when she means no."

Father Sam replies, "Write down everything—questions, answers, any form of response she gives."

Sheriff Marcus pulls up at the House of Wonder. "You're comin' in with me, aren't ya?"

"I, uh … Yes, of course," answers Father Sam.

"You ever been in this place, Father?"

Father Sam gives him a look.

"Some souls need savin' around here, I'll tell you what." They enter the busy atmosphere. Sheriff Marcus points to an empty card table. "That's Bertha's table over there. More than likely she'd be dealin' on the night shift though." He leads the way to Barkeep Bobo. "The man behind the voice. How are ya, Bobo?"

Barkeep Bobo responds, "What can I do ya for, boys?"

Sheriff Marcus says, "Just lookin' for Big Bertha and that little darlin' of hers. Gotta couple questions for little Fanny."

Barkeep Bobo isn't much help. "Good luck with that, Sheriff. Big's shift starts later, if she gets back today."

Sheriff Marcus plays dumb. "Gets back?"

"Yep. Fanny's shootin' in some to-do over at Johnson's Creek," answers Barkeep Bobo.

"Johnson's Creek. That's only about an hour west from here. About what time would later be?"

"Eight or so. Like I said, if she rolls in on time."

Sheriff Marcus tips his hat. "Alright then. Thank ya kindly, Bobo, we'll check back a little later."

CHAPTER 28

The Antagonist of
The Antagonist

B ouncer Bill's Land Rover is parked and idling in a clearing near an overgrowth of blackberries at the junction of Biggs Highway and Blue Gopher Road, before the steep, rough climb to McGuffin Ridge. Mayor Swenson climbs out of the Land Rover and finds a place behind the blackberries to stay out of sight.

Soon, a stretch limousine slows down as Circuit Court Judge Schmidt's driver peers out the windshield, searching for the Land Rover.

Bouncer Bill sees the limo and pulls out to the road where its driver can see him.

No limo could navigate the old road from that junction all the way to McGuffin Ridge. Especially a stretch. The limo stops. The driver gets out and opens the rear door for Judge Schmidt and his new legal apprentice—none other than Miss Matilda.

Judge Schmidt is a stately gentleman of sixty-two. His regular trips to the racquet club keep him trim enough for a man of his age.

As the limo turns around and drives away, Miss Matilda fusses over Judge Schmidt's shirt buttons till they are properly perpendicular, cinches up his tie, and smooths his collar. Bouncer Bill rolls up close to them. She takes the opportunity to look at his side window to check herself in its reflection.

After Miss Matilda finishes primping, she and Judge Schmidt board the Land Rover. Miss Matilda slides close to Judge Schmidt and opens a notepad. She tells him she knows shorthand if he needs to think out loud.

He responds by resting a hand on her knee and settling in for the bumpy ride through the toolies. "What I'm thinking shouldn't be thinked out loud."

Miss Matilda gets his corny playboy-play-on-words and gives him a flirty nudge.

Mayor Swenson watches through low-hanging branches as Bouncer Bill heads up Blue Gopher Road with his esteemed passengers aboard. He steps out from his hiding place when a driver pulls up in a four-wheel-drive SUV. DA Fenton Jones is sitting in the back seat. He pushes the door open, and Mayor Swenson gets in beside him.

DA Fenton Jones pushes a button to open the glass partition that separates the back and front seating compartments and gives an order to the driver. "Let the judge get a healthy lead and drive slow."

Before the glass partition seals shut, Mayor Swenson starts brownnosing. "May I say, Mr. Jones, it is a pleasure to meet you."

DA Fenton Jones changes Mayor Swenson's mind about that. "Your father died in 1960. You were disbarred that same year. You inherited land now known as McGuffin Ridge. And you're running guns. So, who's your buyer, Mayor? Javier?"

This is starting off badly for Mayor Swenson. He's gonna have to do some fancy tap dancing. "I'm doin' what?" That isn't very fancy, but hopefully there's a deal to be made. He's feeling guilty as charged already.

DA Fenton Jones is just getting started. "That new model Kalashnikov is a beauty."

"Jesus, man! You need a cup of coffee?" His defenses completely down now, that is the best Mayor Swenson could come up with.

"My cousin Hubert is undercover with the Jamaicans that you're buying from. But that's between Cuz and I."

Mayor Swenson has no dance moves left. His face goes cold.

DA Fenton Jones presses on, "Now about this little murder case you have on your hands. Your legal position will be that it was self defense. A notorious escaped felon sodomized your client."

Trying to maintain some dignity, Mayor Swenson responds, "That sounds about right."

"Not attacked, accosted, taken-advantage-of, or any other cleaned-up way of putting it. Sodomized. Clear?"

Mayor Swenson gets blunt. "You mean raped, I guess, huh?"

DA Fenton Jones responds, "I sense that we're a team already. This case will go to trial in my city, Mayor, and quite frankly, I want my audience fascinated, so the flashier the language, the better the television coverage."

How am I gonna participate in this legal proceeding? Like you pointed out, Mr. Jones, I ain't been licensed for a good long time now. You gonna do something about that?

"I'll take care of the paperwork that will quietly disqualify you for practicing without a license and later I'll see that we lose your file. And life will go on up here. Sound good?"

Mayor Swenson grovels for a fringe benefit. "How much does that cousin of yours know?" Mayor Swenson assumes he's not going to get an answer but takes a chance and pushes hard. "You say he's working with the DEA? Can they hold off on raiding me till I shuffle my business a little bit, Mr. Jones?"

"I'll see what I can do." A subtle wrinkle in his brow shows. "By the way, who's Fanny and what's this about her photo in a Mexican tabloid?"

It's the first Mayor Swenson has heard of a photo of Fanny in a Mexican tabloid. Now he knows Paparazzi Mickey was holding back, after all. DA Fenton Jones clues him in on what Cuz overheard when Deputy Sydney was jabbering at Mabelline's counter.

Mayor Swenson is stunned and knows he has to move fast.

CHAPTER 29

Saturday Night Meatloaf and Coffee

Mabelline's backroom would normally get set up today for tomorrow morning's bingo parties or the Past 45 Club's bazaar. Right about now, there'd be community folks stacking tables with homemade afghans, rugs, potholders and wood-turned-ashtrays that grandpa carved with his lathe—things folks have an everyday need for.

But the Saturday work squad is setting up for a different occasion. A fancy, formal occasion that will kick-off first thing in the morning.

DA Fenton Jones wants the John Spinks legal proceeding to be vacated from this backwoods whistle stop ASAP. When the day is done, there'll be a murder trial ramping up towards a big city showcase that'll hand John Spinks a one-way ticket to *guilty-as-charged* and the electric chair.

Mayor Swenson takes a break and comes out of the back room. He brings a coffee he's been nursing and his CB just as Father Sam enters through the front door.

Mayor Swenson slides on to a stool. "We'll sit at the counter, Mabelline." He gestures to Father Sam. "The counter good with you, Father?"

Mabelline pours Father Sam a coffee and then offers refills to other customers as he sits down. "Yes, thank you." He's too much in pain to hide his need. He pulls a bottle of prescription pills out and shakes a couple onto his hand, tosses them into his mouth and drinks from the coffee cup.

"What's ailing ya, Father?"

"What's ailing me? Injustice, Mayor."

"Injustice, huh? Well now, more than likely it'll take more than a couple pills to cure that, don't ya know? I guess you're here to talk about the Cleveland Stockton killin'. You go ahead and get it off your chest, then."

While answering Father Sam's questions about the legitimacy of the upcoming John Spinks hearing, Mayor Swenson fishes for information about the previously-unknown photo of Fanny. By now, their coffee cups are nearly empty, and Father Sam hasn't brought up the subject.

"I'm not a legal scholar, Mayor, but I see a strong likelihood that John Spinks was a victim in all this."

"Don't you worry about my defending the rights of John Spinks. It looked like self-defense to me. I'm lookin' to go toe-to-toe with that big-shot DA who's up here trying to make a name for himself."

"I'm not talking self-defense, Mayor."

"Well, what are you talkin' then?"

Father Sam proceeds to make his case. "I'm suggesting that there may have been a witness. In fact, that witness may have been the shooter." He lays out the Mexican tabloid and offers the magnifying glass to Mayor Swenson to help make his case. "I believe this photograph could help provide reasonable doubt. I don't believe John Spinks is your shooter. Take a good look at the dolls in that photo."

At last, Mayor Swenson will be privy to the suddenly

infamous photo that DA Fenton Jones alluded to. He holds the magnifying glass and bends his head down to examine. "Well, I'll be a son of a gun. This here photo by our Mickey?"

"Yes, sir," answers Father Sam.

Mayor Swenson blurts out, "Well, I'd grab him by his ass and haul him in front of the judge in a jiffy, but he got outta Dodge some time ago. He's got a no-account family living somewhere out in the woods. You might find him out there."

There's a table of four in the corner that, by no coincidence, are Paparazzi Mickey's kin. That table of four hear loudmouth Mayor Swenson say Paparazzi Mickey has a no-account family.

"Mickey is not my primary aim here—the subject of his photography is." Father Sam pecks the laid-out photo of Fanny with his index finger. "Quite possibly, Fanny was the shooter. Whoever shot out both eyes of Cleveland Stockton was not comatose. We have reason to believe John Spinks had been unconscious several days prior to the day of the murder … and on the day of the murder."

"So your theory is that Fanny did this. Uh-huh. Look here, preacher, shootin' targets is one thing, shootin' people is another. That looks like Fanny and her dolls, alright. But that's John Spinks layin' there, gun right near his hand, naked as a centerfold. How do ya work that out?"

Father Sam says, "What do you say, we get Fanny's side of it?"

"Fanny's side of it? That'll take somebody some doin'. I've known that baby since she came into this world. Fanny is as dumb as a billy goat."

Mayor Swenson places the magnifying glass in front of Father Sam, leans back, and takes a big puff on his cigar. He signals for Mabelline to refill their coffee cups. "Maybe you and the good Lord can get somethin' out of Fanny. You got my blessings."

"The good Lord and I will give it our best. I understand she's travelled to Johnson's Creek with her mother."

"Her shootin' reputation is gettin' widespread. Fanny Oakley, what a girl. We grow 'em good up here, don't we?"

Mabelline refills their coffee. Mayor Swenson looks up at Mabelline. He points at the chalk board which lists daily specials. "Honey, I'd take one of those Saturday night specials. How 'bout you, preacher, you like meatloaf?"

As Father Sam's eyes divert to the chalkboard, Mayor Swenson *accidentally* bumps his fresh poured cup of coffee. It soaks the Mexican tabloid photo. "Watch it! Look out now, Father, that's hot coffee! Mabelline, honey, gimme a towel here!"

Father Sam desperately dabs the tabloid photo with his sleeve.

"Will ya look at that? Dammit, anyway, Father! I sure am sorry. Doggone it, I hope you got backup copies of that."

Father Sam doesn't respond to Mayor Swenson's last remark. He's still trying to save the original. He finally gives up and leans back in his chair, ruminating on what's left of his options and massaging his temples, feeling a pain coming.

Mayor Swenson leaves him to his ruminating for a moment. Then he repeats his inquiry, "I, uh, I hope you got a backup copy of the photo, Father."

Father Sam is damned near catatonic right now. "No, I don't."

Feeling the weight off his shoulders, Mayor Swenson calls out to Mabelline. "Honey, bring us each the full-course meat loaf special."

Trying to snap out of it, Father Sam asks, "When do they return?"

"Fanny and her mama? Maybe tomorrow afternoon, maybe next week. Hell, I don't know. Go on over to Johnson's Creek and catch her act. You got my blessing. Go talk to her."

Father Sam is having a hard time *loving thy neighbor* right now. He rolls up what's left of the tabloid and sticks it into his left jacket pocket, gets out of his chair, and walks away, not mindful that he doesn't excuse himself. His hand is on the door, about to push it open, when the nickering of the horse startles him. He jerks his head to the right to see if the horse is standing in the middle of Mabelline's Café. Suddenly embarrassed at his loss of control, he pushes the door open and trudges out, no longer in possession of the photo-evidence and barely in possession of his physiological, not to mention, his ecclesiastical, equilibrium.

The horse and the headache show up like Bonnie and Clyde and try to rob him of the will to go on. He has enough wits about himself that he is able to stay upright all the way to his house. He climbs onto the porch, gets through the front door, and collapses.

CHAPTER 30

Tracking The Mayor

That soaked-up tabloid hanging out of Father Sam's left jacket pocket was easy picking for one of Paparazzi Mickey's brothers sitting near the door. At the counter, Mayor Swenson wolfs down his plate of meatloaf, potatoes and gravy. His coffee's all gone, so he picks up Father Sam's full cup. He leans back, guzzles it down and does some thinking. *It'd be a damn shame if those two clowns catch up with Fanny and get a half-ass deposition out of her. They be makin' my life miserable tomorrow, no doubt about that.* He spends a thoughtful moment on that subject, checks his watch, then picks up his CB. "Bouncer Bill, Bouncer Bill. You out there yet?"

Bouncer Bill responds, *"Yes, sir. All set up."*

"I'm on my way. Finishin' up my supper."

He soaks up the last of the gravy from his plate with a dinner roll and shoves it in his mouth. He gets up and ducks his head inside the back room and barks at the set-up crew. "Hey y'all, I want all those tables laid out like I diagrammed 'em. Bring over some black boards, white tablecloths, dust off the silver and crystal—y'all know what I'm talkin' about, and get everything else spit-shined real good before you leave tonight. Important folks'll be in here early tomorrow morning."

The DEA isn't the only suspicious party taking a look at Mayor Swenson's shenanigans. They may be looking at his trade deals between the Jamaicans and South Americans, but the family of Paparazzi Mickey has a more personal reason for tailing him.

Mickey's pa and his other three sons only want to know about Mayor Swenson's connection to the disappearance of Paparazzi Mickey, the youngest and most reckless of their brood. The four men divert their attention back to their half-eaten Saturday night specials and start talking about the weather as Mayor Swenson passes by their table. They haven't rubbed elbows with Mayor Swenson in a way that would make them recognizable to him.

Back when word got to Mickey's pa that Mayor Swenson had made disparaging references to the family, it gave notice to him that Mayor Swenson was not an honorable character. He knew of the close relationship of his young son with Mayor Swenson but had decided a long time ago to not get in the way of his boy's photography ambitions.

Now, with their own ears, Mickey's pa and brothers have heard their family honor disparaged again. That is enough to embolden Mickey's Pa to pay close attention to what Mayor Swenson is up to. It's been too long now since Mickey's pa has seen his boy come home. He aims to clear his fatherly mindset one way or the other as to what Mayor Swenson's connection is to his son's disappearance.

Mickey's pa owns a wide swath of mountain land outside of McGuffin Ridge, which grows that valuable root known as American ginseng. He's cultivated a strong business agreement with Asian brokers who export it for him. That business, along with the trapping and hunting and some logging on his land, keeps his extended family and some of the local Cherokees earning a good living pretty much all year around.

There's a fair amount of family pride sitting around that table in the corner. Paparazzi Mickey might be the black sheep of the family, but there is no shortage of familial love for him.

Mickey's family takes a close look at the soaked Mexican tabloid to figure out why Mayor Swenson intentionally ruined it. There's nothing left to see on the soaked page.

Mickey's pa never heard a word from his son about photographs of that murder over at the Cozy Inn Cabins. But he knows Mayor Swenson has dirty doings there and in plenty of other places. He also knows his boy lived in one of the cabins where that crime was committed. Hearing that heated conversation between Father Sam and Mayor Swenson about his son's photography gives Mickey's pa plenty more incentive to keep tracking Mayor Swenson.

CHAPTER 31

Real Damn Fishy

Still licking gravy from his fingers, Mayor Swenson exits Mabelline's Café and heads east of town where, slivered in a cleared-out area of forestry, lies a hard-grass airstrip. A camouflaged warehouse conceals equipment used for Mayor Swenson's brokering operation—shipping and receiving guns and drugs.

As Mickey's pa and his boys followed Mayor Swenson from Mabelline's Café eastward out of town, he contacts his Cherokee brothers by CB. They know the lay of the land and tell him about that airstrip. They know because members of the tribe were hired to clear trees to accommodate the airstrip. There's nothing else out there except scenery. That leads Mickey's pa to figure the airstrip is Mayor Swenson's destination. He knows his way around the backroads, so he detours from the main road to avoid coming up behind Mayor Swenson and heads for the airstrip.

Bouncer Bill arrives early to set up the control panel that attaches to underground cables that lead to the runway lights. He pushes a throttle on the panel, which cranks up the generator and brings up the lights. A nighttime landing on an unlit airstrip surrounded by wilderness would be nearly impossible.

By the time Mayor Swenson arrives at the airstrip, Mickey's pa, his three sons, a couple more family members, and his Cherokee brothers are united and find a vantage-point hidden in the dense edge of the forest. Mickey's pa peers through a scope mounted on his .30-30. He watches a cargo plane land easily and come to a stop like it's landed here a million times. Señor Javier and two armed guerrillas climb out as the pilot shuts down the engines.

The guerrillas unload bundles of cocaine through the cargo door as Mayor Swenson admires the haul.

Bouncer Bill drives a forklift carrying a pallet from the opened warehouse door. On it are two small crates of Kalashnikov shorties—modified AK-47 assault rifles.

Señor Javier opens a crate, picks out one of the weapons and tests it's adjustability.

Mayor Swenson extols the collapsible stock. "Fold it up and take it anywhere. Nobody's got these but me, Javier."

"And now me, Señor."

"Yep, you're the man, my friend. Say, Javier, I got another first look for ya. C'mon with me, I'm gonna show you a little somethin' that'll make you glad you was born."

Mayor Swenson and Señor Javier board a four-wheeler and drive away. Bouncer Bill and the guerrillas stay with the guns and drugs.

Mickey's pa turns to his entourage. "He's breaking a shitload of serious laws, ain't he? I believe my boy got in a little too deep with that fat rat. I feel he did Mickey some harm. Y'all keep an eye out. This evening's activities ain't over. I'm gonna tail those two, see if I can learn something. We gonna find Mickey if we keep at it."

A sudden cloudburst showers down as Mickey's pa follows them to the House of Wonder where they park the four-wheeler. Mayor Swenson and Señor Javier don't enter the front door. Instead, Mayor Swenson pulls out a big umbrella to huddle under as they trot along a muddy pathway that leads to the back where the hatchery is located.

Mickey's pa disappears into the unlit perimeter of the property and follows close enough to keep an eye on them through the scope of his .30-30.

It'd be a surprise to most anyone to know that Big Bertha is the caretaker of the hatchery and a darn good breeder of gamecocks. She knows all about selecting young roosters that have naturally bad attitudes—a bad attitude is a virtue amongst roosters. Growing them into killer roosters as hostile as Blackjack takes some time and skill.

Big Bertha is also a self-taught, hands-on scholar on the subject of drugs—which ones to inject into the young roosters-in-training to make them bleed less during fights; which ones to make their muscles resilient; which ones to boost their homicidal temperaments. No restrictions against PED's in this sport.

Earlier that day, Big Bertha and Fanny arrived from Johnson's Creek. They didn't know it was going to be their last day in McGuffin Ridge. Mayor Swenson had ordered Bertha to tend to her duties in the hatchery and keep Fanny with her. He told her to be prepared to show off the prize babies if they hatched.

Big Bertha is sharpening spurs that will fit snugly onto the nubs on the back of the roosters' legs when Mayor Swenson walks in with Señor Javier. Putting on a grand manner he says, "Big, you go ahead and shine a light on the new family to-be for my amigo here to appreciate."

Big Bertha does as she's told and points a flashlight beam at a nest of eggs.

Mayor Swenson points. "That one there. See that?"

"Si," answers Señor Javier.

"Those veins running inside that egg there? Swellin' up like that?"

"Si, señor."

"It's 'bout done incubatin.' Gonna hatch any day. All them chickies are the bloodline of—guess who?"

Señor Javier's hopes are up. "Blackjack, Señor?

Mayor Swenson grins like an encyclopedia salesman.

"How much?" asks Señor Havier.

"They're yours. I won't take a red cent, but I need a little favor real bad."

"I'm listening, Señor Mayor."

"This lady right here raised Blackjack herself. You know Big Bertha from the cockfights. How can ya miss her? Real honest gal holds everybody's money like she's the dog-gone escrow itself. Well, she nurtured and fed Blackjack just the right amount of steroids and food from when he was peepin' like a mouse right up to when he … well, you know."

Yes, Señor Javier knows. He recalls how his prize Yellow Leg Hatch was annihilated by Blackjack.

"Well, Javier, Big Bertha and her sharpshootin' daughter, Fanny Oakley, are both part of the deal. I want you to fly them on out of here when you head south. I expect you'll give Blackjack's babies a good home and the ladies, too. How's that set with ya?" He hasn't checked with Big Bertha as to how it set with her.

"They will love my country, Mayor."

"One thing—y'all gotta go tonight, rain or not." He stoops down to look outside through a window. "And will you look at that, Javier, the rain stopped. Mother nature's bein' good to us."

Señor Javier's no fool. He senses desperation is driving Mayor Swenson. So, he holds back to make like he is considering the potential danger. "But for how long will the skies welcome us, Señor?"

Mayor Swenson sweetens the deal. "Did I forget to mention?"

Señor Javier's got him now. He hopes what Mayor Swenson *forgot to mention* is …

"Blackjack. You son of a pistolero, I know what you're doin'. But alright, Javier, Blackjack will be part of the damn deal, too. You happy now, amigo?"

Señor Javier knows his pilot is first class. Rain, thunder, lightning, federales, none of that is a problem for his man in the cockpit.

Mayor Swenson anticipated making this deal, so he's already had some men stack the belongings of Big Bertha and Fanny on a pickup truck with bed rails, including Fanny's dolls. When he orders Big Bertha to get into the truck, she hustles up a few personal items laying around her work area, gives her protégé, Maria, a hug and an adiós, grabs Fanny's hand and does as she's told.

After Maria sees off Big Bertha and Fanny and returns to her duties in the hatchery, she sees Big Bertha forgot her leather Chi-Rho. The loaded pickup is creeping very slowly over the uneven terrain. Maria plucks the Chi-Rho from the nail and sloshes along the muddy tracks of the pickup till she catches up and manages to give it a desperate toss onto the top of the pickup's load.

One look at that overloaded pickup tells Mickey's pa he's on to something. But will it lead to his boy? He's not interested in meddling with Mayor Swenson's private business. He's interested in Mickey coming home. Seeing something tossed onto the pickup by the Mexican lady and then watching it fly off the top of the cardboard box and land in the freshly stirred up mud doesn't interest him either. He heads back to the forest.

After Mickey's pa gets back, he and his entourage watch from their hiding place as the pickup arrives, followed by Mayor Swenson's four-wheeler. The guerrillas unload the pickup and transfer Big Bertha and Fanny's belongings to Señor Javier's cargo plane.

As Mayor Swenson walks the ladies toward the aircraft, Fanny spots her doll pals and runs to rescue them. She grabs them from one of the Latin gunmen. He backs away and lets the child be a child. Just then, the airplane engines start up, scaring Fanny. She bolts, screaming, her thin arms wrapped around the dolls.

One of the guerrillas catches her and tries to force her on board. Fanny won't have it. Her screaming gets louder.

"Hold on," yells Mayor Swenson. He reaches into the aircraft's cargo door and pulls out one of the AK-47 shorties. Fanny sees the weapon and instantly zooms in on it, but won't let go of her dolls. "That's all right, she can have the dolls and the gun," yells Mayor Swenson over the engine noise. "Make damn sure it ain't loaded." He tussles Fanny's hair, "God bless ya, darlin'" A calm comes over Fanny. Big Bertha guides her into the aircraft cabin. Mayor Swenson winks at Señor Havier.

At the edge of the forest line, Mickey's pa and the entourage move out in silence. "Real fishy," he mutters. "Real damn fishy."

CHAPTER 32

Firewater and
Children's Class

Waking up on a Sunday morning is normally a delight for Sheriff Marcus. Filling his thermos and moseying over to Father Sam's to watch him set up for his English class, shootin' the bull, giving Molly a good morning scratch behind her ears and seeing the glowing faces of those Cherokee young ones when they race into the back yard—that's the norm on Sunday mornings.

This morning is a different kind of Sunday morning—not the norm. He thinks back to last night when he dropped by the House of Wonder to see if Big Bertha and Fanny had showed. It was the usual busy evening with mountain boys and ladies gambling and horsing around on the dance floor … and Big Bertha's table empty again.

Sheriff Marcus fills his thermos with hot coffee and heads for Father Sam's back porch. During the walk over, he starts putting together an afternoon strategy. *It's the last day to find Fanny, even if it means fillin' up the gas tank and driving the old Jeep to Johnson's Creek.*

In Father Sam's backyard, the red and blue children's benches are lined up in fine order in front of the chalkboard.

Molly is dozing in her sunny spot near the wickiup. One eye opens periodically to check the corner of the log house where the kids appear when they come running to play with her. She knows the signs. When the red and blue benches and the chalk board go up, her little buddies will soon storm into the backyard.

There's a noise. Molly perks up and gives her attention to that corner. Sheriff Marcus carrying his thermos comes round the bend. Molly goes back to dozing. Sheriff Marcus calls out, "Father?"

The screen door squeaks and out comes Father Sam with his empty cup in hand. He is a mess, and his face hasn't changed much since he collapsed on his floor last night. They sit down on the wood stairs, and Sheriff Marcus pours.

Sheriff Marcus has seen that face before. "What'd you do, sleep in your clothes?"

"Yep."

"That old horse been keepin' you awake?" Sheriff Marcus says.

"I started seeing the damn thing last night. Hallucinations."

"Well, it got ya to cussin' on a Sunday morning. That's a good sign. What's it look like?"

"Appaloosa." Father Sam polishes off his coffee. "Something to do with my Cherokee grandma."

"That's too much symbolizin' for me. Let me refill that for ya."

"Swenson sabotaged me at Mabelline's." Father Sam holds out his cup

Sheriff Marcus pours and waits for the rest of the bad news.

Father Sam gives it to him. "He spilled a full cup of hot coffee on the tabloid photo. Ruined it accidentally on purpose."

Sheriff Marcus says, "Damn. Ya got me Sunday morning cussin' now. Gotta wonder what's up. We got to find Fanny and her mama today. That fancy legal proceeding will be startin' up first thing tomorrow morning."

Father Sam agrees. "I know." He swigs down the second cup fast. "Watch for the kids and Dr. Blackfox, will you, Marcus? I need to wash my face and straighten myself up." He stands and before he can move to the back door, a headache hits him, and the Appaloosa raises hell with his brain. "Ohhhh, God." He braces himself against the wobbly-legged table.

"Splash some cold water on your face," yells Sheriff Marcus.

Father Sam pulls open his screen door and lurches inside. In his kitchen, he reaches into a cupboard for a bottle and pours a straight shot into a small glass. He'll need more than a splash of cold water to get through the day.

Outside, Molly gives a muffled whoof, jumps to her feet, and here comes the kids. Dr. Blackfox comes around the corner behind them.

The children play as Dr. Blackfox accepts Sheriff Marcus's offer of a cup of coffee. "Let me go get you a mug?" Sheriff Marcus lifts himself up part way when Dr. Blackfox stops him by pointing to the screw-on thermos top.

"That'll do fine. Half-a-cup." says Dr. Blackfox.

Sheriff Marcus sets himself back down and pours coffee into the thermos top and hands it to Dr. Blackfox.

As they sit watching the little ones play with Molly, Dr. Blackfox informs Sheriff Marcus that he was notified by the Office of Indian Affairs that a young tribesman has discovered some human remains and scraps of clothing while setting traps in the wilderness. A part of the forest not on the reservation. "Your jurisdiction, if I'm not mistaken," he says to Sheriff Marcus.

Sheriff Marcus has been around mountain life long enough to know about the brainless villainy that can lead to such an inglorious end—a shallow grave in the woods. It might be as cuckoo as a birdbrain playboy that couldn't outrun the shotgunner at his shotgun wedding, or a moonshiner who got caught pouring bull's urine in his rival's distillery.

Dr. Blackfox adds, "They asked me to bring the young Cherokee to you, Sheriff. He can tell you more. I'll translate for him."

The screen door squeaks, and Father Sam walks out. A stride and a stumble and his knees buckle. He gets to the steps and starts to sit down. He doesn't make it and keels forward. Dr. Blackfox breaks his fall and holds him steady on his feet.

"Thank you, Joe, thank you."

Dr. Blackfox looks into Father Sam's eyes and smells the corn whiskey on his breath. Father Sam's pained eyes shows he's not hiding it. "I'm sorry."

Dr. Blackfox gives him a moral boost. "My friend. Don't worry about it."

Father Sam turns to Sheriff Marcus, who is holding out a fresh cup of hot coffee. He takes it and walks to the kids. "Okay, children, time to sit down. Let's learn some new words."

Sheriff Marcus and Dr. Blackfox sit down on the porch steps. It looks like class is going to proceed just fine.

CHAPTER 33

A Useless Clue

After the kids and moms leave the Sunday morning school session, Sheriff Marcus and a fading Father Sam head for the House of Wonder. When Sheriff Marcus pulls his Jeep in and parks, Father Sam gets out as fast as his weary legs will let him.

"Sorry, Marcus, I drank too much coffee and uh ... I'll be back in a minute."

Father Sam heads to the back of the House of Wonder to find a clump of bushes to get behind to relieve himself. He still isn't walking a straight line.

Sheriff Marcus leans back against the front-end of his Jeep and absorbs some engine heat for his osteoarthritic backbone. He knows he ought to be cuddled up to the grille of his old Franklin stove instead of the grille of his old, beat-up Jeep, but he's got a fractured priest on his hands, and if that priest can go on this hunt, and be by his side, he ain't gonna let him down.

After about five minutes of waiting, Father Sam yells from the back of the House of Wonder, "Marcus, Marcus, come here." He is half-yelling and half-whispering.

Sheriff Marcus figures Father Sam got disorientated and heads in the direction of his wilting voice.

"Look." Father Sam is standing, huffing and puffing in

the middle of a stretch of wet dirt and old grass. He's holding a small square of leather—the Chi-Rho Maria tried to pitch onto the top of the truck load. "I got a little disoriented. But look. I found it over here." He leads Sheriff Marcus to a muddier area.

"What is it?" Sheriff Marcus asks.

"I guess Bertha Stockton was a Catholic," Father Sam answers.

Sheriff Marcus waits for the punchline. He doesn't get one.

Father Sam has just stumbled upon a real clue. "This is a symbol of …" It's hard for Father Sam to be excited and get through a full sentence at the same time without stopping to draw new breath. "… of Christ, Marcus. To Catholics, mainly."

"What's her being a Catholic got to do with anything?" Sheriff Marcus asks. He had seen the blood stains on the wall on the day of the murder, but the leather wall hanging next to the blood stains didn't get his attention.

Father Sam gathers himself. "It was hanging … on a nail in the cabin." He punctuates. "Her cabin."

"Hmm. You don't say. What the hell is it doing here in the mud?"

The leather is wet and dirty on the side that was in contact with the mud—the top side is dry and clean.

Just then, Maria, now newly in charge of the hatchery, comes out to greet them. Mayor Swenson had instructed her to make no comments about Big Bertha to anyone—strict no-no.

Big Bertha had informed Mayor Swenson that he shouldn't move the eggs around at this stage of the incubation. Lack of temperature and humidity control would destroy them. So, Big Bertha told him, they need to be kept safe right here at the hatchery.

When Big Bertha was shanghaied to South America, Maria was put in charge of the incubation-watch. She'll prepare Blackjack and the chicks for safe travel once they come into the world.

Father Sam looks Maria in the eyes and speaks Spanish. He asks about Big Bertha and Fanny's whereabouts.

Maria respects the priestly collar—fears it even. But she humbly remains unresponsive.

Father Sam shows her the leather Chi-Rho and asks where it came from. Maria stares uncomfortably at it. Still mum. Father Sam's hand is shaking uncontrollably as he pushes the question. She knows that's a sure sign the Holy Spirit is animating him. What to do, she worries. A priest divined by the Holy Spirit stands before her, expects the truth. Maria is torn.

He asks, "Who does the leather wall hanging belong to?"

She knows God instructs her to dare not tell a lie. But she knows Mayor Swenson instructs her to dare not tell the truth. What's more important right this minute: going to heaven or feeding her kids?

Father Sam's face frowns before Maria.

She fears he is possessed by St Dionysius—the truth saint. This means Father Sam is for sure a human lie detector.

Then he fine-tunes the inquisition. "Does this Chi-Rho belong to Big Bertha?"

Maria tries to obey both God and Mayor Swenson at the same time. She nods at the leather wall hanging and gestures for him to turn it over and examine the back of it. She hasn't had to speak a single non-truth.

Steven Boergadine

Father Sam then turns it over. It's dirty. He is not all the way cogent right now. So far, he has not learned much from Maria that helps explain the disappearance of Big Bertha and, more importantly, Fanny.

There's a light going dim in his eyes that tells Maria he's off reporting to God, so he's not altogether on the earthly plane. Father Sam fixes his weary gaze on the leather wall hanging, dry and clean on one side, wet and dirty on the other.

Maria prays a silent prayer that Father Sam can figure things out. She helps the prayer along by giving a nod to the muddy surface of the leather, and then gently takes the leather piece, bends over to a patch of wet grass, and rubs the dirt off the back side of it. She places it back in Father Sam's hand.

When he looks at the cleaned-off back side, he blinks a couple times to get his focus, then finally sees it. "Marcus?" He hands it to Sheriff Marcus.

On the back side of the leather are the words that were engraved by the pawnbroker for Paparazzi Mickey: "For my Bertha baby. Your Mickey."

Maria doesn't speak or read English, so she doesn't know what words are engraved on the leather. She is happy about that. Ignorance is God's grace. Now, she's pretty sure she probably won't get sent to purgatory and probably won't get fired.

Sheriff Marcus reads the engraving and says, "Well, looks like you're right. This here was Bertha's."

Father Sam backs up against an upright fence post to keep himself in the same position as the fence post.

Maria sees him trying to hold himself up. His face is made of pain and sweat right now. She offers a clean hankie from her apron pocket. Father Sam wipes his face, then gives it back to her with all the gratitude he can muster up in a little smile.

Sheriff Marcus sees that Father Sam is near a dead faint. Sure enough, he gets wobbly and is about go down. Sheriff Marcus and Maria stabilize him and walk him to the Jeep.

Maria watches with worried eyes as the Jeep putts out of sight. She holds the soiled hankie in her hands and feels blessed.

As Sheriff Marcus points his Jeep away from the House of Wonder, he mulls over what they've just learned. It doesn't take long to understand the significance of the Chi-Rho being wet and dirty on one side but not the other. He figures Big Bertha and Fanny were on that property sometime after yesterday's rain.

CHAPTER 34

No Clues At Mabelline's

A fter Mayor Swenson eliminated Father Sam's pho-
tographic evidence and then arranged the get-
outta-town-fast flight for Big Bertha and Fanny, he
upped his advantage over Father Sam and Sheriff Marcus
by influencing DA Fenton Jones to influence Miss Matilda
to influence Judge Schmidt to start the John Spinks hearing early, even though it is a Sunday. It's not the first time
pillow talk influenced politics. Miss Matilda's mama would
be proud. Sheriff Marcus and Father Sam are in the dark—
convinced the hearing will be held Monday morning.

As for John Spinks, he won't speak to Father Sam or
Sheriff Marcus. John is turned off to any discussion about
his case. He wouldn't talk to a lawyer if one dropped by—
why would he?

John's last memory of his overturned life is the memory
of huddling behind pieces of a billboard in a Texas desert
rainstorm. He doesn't remember being hit by the flying
timber from the falling billboard. He has no recall of being
picked up by Cleveland Stockton, being transported and
assaulted, crawling out of the bathtub, gunshots, nothing.
He is incarcerated against his will.

Deputy Sydney takes meal trays to John's cell from
Mabelline's and sets them on the flat top of a short step-

ladder. The trays are reachable through the food slot. Most of the time, John doesn't reach for them. Deputy Sydney figures John must be pretty darned depressed to not want to eat Mabelline's cooking.

EARLY IN THE MORNING, ONE OF PAPARAZZI MICKEY'S brothers saw a horde of slick city folk—a judge, DA, executive secretary, court stenographer, a couple clerks, and a newspaper reporter—march down the old wood sidewalk on Main Street, with Mayor Swenson leading the way.

For Mickey's pa, it's not hard to work out that Mayor Swenson is pandering to County officials who've never set foot in McGuffin Ridge till now, and that his authoritarian rein over this neck of the woods is slipping.

Paparazzi Mickey's family wait for the parade to find its way to Mabelline's back room and then they entered, take the table near the blue gingham curtains, and ordered coffee and pie.

A distinct tone of argument spills through the swinging doors that separate the coffee shop from the back room. Mickey's pa pours most of his cup of coffee into a potted plant within arm's reach. Then he takes his empty cup to the coffee station near the swinging doors to refill and eavesdrop. The coffee station is near the swinging doors. He takes his time picking up the coffee pot and dribbling a refill into his cup. He hears a lot of pontificating from the back room and loses interest. Legal babble doesn't interest him, so he returns to his family. "Nothin' about Mickey being said in there."

WHILE PAPARAZZI MICKEY'S FAMILY ARE BROODING IN the corner booth of Mabelline's Café, Sheriff Marcus looks over at the Chi-Rho on the lap of Father Sam, who is nodding off and on, hoping his ailing buddy's head isn't about ready to explode when it thumps against the glass every time his old Jeep encounters a bump on the road.

The old Jeep needs new shocks. It was abandoned by a couple of drifters a few years back—before Father Sam moved to McGuffin Ridge. Sheriff Marcus hadn't turned over a new leaf yet, as his dealings with the drifters would show.

The two drifters had eaten a big lunch at Mabelline's and then pulled the old Tennessee tennis shoe on her. That is, they ran out of her place without paying and jumped in the Jeep to skedaddle, but the engine wouldn't start, and out came Mabelline. It all took place as Sheriff Marcus watched from the window of the jailhouse. It looked like Mabelline would be able to handle the two drifters as she stood at the passenger-side window and scolded them. But Sheriff Marcus saw an opportunity to run an easy scam on the two nincompoops. So he walked across the street, and thanked Mabelline for her citizen's arrest, booked them, and put them in his jail.

After a serious talking-to, those two hungry drifters needed a break in Mabelline's view, which she shared with Sheriff Marcus privately. She wasn't about to press charges. Sheriff Marcus didn't tell the two drifters about her charitable concern. He also declined to inform them they were free to go.

Mabelline went back to her kitchen to fix up boxed lunches for the two drifters to take with them. It was the least she could do. She learned they were brothers who'd been on the road several days. The only food they'd eaten were those hot beef sandwiches they'd just wolfed down at her counter. Not being natural thieves, they figured they'd get caught but desperation had driven them to her door. Those hot beef sandwiches took away the taste of gasoline on their lips that was makin' them sick to their stomachs. They'd been siphoning a little gas here and a little there, just enough to keep their old Jeep going so they could get home to their mama who was infected with TB and about to give up the ghost.

Brothers? A sick mother? Sheriff Marcus had looked at their identification when he confiscated their personal belongings and saw they had different last names. Obviously a cheap attempt to play with Mabelline's generous nature. Sheriff Marcus decided to pull some trickery in return. He told them bail was set at a hundred dollars each. He knew they didn't have enough to pay for hot beef sandwiches, so a hundred dollars bail? It was gonna have to be the end of the road for their old Jeep, he guessed.

Since they didn't have any money to bail out on, Sheriff Marcus agreed to take the old Jeep as collateral. He told them that the town's judge was booked solid for the next three months. "And by the way, he's Mabelline's sugar daddy, so don't expect a slap on the wrist."

The two drifters eagerly handed over the Jeep, and Sheriff Marcus set them free. He was pretty sure they wouldn't be back in three months. He told them about the railroad tracks that led to the stockyards where the cattle cars were loaded. There was a train full of Guernseys loading soon and it'd be headed in the general direction of their dear momma's bedside. It wouldn't be the most fragrant mode of travel, but it would be free. Sheriff Marcus picked up the boxed lunches Mabelline had offered, walked them to the train tracks, handed over the boxed lunches, and pointed them in the direction of the stockyard.

Back when Father Sam moved to McGuffin Ridge, Sheriff Marcus ended his nefarious ways of thinking and doing. Getting to know that good-hearted priest led Sheriff Marcus to want to change himself.

Not coming back to the jailhouse empty-handed feels good to Sheriff Marcus. Having that leather wall hanging gives him and Father Sam a sense of makin' headway. *But it ain't worth much*, he thinks. *That Chi-Rho ain't much as evidence, but at least now we've got a clue that Big Bertha and Fanny are somewhere near by. But where the hell are they?* He guesses they're parked in a room upstairs at the House of Wonder. He'll be going back there in the morning to check it out. But right now, he needs to put Father Sam to bed so he'll be rested and ready in the morning to conduct that interview of Fanny.

Sheriff Marcus pulls up to the jailhouse and turns off the key. The Jeep's final lurch arouses Father Sam from his bumpy slumber. "If you got a headache, it wasn't the Appaloosa," jokes Sheriff Marcus.

The nap during the ride home has repaid some of Father Sam's sleep debt. He manages to climb out of the Jeep, albeit with limited agility.

CHAPTER 35

Another Clue

F ather Sam slides out the passenger door of the Jeep
and assumes a standing position gripping the top of
the open car door with one hand until he's sure he's
all right and upright.

Dr. Blackfox and Little Wolf, the young Cherokee trapper are waiting outside the jailhouse entrance. Little Wolf is
clutching a dirty, rusted camera. He's nervous about being
away from his tribal home base in the denser part of the
mountain range, but he has a duty to perform.

Sheriff Marcus's greeting is a slight apologetic nod to
Dr. Blackfox and his young Cherokee friend as he circles
the front of the Jeep to make sure he's there to catch Father
Sam if he gets weak in the knees again.

Father Sam sees Dr. Blackfox walking toward him and
Sheriff Marcus. He's mostly got his balance now, shuts the
Jeep door, then extends both hands to grasp Dr. Blackfox's
hands. "How are you, Joe?"

Dr. Blackfox's expression of good will and kindness
sparkles in his eyes. He finds Father Sam's hands cold and
weak and notices that he's pressing his left hip against the
right fender of the Jeep for support.

Dr. Blackfox reflects on the incident at the Sunday
morning children's class. "It's been a long day, Father."

Sheriff Marcus remembers that Dr. Blackfox had promised to bring the young Cherokee. Something about the Office of Indian Affairs. "Howdy, Dr. Blackfox," he says.

Dr. Blackfox turns to Little Wolf and gives him a supportive nod to speak to the Sheriff in his own tongue.

The young Indian is not as confidant as he wants to be. He doesn't have any experience meeting with white folks, especially white folks who wear sheriff's badges.

Across the street from the jailhouse, Mickey's pa finishes off the last piece of apple pie. He glances through the parted gingham curtains and sees the street-side encounter between the Cherokees, Sheriff Marcus, and Father Sam. He notes a serious demeanor amongst the four men. More than a howdy-do moment.

Mickey's pa knows Dr. Blackfox. They're both members of the same operations group of the state's Air National Guard, although Dr. Blackfox is one rank above him. They both maintain small hangars at a co-op volunteer airfield along with a couple other pilots. He can't get a good view of the younger Cherokee because he's mostly hidden by the others.

Mickey's pa watches Dr. Blackfox turn and place his arm across Little Wolf's shoulders in a gesture of encouragement. Little Wolf comes into view. "Look at that there." Mickey's pa jumps out of his seat. He just got an unobstructed look at Little Wolf and the battered camera in his hands.

Mickey's pa expends little more than a single move to reach into his pocket, pull out a wad of cash, toss it on the table and bail out of Mabelline's Café. He leads his menfolk across the street. "You wait a damn minute." He rattles off in perfect Cherokee, "Where did you get that, boy?" It's not anger that brings this consternation to Mickey's pa—it's recognizing what Little Wolf is holding in his hands and fearing the implication of it.

Sheriff Marcus is taken by surprise by the sudden swarm of Paparazzi Mickey's kin. "Whoa, now wait a minute, Mr. Stollard, you settle down. Everything is real fragile right now. What's on your mind?"

Mickey's pa tries to calm down. "That's Mickey's camera, Sheriff. What's he doin' with it?" He points at Little Wolf.

Dr. Blackfox intervenes. "Mr. Stollard, I'm here to translate for Little Wolf. The Bureau wants some answers, too. Little Wolf found the camera in the woods, sir. If you can identify it, we'd appreciate your help."

Sheriff Marcus is shocked. "Are you sure this camera belongs to your son?"

"I damn sure am sure. Mickey's initials are on the camera bag. You got the camera bag somewhere, son?" He switches to the Cherokee tongue and demands that Little Wolf tell him where the camera bag is.

Loud nickering from the Appaloosa staggers Father Sam. The pulsating pressure in his cranium causes him to sway slightly as he backs up to the grille of the jeep and holds on.

Everyone's attention diverts to Father Sam.

Undue attention doesn't appeal to him even though he's on the verge of a medical emergency.

"I'm sorry." He pulls through it. His eyes smile. "It's a difficult day, Mr. Stollard. For all of us, I suspect."

Sheriff Marcus directs his remark to Mickey's pa, "Let's take care of this little matter of whether that's Mickey's camera or not—where did he say he found it, Dr. Blackfox?"

"Out in the woods near Swenson's airfield. Little Wolf will show the way," answers Dr. Blackfox.

"I suspect Little Wolf is trying to do the right thing, or he wouldn't be here," says Sheriff Marcus. "We are gonna follow him to where he found the camera. Ya mind followin' us? Maybe we can find that camera bag and settle this thing." He directs that invitation to Mickey's pa.

Mickey's pa gives little more than a blink of his eyes in agreement. "I know about that airfield."

Deputy Sydney is standing behind the window watching and listening from inside the jailhouse.

Sheriff Marcus yells, "Sydney, come out here."

Deputy Sydney hurries out to the crowd.

"I want you to put this evidence inside." Sheriff Marcus gestures toward the camera that Little Wolf is still holding.

Deputy Sydney steps toward Little Wolf to receive the camera.

Little Wolf backs up a step, not relinquishing it. He looks at Mickey's Pa, who is still trying to find a calm heart, and hands the camera to him.

Restrained anguish haunts Mickey's pa. He's not a man who would cry when people are around, so he wishes he were alone right now. He holds the camera with the grandfatherly care he would hold Paparazzi Mickey's firstborn. Despair of what's coming puts itself on his face. He's been part of mountain life as long as anyone. He knows about shallow graves, and he suspects the dirt on the camera is from one. And he knows the odds are he'll find his son there, too. He hands the camera to Deputy Sydney.

Sheriff Marcus wants to move things along now. They might still have time to find Big Bertha and Fanny. "Okay, folks, let's go."

CHAPTER 36

Shallow Grave

Mickey's pa follows Dr. Blackfox and Little Wolf to familiar territory. Sheriff Marcus and Father Sam are not far behind.

Mickey's pa had been at the airfield when he watched Mayor Swenson's guns for drugs deal go down. The deal was no business of his. It was between Mayor Swenson and his partners in crime. Watching Big Bertha and Fanny through the scope of his .30-30 get flown out of the country on that twin-engine aircraft? That wasn't any of his business, either. He has been tracking Mayor Swenson only to get a clue that would lead to his Mickey. People and things that interfere with Mayor Swenson's world stand a good chance of getting tainted and tossed. Now, out here, close to Mayor Swenson's airfield, Paparazzi Mickey's camera has been lying on the forest floor long enough to get rusty. To stay on Mayor Swenson's tail—that was the gut feeling that'd been churning in Mickey's pa all along. Did his boy get sucked into Mayor Swenson's world, tainted and tossed onto the forest floor?

They all huddle together after they get parked. None of them are armed with any weapon that you can see, but Sheriff Marcus and a couple of Paparazzi Mickey's brothers are holding flashlights.

Sheriff Marcus hands his own flashlight to his foggy-eyed friend. "Here you go, Father. Watch your step out here. Not much sunlight gets down to the forest floor." He knows Father Sam didn't get any sleep on the way out here.

Mickey's pa gets right to the point. "Where'd ya find that camera?"

It won't take long for the young Cherokee to relocate the site. He knows the terrain well.

The group trudges behind Little Wolf until he stops, points, and murmurs in Cherokee, "That is the place." Visible in the dirt is a partially dug-up grave with remnants of Paparazzi Mickey's city-slicker clothing and a shoe. Emerging from the dirt is the strap to a camera bag. Little Wolf speaks his native language to the group.

Dr. Blackfox translates, "He found the camera here. Animals have been digging."

Sheriff Marcus reaches down to pull on the strap. "Might be a camera bag."

Mickey's pa remains stalwart, but not easily. His boys bow their heads. "Don't do that, Sheriff." Heavy silence sets in. Sheriff Marcus stops his reach for the strap. They all know it's a grave. And they all know who's buried in it.

"That there is Mickey's shoe. I bought 'em for him when he was a young 'un. Before he grew into his feet," says Mickey's pa. "If you're gonna do any more digging, we'd like to leave first."

Father Sam clicks on his flashlight and finds his way to the airfield to distance himself from the painful human tribulation before them all. He closes his eyes and prays, then opens them and observes the airstrip. He wishes God would send the Appaloosa down for a four-point landing. He'd climb on and ride him out of this hell.

Dr. Blackfox and the young Cherokee walk up behind Father Sam. "Father?"

Father Sam is jolted from his abstracted muse.

Dr. Blackfox inquires, "You've been looking for the little sharpshooter?"

Father Sam's heartache lightens. He peers at Dr. Blackfox's face. No words come—only hope and heartache at once. He can't take it standing. There's a knee-high stump just right for sitting about two feet away. He asks, "Do you mind?"

Dr. Blackfox helps Father Sam sit on the stump and then defers to the young Cherokee, who speaks in his native tongue as Dr. Blackfox translates. "This is a place of trade for the Mayor's partners. Sometimes a plane lands and unloads boxes of guns. Other times a different plane lands and trades boxes of drugs for boxes of guns. Then other planes land and pick up boxes of drugs."

Sheriff Marcus enters the picture and listens in. He is compelled to unload his troubled mind. "Yep, the Mayor brokers drug and gun deals, all right." The group turns to him to hear what he has to say. "I'll tell ya a story and trust y'all to keep it to yourselves. I came upon his crookedness out here years ago. I hid out here and spied on what turned out to be one of those Colombian cartel groups in action, but I got caught watchin'. The Mayor rolled in when I was this far from having my head taken off." Sheriff Marcus holds up his thumb and finger. Then he points to the tree stump Father Sam is sitting on. "They had me on my knees, and my head was pushed down on that stump you're sittin' on, Father. Mayor Swenson stopped 'em. Told 'em he owned the badge I was wearin' and to put down that machete. And I've been lookin' the other way ever since."

Silently, Mickey's pa has appeared behind them. He has cleared his head for now. "We all got somethin' to hide, Sheriff."

Father Sam nods. "Yep."

All the clues start to add up as full-on contrition spills out of the impromptu powwow.

Little Wolf describes what he saw. Dr. Blackfox translates, "Big woman. Little girl. Dolls. Clothes. Machine guns."

Father Sam winces. "That's Bertha. And Fanny. What about them?"

Little Wolf goes on as Dr. Blackfox translates, "Big woman cry. Little girl fight."

Sheriff Marcus thinks he gets it. "He damned sure put them in the ground, too. I'm 'bout ready to throw this badge in the river and get my gun."

Mickey's pa adds his eye-witness account to Little Wolf's report, "Nope, they're not dead. But they're gone, Sheriff. The ladies got flown out. I saw it myself."

"Flown where?" Father Sam asks. He knows *where* doesn't matter. They're gone, and John Spink's best chance at freedom is gone with them.

"That big cargo plane will carry 'em pretty far south of the border, I'd say," Mickey's pa informs them.

"Why?" Father Sam's question can't be answered by anyone here.

Mickey's pa finalizes his participation with them. "We're way past why, and we know who." He walks away—stops, turns. "Sheriff, I'm gonna be honest with you. I'm plannin' on doin' somethin' about my son bein' killed 'cause of that man, and you might as well get used to lookin' the other way." He gives them all a long look—then keeps on walking.

Sheriff Marcus has an idea what that somethin' is. A slight resignation registers on his face as his thoughts roil inside him. *Maybe I'll join up with ya when you do.*

Dr. Blackfox gives Father Sam a commiserating pat on the shoulder. Then he and the young Cherokee walk away.

It's just Father Sam and Sheriff Marcus now.

All that's left in Father Sam's mind is knowing he has to free John Spinks. He hopes that is okay with God because he's gonna do it, even if it isn't.

Just then, the Appaloosa shows up. Father Sam's head pain bends him over. "C'mon, c'mon, give it to me," he cries out to the dark sky, as if God might be up there orchestrating his lousy life. He welcomes the pain right now. Pain takes away the anguish of thinking. Pain allows irrationality. He rises from the stump, stumbles onto the air strip, and kicks the first runway light till it's scattered in pieces and he's fallen to the ground.

"C'mon, my friend. Let's go home." Sheriff Marcus helps him to his feet.

But Father Sam isn't done. He pulls away from Sheriff Marcus, goes to the next runway light, and kicks it to smithereens. Then on to the next one.

Sheriff Marcus doesn't stop him. In fact, he thinks it's not a bad idea. He goes to the other end, kicks and stomps runway lights into little pieces, one after the other, until he meets Father Sam in the middle. They're both dripping with sweat, exhausted.

Sheriff Marcus slings Father Sam's arm around the back of his shoulders, and they walk to the Jeep. Useless clumps of wire, metal, and broken glass decorate the perimeter of the hard-grass airstrip.

The hearing begins tomorrow, figures Sheriff Marcus. *What's left to do? Getting a good night's sleep would be a good start.*

Sheriff Marcus helps his worn-out buddy into the Jeep, cranks it up and heads for home.

CHAPTER 37

A Good Night's Sleep Will Have To Wait

Twice today Sheriff Marcus has driven the old Jeep back to town with Father Sam barely lucid. He pulls up in front of the jailhouse and switches off his headlights.

Deputy Sydney comes out of Mabelline's Café, admiring a fan made of dollar bills spread out in his two-handed grip. He doesn't notice the Jeep until he hears the transmission thump when the ignition turns off. He looks up and stands proud as he shows off his evening take to Sheriff Marcus.

Father Sam struggles to sit up and open the passenger door of the Jeep. Sheriff Marcus tells him, "Hold on, I'll help ya."

As Sheriff Marcus climbs out of his Jeep, he asks Deputy Sydney, "Mabelline got a poker game goin' this evening?"

"Mabelline hired me to help out today for a fancy meeting and looky here." Deputy Sydney waves his handful of bills.

Father Sam manages to get out of the Jeep by himself. As Sheriff Marcus gets caught up in Deputy Sydney's description of the backroom activity in Mabelline's Café, Father Sam overhears him.

"What kind of fancy meeting?" Sheriff Marcus asks, paying more attention to Deputy Sydney than to getting the door for Father Sam.

"A whole room full of well-dressed folks. Mabelline said the old guy is a judge from the big city." Deputy Sydney folds up his bankroll and shoves it into his pocket. "Goin' up to the *House*. Double my money."

"Damned idiot." Sheriff Marcus watches Deputy Sydney make his quick exit and gives some thought to what he just said about the judge and the meeting.

Father Sam stabilizes himself by leaning on the Jeep as he makes his way around to the back end of it and pushes off into the street toward Mabelline's.

The court procedure has already started? Dire thoughts fill Sheriff Marcus's mind. *We've been blindsided.*

The same woeful conclusion comes to Father Sam. His knees get wobbly before he makes it half-way to Mabelline's Café, and he no longer has the Jeep to lean on. On top of that, the Appaloosa starts kicking the hell out of the inside of his skull. Father Sam grasps both sides of his head to keep it from breaking in half and teeters backward.

Sheriff Marcus turns his head and sees Father Sam about to tip over. "Wait a minute." With a couple fast steps, he catches his worn-out buddy before he goes down and guides him to the jailhouse.

"Where's your pills? You need 'em, don't ya?" Sheriff Marcus yells in Father Sam's ear as he opens the door with his free hand, then knees the door open wide enough to get his pal inside.

"I need a drink." Father Sam's chest heaves, his sweating won't stop, and the agitated tumor in his skull is letting him know it's going to be a long night. He doesn't usually cry, but he can't stop the involuntarily gush of tears that roll from the corners of his eyes.

"You don't need a damn drink. You need your pills, don't ya?" Sheriff Marcus has got to stop his old pal's pain. "Where do you keep 'em?"

"Kitchen," moans Father Sam.

Sheriff Marcus snaps on the lights and helps Father Sam lie down on a cot near the stove. "Where in the kitchen? Never mind, I'll find 'em." He dampens a cloth, lays it across Father Sam's forehead and sets out for Father Sam's log house.

The ceiling light is too much for Father Sam's pained eyes. He raises himself to a standing position to reach the light switch, then changes his mind and makes for Sheriff Marcus's bottle of whiskey. He twists the cap off and lets it drop onto the floor. A couple swigs later, mobilized and inspired, he lurches to the cell block door. A key hangs beside it. He unlocks the cell block door and inside he goes, whiskey bottle in one hand, key in the other.

John watches the red-eyed priest enter and wobble towards him, and backs away. "Get outta here!"

Father Sam doesn't hear anything but the roar of malignant neurons in his head. He holds himself upright against the jail bars till he can't. He slides down to his knees and drinks from the whiskey bottle. "They'll railroad you, Johnny." He holds himself in a kneeling position, puts the bottle on the cement floor and gives the whiskey a push between two bars as far as his arm can extend. John drop-kicks the bottle against the bars. "I ain't no damned Johnny, you drunk phony." The bottle shatters on his side of the bars—no damage done to Father Sam except for getting splattered with glass and whiskey. He doesn't flinch or care.

John's rage bursts. He presses his face between the bars and drops to his knees, nose to nose with Father Sam. "What's a goddamned bottle of whiskey supposed to do for me? I want outta here, I want outta here!" The pain in his eyes is not unlike the pain in Father Sam's.

Sam looks long and hard at John. "So do I." Then he pulls himself up to a standing position and inserts the key into the cell lock. It doesn't fit the cell door.

"Wrong key, Father." Sheriff Marcus had watched everything from behind. He even got the whiskey shower.

Father Sam doesn't turn around. He tries the key a couple more times.

Sheriff Marcus keeps talking, "It'd be right. But it wouldn't be legal. We'd both go to jail."

Father Sam doesn't care what's legal. He's already dared God to stop him from setting John free. He's on his own— his own damned-by-God self is all there is now. He leaves the key in the lock, turns, and stumbles past Sheriff Marcus and out the cell block door.

"You need to lay down and shut your eyes," Sheriff Marcus yells after him. "I got your pills."

"I'm sorry, son," Sheriff Marcus says as he lifts a broom off a hook and makes a few passes over the wet glass on his side of the jail cell. "If you got broken glass on your floor sweep it out of there if you want to." He places the broom between the bars and makes a little more small talk. "I better see how that damned priest is doin.'"

John isn't listening. He's curled into a fetal position on his bunk with a wool blanket pulled over his head.

Sheriff Marcus pats his chest pocket and feels the pill bottle. He opens the cell block door.

Father Sam is long gone.

CHAPTER 38

Back-Room Railroad Party

In the back room of Mabelline's Café the hearing to gather depositions from local witnesses progresses to its foregone conclusion—an order by Judge Schmidt for the arraignment of John Spinks in the big city.

The little jurisdiction-nudge Miss Matilda wants for DA Fenton Jones's political showcase? It'll be a done deal by the end of the day.

In Father Sam's and Sheriff Marcus's minds, however, there are no legal grounds for John's arraignment for anything, anywhere.

In Mayor Swenson's mind, the sooner the John Spinks business is vacated from McGuffin Ridge, the better. DA Fenton Jones guaranteed as much when he said, *I'll take care of the paperwork that will quietly disqualify you for practicing without a license and later I'll see that Miss Matilda sweet talks the judge into expunging your file from the system. And life will go on up here.*

In DA Fenton Jones's mind, it's all about being seen on the evening news, spouting clever homophobic one-liners, and dancing the eye-for-an-eye, tooth-for-a-tooth dance. The Bible-Belt couch potatoes will follow his lead and dance all the way to the voting booths.

Father Sam and Sheriff Marcus know that the defense

and prosecution are on the same team. The show goes on as Manager Salvo is sworn in and gives his deposition. He saw John Spinks, bloody and out cold in the front seat of Cleveland Stockton's stolen Mercury while he held a shotgun on Cleveland Stockton. But those facts will not be included in his testimony.

DA Fenton Jones pours it on. "Is it your sworn testimony here before Judge Schmidt that you rented Cleveland Stockton and John Spinks a room with only one bed, Mr. Salvo?" A cheap shot, but for an anything-goes political campaign—anything goes.

A freelance newspaper reporter scribbles down word-for-word the cheap shots. Cajoled to get on board by Miss *Mama-Look-At-Me-Now* Matilda, how could he not. He jots down Manager Salvo's flip response.

"I always fix a customer up with what they ask for, you're damn right," answers Mr. Salvo, sounding convincingly plainspoken.

WHEN SHERIFF MARCUS LEFT JOHN IN HIS JAIL CELL huddling under his wool blanket and then saw that Father Sam was gone, the first thought that came to him was, *Oh Lordy, we're all gonna end up in handcuffs.* He figured Father Sam had gone to Mabelline's to crash the John Spinks railroad party.

At said party, DA Fenton Jones finishes up with Mr. Salvo. "Do you rent rooms with two beds, Sir?"

"Hell yeah, I got rooms with two beds." Sounding like a regular Joe, Mr. Salvo keeps his every lie as real as can be. "None of my business to judge why someone wants one bed or two beds or anything else. I'd throw in spurs and chaps if they want to pay for 'em."

Sheriff Marcus rushes in to Mabelline's to stop his buddy from making a damn fool of himself. He stops by the coffee urns and peeks at the proceedings. No sign of Father Sam, so he doesn't stay long. He's more interested in making sure his meandering friend gets his medicine than he is on eavesdropping on DA Fenton Jones.

He turns away from the door as DA Fenton Jones makes it easy for Manager Salvo to remember his lines. "So, Mr. Salvo, you are stating for the record that Cleveland Stockton paid for a room that had only the one big bed."

CHAPTER 39

Another World

S omewhere between the jailhouse and his log house, Father Sam experiences either a prophetic vision or a nervous breakdown. Approaching his front entrance, he recognizes Saint Peter. It only takes a moment of scrutiny to observe that Saint Peter is sleeping on the job. Normally, he guards the gates of heaven, but he's taken a couple days off to lend a hand to Father Sam. Who knows how many sinners may have slipped into the living room, while Saint Peter has been sleeping on the job.

Father Sam tippy-toes past Saint Peter, forgiving him as he passes. *Let him rest, oh Lord.*

Father Sam's cerebral front room is packed with unwelcome guests—the ones who slipped by Saint Peter. With hyper-malignant perceptibility and without time and space defining Father Sam's world now, the souls who got past Saint Peter, are in for a dusting.

Moments after Father Sam gets home, Sheriff Marcus knocks on his front door and then lets himself in. He doesn't see Saint Peter dozing at the door, but he sees that Father Sam's eyes are the size of fruit jar lids.

Father Sam's reality is shattered. A shrink might say it's a full-blown hyper-religious psychotic episode. Sheriff Marcus might say it's that Appaloosa or lack of sleep or the corn whiskey—or all of the above. But Father Sam knows it for what it is—*hellfire.*

As soon as he enters his log house, Father Sam notes that Judge Schmidt is there. So are DA Fenton Jones, Miss Matilda, Mayor Swenson, Johnny and Gladys Spinks, Cleveland Stockton, Big Bertha, Fanny, Paparazzi Mickey, and even Mabelline. All crowded into his living room and surrounded by hellfire.

He looks for his grandmother and spots her outside the wall of flames. He calls out, "Grandmother, why are you on the other side?"

Father Sam confusing him with his grandmother gets Sheriff Marcus to thinking. *All these years hearing and seeing an Appaloosa that ain't there. That's one thing, but seeing his grandmother that ain't there? There's a whole lot more than just a big headache goin' on with him.*

Right now, though, Sheriff Marcus is gonna try to fix the problem with the pills and some water to wash them down with, so he'll go along with Father Sam's delusion. He yells back, "I got your pills. Relax." Sheriff Marcus walks to the next room.

Father Sam watches his grandmother walk away. "Where are you going?"

Sheriff Marcus yells back, "To the kitchen. You need water for the pills, and then you need to lay your ass down and rest, like I told ya to do back at my jailhouse."

Judge Schmidt gets Father Sam's attention. *Unless there is more than one priest in this mountain town, my guess is that you are …*

Father Sam ignores Judge Schmidt's conciliatory tone and yells toward the kitchen, "Grandmother?"

Sheriff Marcus answers, "I'm coming."

Steven Boergadine

DA Fenton Jones speaks up, *Your Honor, I smell a …*

Father Sam whirls toward DA Fenton Jones and interjects, "Sulfur, Lucifer. You smell sulfur!"

DA Fenton Jones finishes describing what he smells … *a rat in a frock.*

Father Sam addresses the court. "The hearing is scheduled for tomorrow, Judge."

Mayor Swenson interjects, *Preacher, I told Bouncer Bill to inform the good sheriff we'd be starting John Spinks's hearing a day early.*

Father Sam stares at Mayor Swenson without a blink. "You're infested, Swenson. Lies fly from your mouth as flies fly."

Mayor Swenson shivers his head and frowns to imply his confusion over Father Sam's strange charge.

Judge Schmidt interjects, *You must be Father Westburn.*

Father Sam ignores Judge Schmidt again and yells at Mayor Swenson, "Where are Fanny and her mother?"

Mayor Swenson points to the side of the courtroom. *Mabelline's got a little something for you.*

Father Sam remains stoic. "I'm not ordering pie. I'm ordering Fanny's deposition." Something catches the corner of his eye, and he looks in the direction of Mayor Swenson's pointed finger.

There she is—Mabelline holding an extra-large cut of his favorite cherry pie. She winks at Father Sam. *Cherry pie, for my sweetheart. And no lumberjacks with noisy saws to interrupt you from having all you want.*

Sitting next to Mabelline are Big Bertha, Paparazzi Mickey and Fanny.

Big Bertha speaks up, *You stole my Chi-Rho, Father.* She lifts the cherry pie off Mabelline's plate and eats it. *We all even now.*

Fanny waves and asks, *May I play with Molly?*

Paparazzi Mickey raises his camera and shoots a flash of Father Sam. *I got a good shot of you and Gladys out there in the woods. I hung it up in your wickiup.*

Gladys hasn't changed. Neither has her sultry, seductive tone as she moans, *I like it when you crave over me, Sam.*

Cleveland Stockton is wearing sunglasses and leaning on the armrest of Old Sparky, the infamous electric chair. *Johnny has some last words for you.*

Johnny Spinks is strapped down and ready to go to heaven.

Stockton turns to Johnny and says, *Happy Birthday, little guy. Nine years old now. What's 'yer final meal gonna be?*

Johnny is wearing the metal cap that will ground him while the 2300 volts of electricity fry him. *Red licorice, Daddy.*

Gladys rips the metal cap off Johnny's head and bashes Stockton with it. She screams at him, *You are not a daddy, you sick monster!*

Johnny yells, *Give me back my hat. I ride the lightning, Mama. It's my job. I'm a big circus act.*

DA Fenton Jones can't sit on his hands any longer. *I have voters weepin' and wailin' and waitin'. And we're poking along here.*

Judge Schmidt answers, *Patience, Mr. Jones. I have served these rural communities for a good while. I will allow events to poke along as I deem necessary.*

Sheriff Marcus stands in the doorway of the kitchen, holding the glass of water. His heart aches as he watches his best friend go beyond the boundary of a sane mind.

Father Sam's face glows at the sight of his grandmother standing in the kitchen doorway with a glass of water. He holds out his hand and pleads, "Water, please, Grandmother, and my medicine. My head hurts."

"All right, all right, hold your damned horses." Sheriff Marcus walks toward Father Sam with water and the bottle of pills in hand.

Judge Schmidt gives Gladys a suggestion. *Say something nice to him, Mrs. Spinks. You know what I mean. Something carnal. He never got his share.*

Gladys blows a kiss at Father Sam. *I've been feelin' your eyes on me. Can I tempt ya, Sam?*

Sheriff Marcus holds out the glass and pills for Father Sam. He tries to ignore Gladys as he reminds Sheriff Marcus. "She's doing it again."

"Who's doing what?"

"She's tempting me, Grandmother. Don't let me fall again." Father Sam sees his grandmother standing there with the glass of water. "Thank you for the water, Grandmother." He downs the glass of water along with what's left in the pill bottle. He hands the glass and bottle back to his grandmother and thanks her in Cherokee. "Wa do. Wa do. Will you stay?"

Sheriff Marcus takes the glass and bottle. "Your grandmother is with you, pal. She's always with you." He pats Father Sam on the back and mutters to himself, "What the hell am I gonna do with you?"

If he could call for the men in white coats, he'd probably do it. But Sheriff Marcus is stuck—until he remembers that Joe Blackfox could fly Father Sam to those men in white coats. But how to contain Father Sam right now? He's under a mental spell that might not end till his brain gives out on him altogether.

Is there anything else? Judge Schmidt gets Father Sam's attention.

Father Sam's psychotic soliloquy continues as Sheriff

Marcus eases away from Father Sam and picks up his walkie-talkie. He ducks into the kitchen.

"Your Honor," answers Father Sam, "there is circumstantial evidence that Fanny Stockton is the shooter—not John Spinks. I brought a photograph that will tell you everything."

DA Fenton Jones roars with laughter. *That will tell us everything? He brought a talking photograph? Where is it? Where's your photograph that tells us something? I'm the only person who has photographs that speak louder than words. That's right, photographs that show and tell, photographs of both men naked as jaybirds, when they were found by Mr. Salvo in that room.* He slaps a handful of photographs on the table for Judge Schmidt to see. *There are some talking photographs for you, Your Honor! In addition to a ballistics test that proves the gun in John Spinks's hand was the murder weapon. Is that circumstantial enough?*

Judge Schmidt bangs the back of a spoon on a table three times. *Mr. Jones, settle down.*

DA Fenton Jones doesn't settle down. He continues his rant. *Clarence Darrow here wants us to believe that he has a talking photograph that proves an adolescent deaf-mute shot her daddy.*

Father Sam points to Fanny, who is quietly sitting with Big Bertha. "She is an autistic savant, Your Honor. Not deaf and not mute. A prodigious shooter. She is my evidence." He goes to Fanny's side. "So, you see, Judge, a photograph that tells the truth. This is the photo of Fanny. It will clear John Spinks." He points to Fanny. "She shot her father in each eye, and she'll tell you so, won't you, Fanny?"

Fanny pipes up, *Yeah, Judge, you ever heard of me? I'm Fanny Oakley. I shot my daddy in each eye, and I'm tellin' ya so.* Fanny stands and yells, *I am the only photograph that matters!*

Judge Schmidt glares at Cleveland Stockton. *Approach the bench now, Mr. Stockton.* Stockton walks across the courtroom and presents himself, as ordered. *Remove your sunglasses,* barks Judge Schmidt. Stockton removes his sunglasses. Judge Schmidt looks closely at the two holes where his eyes should be and asks, *Mr. Stockton, is the shooter in this room—the shooter who shot your eyes out?*

Stockton puts his sunglasses on. *Yes, Your Honor.*

Point to the shooter, says the judge.

Stockton blurts out, *My eyes was shot out. I can't see. How'm I gonna point to the little deaf mute who shot 'em out, Judge?*

Don't get smart with me, Mr. Stockton.

"That's it, Your Honor, there's the account from an eyewitness, Cleveland Stockton," yells Father Sam, "You heard him."

Stockton whisks his sunglasses off and mugs toward Judge Schmidt. *"I had eyes once before the little deaf mute left me with black holes."* He starts making sobbing noises as he directs his remark in Fanny's direction. *"Why won't ya call me daddy?"*

"Don't you call him that, honey," orders Big Bertha.

Fanny lifts a pistol and shoots twice. The bullets whiz through her daddy's black holes.

Stockton is still standing. *"Ya see, Judge? She did it to me again"* Stockton stamps his feet like a little boy having a tantrum. *"Call me daddy, call me daddy, it's no fair."*

DA Fenton Jones jumps to his feet and yells, *"Theatrics, nothing but cheap courtroom theatrics. How's he possibly going to be an eye witness? He's got black holes?"*

Judge Schmidt stands and bellows. *Shut up, Fenton. The deaf mute did it. Self defense.* He bangs the back of the spoon on a table. *The party's over!* Judge Schmidt whacks the table with the spoon one final time. *Case dismissed!*

The hellfire fades as Father Sam's brain reverberates with the sound of the steel spoon hammering the oak table. He quiets down and his eyes close to the world of delusion that has kept him from sleep. He falls to his knees. "Take me. Grandmother, it's done. He's free. I'm so happy, Grandmother. Now me. Where's my Appaloosa? Praise the Lord, take me!" Common sense seeps into his mind. He suddenly realizes for an instant that he is sick and needs to stop his sickness. He squeezes his eyes shut, begging darkness to come, squeezing harder, trying to shut down his wild schizophrenic ride, using every muscle in his face to squeeze his eye lids together, the pressure so forcible that the blood flow to his optic nerves stops. The optical flagellation causes him to suffer an eye stroke.

Father Sam slumps to the floor, twitching and jerking. Finally, he becomes still.

Witnessing the indefinable freak show from the kitchen, Sheriff Marcus holds the talk button on his walkie-talkie. "Oh God, our friend just died, Joe. He's dead." Sheriff Marcus runs to Father Sam's body. "No, he's breathing, not dead," he yells into the walkie-talkie.

Sheriff Marcus has just watched the complete mind-crash of the finest human being he's ever known while he made a distress call to Dr. Blackfox. He's certain Father Sam has gone insane and maybe he would have been better off dying. He disconnects from Dr. Blackfox and contacts Deputy Sydney. Then he runs into the kitchen, brings a soaked dish towel to Father Sam, and gently wipes his brow.

CHAPTER 40

Father Sam's Flight For Life

I n Mabelline's backroom, the actual hearing is winding down. Fake attorney, Mayor Swenson is presenting the obligatory defense authored by DA Fenton Jones. It's time to call on a witness who'll provide expert testimony from a medical doctor's perspective. "Your Honor! I would like to bring Dr. Willard forward, my client's attending physician."

Judge Schmidt is impressed. "I understood him to be away for family matters." He admires Doc Willard, who is about to put his hand on a Bible at the clerk's table.

Mayor Swenson puffs up the room. "Dr. Willard has cut his out-of-town business short and returned to McGuffin Ridge to do his civic duty, Your Honor."

Just then a frantic CB call shakes up the proceeding. *Stork chaser, Stork chaser, you out there? SOS, Doc. This is Jailbird Two.*

Doc Willard picks up his CB. The volume is loud, so everyone listens. "What is it, Sydney? I'm at Mabelline's. Over."

Deputy Sydney is hysterical. *Father Sam is dying, Doc! Sheriff Marcus is trying to revive him! Come outside, will ya?*

Doc Willard doesn't bother excusing himself. His black bag is never far. He grabs it and dashes out the door.

Judge Schmidt watches Doc Willard's unapologetic exit. "The good doctor's priorities need no discussion here. We all heard the call. We will adjourn until the good doctor returns to this legal proceeding."

Deputy Sydney is behind the wheel of Sheriff Marcus's Jeep, taking his responsibility serious. He even has the flashing red light placed on the roof.

Doc Willard jumps on board. They speed up the street.

Deputy Sydney had just come down from the House of Wonder when Sheriff Marcus called him to bring the Jeep to Father Sam's log house.

Deputy Sydney skids the Jeep to a stop. The two men disembark and gallop into Father Sam's, leaving the red light blinking.

Doc Willard runs to Father Sam's side and does a quick check. "What happened?"

Sheriff Marcus explains all he knows. "He was goin' on and on like he was in another world, sometimes talkin' to this person, sometimes to another, callin' out to his dead grandma. I guess he was makin' a lot of sense to himself. But there was flat-out craziness in his face … like he was hypnotized."

Doc Willard asks, "How'd he end up unconscious on the floor?"

"He started shiverin' and twitching and jerkin' and just fell, and then nothin.'"

Doc Willard tries to figure it. "Grand mal, maybe—epileptic seizure. Hard to tell about the rest of it."

"Well, Doc, you know he hears that horse a lot when there ain't one around, but he never talked to it like he was talkin' tonight. And he's got those damn headaches that drive him to drink. Lately, he's been goin' toe-to-toe with his idea of the devil, seems to me."

Doc Willard removes the white collar from Father Sam's

neck, unsnaps a couple buttons at the top of his shirt and turns his head to one side.

Sheriff Marcus puts a pillow under Father Sam's head. "I hope he can be moved without doin' him harm 'cause I got Dr. Blackfox about to land nearby to fly him to a hospital."

"Very good, Sheriff. Very good," says Doc Willard.

They all hoist Father Sam up and carry him to the Jeep. The Jeep heads to the hard-grass runway.

The runway has no lights due to the earlier mischief of Father Sam and Sheriff Marcus. No problem, thanks to the full moon, Dr. Blackfox brings his Cessna 340 in for a perfect landing, turns it around and waits, engines purring.

Sheriff Marcus pulls his Jeep in as close to the airplane as he can. All four men hustle Father Sam onto the airplane.

Dr. Blackfox tells them, "I've alerted Emergency at the hospital. An ambulance will be waiting at the airport."

Sheriff Marcus gets on board. "I best go along. He might wake up and throw a fit."

Just in case a drifting cloud blocks the moonlight, Deputy Sydney lines the Jeep up beside the airplane and points its headlights down the runway. He and Doc Willard watch it successfully take off.

Sydney maneuvers the Jeep off the field as Doc Willard and him head back to town.

CHAPTER 41

Deputy Sydney Hunkers Down With John

Deputy Sydney parks the Jeep in front of the jailhouse as Doc Willard grabs his black bag, climbs out, and heads across the street to Mabellines to give his deposition.

"Are you 'bout to go say somethin' that'll set John free, Doc?"

"I'll do my darnedest," answers Doc Willard.

"I know ya will, Doc." Deputy Sydney turns, mopes toward the jailhouse, and talks to himself as he unlocks the door, "I sure hope ya do. I like that John. He wouldn't hurt nobody."

He flicks on the lights of the jailhouse office. He's the man in charge while Sheriff Marcus is tending to Father Sam's meltdown, so he'll brew up some coffee and check on his prisoner.

John has not become friendly toward Father Sam or Sheriff Marcus. He chooses to stay quiet most of the time.

Deputy Sydney cleans up around all four cells on a regular basis. And every now and then, he pulls the old wooden chair over to cell number one and plops down on the torn-up wicker seat. He asks John if there's anything he can get for him, and John usually asks for a cup of coffee.

They sit with those bars between them, drink their coffee, and don't say much, sometimes don't say anything. When they do talk, it's mostly Deputy Sydney rattling on and John taking it all in.

A while back, Deputy Sydney talked about the stray cats he feeds every day. On occasion, field mice get into the cell block, so John mentioned that he wished he had a mouser that'd get rid of them. Deputy Sydney brought in a big Siamese named Max who can catch a field mouse's scent in less than a minute and then catch the mouse quicker. John wishes Max had a more sociable disposition, but Max is all business. He lurks under the bunk in cell number four, where he can get-the-drop on those unsuspecting rodents.

Deputy Sydney has a big stoneware mug with his name on it. It's steaming with fresh coffee. He'll take it in to the cell block with him. John has a tin cup that Sydney can fill up from the mug. It holds plenty enough to share.

The broom that Sheriff Marcus left leaning near John is just the right length for what he needs it for. A security lamp at the end of the cell block glows 24/7. John can see well enough to use the broom to reach a piece of glass and rake it into his cell. It is a big piece that survived the smashing. Sheriff Marcus missed it when he did some sweeping earlier. John gets a firm grip on it. Now all he has to do is decide he doesn't want to live anymore as he scratches a faint indentation across his wrist. He doesn't draw blood, but he's working up to it.

Hot coffee in hand, Deputy Sydney steadies his elbow against the cell block door and pushes it open, then turns on the overhead lights with his free hand. It is that moment that he sees John aiming at his wrist with that broken glass. "No, no, no, John. You put that down now." He flies to the bars. "Lookie here, I brought you in some coffee, buddy." He pushes the steaming mug through the bars.

John keeps looking at the mark he's etched across his wrist and stays poised with that piece of glass in his other hand.

Deputy Sydney gets emotional. "I liked what ya told me 'bout that pretty baby of yours, and I sure wouldn't want her to hear ya did this to your own self. Come on now. She's gonna think she weren't enough for Daddy to live for." Deputy Sydney is trying to keep calm. "John, I jes been through seein' Father Sam near dead. Ya ought to know that. Tried to save you in his own personal way."

After a long moment goes by, John hands the broken glass to Deputy Sydney. Then he asks, "His own personal way?"

John looks around for his tin cup. Deputy Sydney nudges him. "Here. You pour it," he says and lets John take the stoneware mug while he pulls up the old wicker chair and sits down. John fills up his tin cup and returns the rest of it to Deputy Sydney.

Deputy Sydney sits back, drinks from the mug, and talks to John in a gentle tone. "The way I see it is, Father Sam drowned in his own mind 'cause his mind is so danged deep. Ya know, God-almighty deep? Not like the rest of us. God-almighty deep."

John gives some thought to Deputy Sydney's words and then answers, "I'm somebody's ticket to some high idea of themself. The priest can't stop 'em." John drinks the last of his coffee. "Why is he near dead?"

Deputy Sydney only knows what he overheard when they picked up Father Sam and drove to the airstrip. "The Sheriff said Father Sam had a brain attack while he was conversin' to imaginary people. See, ya got friends, John.

I want ya to know that for sure. And that priest, well, he's been yer best one all along."

John doesn't register any hope in his eyes regardless of the good-hearted intentions of Deputy Sydney.

Deputy Sydney drains the mug, gets up from the old chair, and points to the broom, meaning he needs to use it now. John sticks the broom handle through the bars, then lies down on his bunk, and stares at the ceiling.

Deputy Sydney sweeps up the glass and mops the whiskey-sticky floor.

CHAPTER 42

Lies Rule The Day

Doc Willard is concluding his deposition. "About the only thing left to tell you is that John Spinks was in a progressive stage of volume shock. That, Your Honor, was because of extreme blood loss, partly due to a severe blow to his head—I'd say two or three days earlier. Upon examining that gash, I could see it hadn't been treated and, mind you, he showed all the symptoms of having been unconscious since receiving that blow—malnutrition, dehydration, blood loss, infection. Possibly the two of them had been fighting against someone or each other before they arrived at McGuffin Ridge. Your guess is as good as mine."

DA Fenton Jones stands up. "We are not here to guess, Your Honor."

Judge Schmidt knocks down the argument. "Mr. Jones, I will hear the good doctor's deposition in whatever way he wishes to characterize it. Sit down and wait your turn."

"Thank you, Your Honor," says Mayor Swenson and then continues, "So John Spinks had been knocked out? And he was out cold for several days, Doctor?"

"More like a comatose state," answers Doc Willard.

"Are you sayin' he was in a coma? Explain what could drive a man to snap out of a coma to defend himself with a firearm?"

Doc Willard explains the academics to Mayor Swenson. "You don't snap out of a coma, Mayor. There are stages of recovery for comatose patients. Voluntary actions are not possible—not while the patient is in an unresponsive stage."

Mayor Swenson follows up. "And how long does that unresponsive stage last?"

"Hours, days, a week. A few go longer."

"And when a man starts to come out of it, Doctor, is he able to physically protect himself?"

"At a certain stage of the recovery, a man might show some anxiety or movement. But he'll likely be unable to cope during that stage. In John's case, he probably was at the highest stage of responsiveness. Responsive enough— given the situation—for his brain to initiate a fight-or-flight response. The brain is a mysterious organ. In a state of fight-or-flight, the body can trigger hormones very fast and involuntarily. The heart rate, blood pressure—all systems go on high alert."

"Thank you, Doctor." Mayor Swenson turns and addresses the room. "Before we move on, I need to say a word or two. Y'all who came up here to McGuffin Ridge from the city, be aware we'll be talkin' about sensitive goings-on. Such talk don't bother us, but you mind your ears … 'specially you ladies." He looks around to see if his audience is in the palm of his hand yet and continues, "Dr. Willard, please describe John Spinks's wounds and how they occurred."

It's a loaded question that Doc Willard answers straight-forwardly. "Blood loss was due to facial and head wounds as I said, as well as rectal injury. As I inferred earlier, the head wounds and rectal wounds probably didn't occur during the same incident of violence."

"Rectal injury, you say? Let's get to that. Caused from bein' viciously attacked by Cleveland Stockton, sir?"

Doc Willard concedes to that point. "You might say that, Mayor."

Mayor Swenson follows up. "Your Honor, my client, John Spinks, was in imminent and lethal danger. As a result, he had no choice but to act in self-defense."

This much is agreeable to Doc Willard. "Let's put it this way, Mayor. My observation of John Spinks without the benefit of modern efficiencies—a rape kit or even forensic examination—my observation was that he was the victim of considerable bludgeoning as well as sexual assault."

Mayor Swenson grabs the opportunity to accentuate it just the way DA Fenton Jones had instructed. "Sodomized? Raped? Dr. Willard, let's not hold back the gravity of our meaning here."

"Yes, sir," answers Doc Willard.

Back at his table, the reporter is hurriedly filling up his legal pad with flammable quotables.

Judge Schmidt turns to DA Fenton Jones. "What do you have to say to that, Mr. Jones?"

DA Fenton Jones has plenty to say. He struts to the midst of the ensemble, then sneaks a peripheral look toward the journalist. One-liners will be flying, so he doesn't want the journalist to miss any of them.

He begins, "Dr. Willard, are you saying that a cursory examination of John Spinks's wounds was all you needed to determine that they were wounds caused by a nonconsensual encounter?"

"I did not say my examination was cursory, Sir," replies Doc Willard.

"Very well, Doctor. A probing examination, then."

"Mr. Jones, stop," barks Judge Schmidt.

Feeling it was a clever retort, DA Fenton Jones sends a quick wink to the journalist to quote him.

Judge Schmidt growls, "Wrap it up, Mr. Jones."

"Very well, Your Honor." DA Fenton Jones begins his brutal summary. "Dr. Willard, why not admit that you cannot be certain that John Spinks was accosted against his will?"

Doc Willard responds, "Excuse me, Mr. Jones?"

D.A. Fenton Jones continues, "Dr. Willard suggests John was raped and that he lashed out in self-defense after miraculously recovering from a three-day coma. But the evidence suggests John Spinks was the boyfriend of Cleveland Stockton. The evidence suggests a lovers' quarrel ensued, indeed a very violent fight ensued, obviously a very rough lovers' encounter. The evidence suggests that in an alcohol-fueled moment John Spinks backed Cleveland Stockton against the wall and shot him. You heard Bouncer Bill's testimony that John smelled of whiskey. And we've all seen enough photographs. Those photographs speak to us, Your Honor. John Spinks shot his lover, and then he fainted from wounds and blood loss that occured because of drunken fighting and bestial sex. Furthermore, photographs show John Spinks's hand was inches from the stolen murder weapon as he lay flat. He was found near death with his finger practically on the trigger. Is John Spinks guilty of manslaughter as Mayor Swenson seems to suggest, or is he guilty of first-degree murder?" With that and a wink at the reporter, DA Fenton Jones closes the show.

CHAPTER 43

Father Sam Survives Again

It takes Dr. Blackfox about two hours to fly to the airport near St. Mary's Hospital. The EMTs roll Father Sam into the OR.

Sheriff Marcus and Dr. Blackfox sleep overnight in the family waiting area on plastic-cushioned couches till a nurse shakes them awake early that morning.

The neurosurgeon, still in his green scrubs, enters the waiting area to give them an update. "We performed an exploratory surgery. He has a tumor, inoperable but manageable—nevertheless, ultimately terminal. He's been living with it for a long time—perhaps you didn't know. Visible scar tissue indicates that he underwent this kind of procedure some years ago."

Sheriff Marcus is feeling the bite of his conscience for encouraging the drunken confessional that took place in his jailhouse. "He told me a little while back, but other than his migraines and hearing a damned horse in his mind now and then … well, it never got as bad as it did when he … when I witnessed him go stark-ravin' mad the other night."

"I understand it must be hard, sir. The good Father has known since he was a very young man. Frankly, he should know better than to indulge himself as he has been doing."

Sheriff Marcus and Dr. Blackfox have the big question

Steven Boergadine

written on their faces. The neurosurgeon knows the look. But he needs to lay some hard facts on the line before he answers that question. "His liver function tests show borderline alcoholic hepatitis and some side effects of medication overdosing. His homemade herb and nutrition remedies have prevented a worst-case scenario. But heart failure, weakness of the immune system, pancreas problems—they could all come at once. He needs to manage his pharmaceuticals—regular and proper dosages. And no offense, Sheriff, he must stop drinking that moonshine you folks cook up there where you live. It's not called rotgut for nothing. Clear?"

Sheriff Marcus and Dr. Blackfox nod in agreement, but they still have the big question on their faces.

The neurosurgeon responds. "I'm guessing you want to know …"

"How long has he got?" Sheriff Marcus cuts him off.

The neurosurgeon offers a roundabout answer, "The Father's principal antagonist is the same as before—the brain tumor. It's further along, but that is no surprise. The best I can predict is—it's still manageable. But if he starts to develop other organ failures, it'll be psychologically disabling, not to mention physically. It will crush his will to live, and for a man who knows he is dying of brain cancer, depression is the tipping point to suicide. I'm afraid I can't give you a more satisfying answer."

Sheriff Marcus speaks up. "What can we do for him, Doctor?"

"He has to take it easy. Live a quiet life. He's a 'man of the Cloth,' for heaven's sake. A quiet life should come natural to him."

Sheriff Marcus and Dr. Blackfox nod affirmatively.

"We'll keep him here for a week or so. Rehab specialists will be ready to assist if he experiences recovery challenges in his behavior, his thinking, his ability to speak. If such symptoms come up, we'll keep him here longer. Does he have family, Sheriff?"

"Yes sir, there's quite a few of us that are his family. We'll make sure he gets back to his good ol' self."

They stay with Father Sam a few days after he is moved to intensive care, mostly watching him sleep. The discharge nurse isn't about to give a release date, so Dr. Blackfox gives them his phone number, and he and Sheriff Marcus set out for the airport to fly back home. Just before they take off for Appalachia, Sheriff Marcus makes a personal phone call on behalf of Father Sam from the airport.

A few weeks later, the good news finally comes when St. Mary's contacts Dr. Blackfox's tribal office. The neurosurgeon lets him know that Father Sam will be discharged in a few days.

Dr. Blackfox tells the neurosurgeon that Sheriff Marcus has already called an old friend of Father Sam's to be his caregiver, who will be sure to check in with the discharge nurse a little before his release date. The old friend will arrange to pick him up and drive him to McGuffin Ridge.

CHAPTER 44

Father Sam's Surrogate Mom

She hasn't changed a bit, just older. When she shows up at St. Mary's Hospital, driving a four-wheel-drive SUV, wearing a flannel shirt, jeans, and cowboy boots, Father Sam could not be happier to see his caregiver, Sister Marietta.

She comes calling as perky and full of it as if it were just yesterday she was teasing him for staring at Gladys Spinks's cleavage. "Sam, Sam, Sam. Sheriff Marcus told me you made a little trouble for yourself. Always loved that about you, Sam—the way you could serve the Lord and get in trouble at the same time."

Sister Marietta is not the boss of a young seminarian student now. What to do or what not to do isn't her message. She is Father Sam's friend and traveling buddy for the long drive home. She knows the score—the uncertainty of his life expectancy. So why interfere, she decides. But now that things have gotten more dire for him, she might have to nudge him a little if it'll help. She is retired and has spent a good amount of time as a volunteer in a surgical unit at the Good Samaritan Medical Center. When Sheriff Marcus called on her, he didn't have to ask twice for her to come to Father Sam's aid.

Morgan, the hospital orderly, wheels Father Sam outside and officially releases him to Sister Marietta's care. "He'll conk out fairly often today, ma'am, so don't worry if he isn't too talkative and just feels like sleeping."

Father Sam chuckles and buckles up. "Who, me? Sleepy? I'm gonna talk her ear off. Thanks for the thermos, Morgan." He raises the thermos of coffee and salutes to the orderly.

It's a balmy morning when they set out for McGuffin Ridge. It's a good ol' day for a couple of good ol' friends. But first, he can't fool himself, he needs a nap. Morgan was right, coffee-time will have to wait.

Sister Marietta tells Father Sam, "Electronic controls, Sam. Reach down on the right." He finds the button, lowers the back of the seat, and drifts off.

After a long day of driving and talking with Father Sam whenever he is awake, Sister Marietta catches sight of Sheriff Marcus sitting at Biggs Junction. He's in the old Jeep, waiting where he said he'd be waiting, to lead her up the mountain road to McGuffin Ridge.

She parks, gets out, stretches her legs, and while they shake hands, she says, "How do you do, Sheriff? Bless your heart."

Sheriff Marcus lights a smoke. "How's our boy?"

"He's not dead, just taking his fourth or fifth nap."

"Yep, I expect he'll be doing a lot of that for a while," says Sheriff Marcus.

Sister Marietta tries a couple knee bends. "Yes, sir."

"Maybe I can keep up with him now," says Sheriff Marcus.

Sister Marietta's still stretching. "You driving a four-wheeler there, Sheriff? I heard it's hilly once we get off the main road."

Sheriff Marcus backs up a bit in case his smoking is a bother. "Hilly? Yep, it's hilly. I'll manage."

"I'm carrying a towline in the back if you get stuck."

She says as she points to his cigarette. "Can you spare one of those?"

Sheriff Marcus steps forward and shakes the pack. She takes the one that slides out and lights up. "That's real smart of ya, Sister Marietta, carryin' the towline. You still go by the full title or just plain Sister or just plain Marietta?"

"Well, nobody's asked me that. How about you, just plain Sheriff?"

"Hell, we call a fella a mayor up here that ain't one. We go by what we like. Wait a minute, doggone if I didn't just curse in front of ya. I'm real sorry, ma'am. My soul has made some changes toward the good side since Father Sam came to town. I 'spect you'll help me get the rest of the way."

"No, Sheriff, I don't think I'll be changing anyone's ways. I'm just family. You never have to call me ma'am."

"That all sounds good, Sister."

"But call me for coffee when you care to."

They finish getting to know each other and head out. Sister Marietta keeps her SUV right behind the Jeep as it zigzags up the mountain on Biggs Road. She shifts into four-wheel drive when they turn at the unnamed trail and cut through the wilderness. The final turn is where Blue Gopher Road is marked by the worn-out wood sign that is mostly hidden. It's where Cleveland Stockton did his happy dance as John Spinks lay comatose in the stolen Mercury. Sheriff Marcus and Sister Marietta don't stop to do a happy dance, but they're happy to be darned near home. The neon sign is blinking up ahead at the Cozy Inn Cabins. Still no B, though. There's a haunted-house feeling about the place now. A dark and ominous midnight feeling.

Sheriff Marcus slows his Jeep down so she'll remember seeing the Cozy Inn Cabins when they get to talking later.

Sister Marietta had already been apprised of the Cozy Inn's background. She gets the feeling Sheriff Marcus wants her to say a prayer for the ramshackled monument of evil as they creep by it. So she does.

It's midnight. They speed up for the last mile to McGuffin Ridge, her prayin' and him cursin', both of 'em communicating with God in their own way.

As she shifts back into two-wheel drive and eases her SUV along Main Street past the jailhouse and Mabelline's Café, she reflects on the long day of driving and chit-chatting with Father Sam.

She looks at him snoozing on the seat beside her as his stunning revelations churn in her head. She thinks about nine-year-old Johnny Spinks's disappearance all those years ago, where he ran off to, and how he ended up in the McGuffin Ridge jail right under Father Sam's nose. She thinks about the tiny autistic savant who can shoot out the eyes of a mountain lion if it's coming for her or shoot out the eyes of a mountain man if he's coming for her.

She knows the local mayor is as dirty as they get; she knows the now-grown John Spinks is being exploited by out-of-towners with the help of Mayor Swenson. And she isn't surprised Father Sam melted into a psychotic puddle. The headaches, the pills, the nickering of an invisible Appaloosa, the delusions—it all makes sense.

She remembers when it started twenty-four years ago. She whispers to Father Sam as he sleeps on, "It's a wonder you are still alive, you silly rabbit."

She thinks about the good stuff they talked about, too. It sounds divine—beehives, black bears, braided rugs, Sunday morning children's classes, Mabelline's cherry pie and morning coffee. She is already looking forward to sitting on the warm wooden back porch with Father Sam and Sheriff Marcus and Molly, enjoying the jabbering while she takes in the hickory, oak, and poplar trees that skirt Father Sam's back field.

She realizes after that long drive and all the heart-to-heart talks along the way that she wants to be, and probably needs to be, Father Sam's surrogate mom-figure. He's the closest thing to a son she's ever had.

Sheriff Marcus pulls up to Father Sam's log house with Sister Marietta right on his tail. There is a little welcoming crowd—the late hour doesn't matter to them. Dr. Blackfox and his wife, Wilma, Deputy Sydney, Doc Willard, Mabelline, and a few others are there to see that their village priest has come home good as new. Sheriff Marcus escorts Sister Marietta into the middle of all-around welcome hugs.

The only person missing out on the hugging is Father Sam. He is still in Sister Marietta's SUV, tuckered out from today's marathon fellowship. The whole crew goes to the SUV to wake him and welcome him home. Father Sam is a little groggy, so once he is on his feet and safely inside, they say their good nights and see-ya-tomorrows.

Sister Marietta carries Father Sam's few belongings, medical instructions, and prescription medicine into his log house. She feels like she's part of his family circle by the time she brings her own luggage inside. She's an old, retired nun with a pretty good pension and an aim to do some good with it. She figures that is perfect.

CHAPTER 45

Six Months And No Appaloosa

I t's been six months since plain-clothed transport officers chained John Spinks's ankles and wrists, shuffled
him out of the McGuffin Ridge jailhouse and into
an unmarked sedan, and delivered him to the big city.
Same city Father Sam was flown to by Dr. Blackfox and
Sheriff Marcus just days before. Difference being, a few
weeks later, Father Sam went home, but John was put on
trial. He had no chance against an underfinanced public
defender's office, Miss Matilda's love-sick judge and the
Bible Belt jury pool under the spell of DA Fenton Jones's
daily press briefs.

DURING THE SIX MONTHS FATHER SAM HAS BEEN BACK
in McGuffin Ridge, convalescing from brain surgery, he is
slow to recover. Sleep is his refuge—at unexpected inter-
vals. And proper dosages of his prescription meds. And a
permanent seat *on the wagon.*

During Father Sam's waking hours, he doesn't think
about John Spinks's legal plight. He can't. His brain requires
simple neuronal order. His pastoral passion for justice has
not returned to what it once was.

English language class for the Cherokee children now takes place in Mabelline's back room instead of Father Sam's back yard. During winter, Mabelline's Café serves a lot of purposes around McGuffin Ridge, none more noble than Father Sam's Sunday morning English class.

Sister Marietta has been looking after Father Sam since she brought him back to McGuffin Ridge a half-year ago. She doesn't plan on moving out of his house, and he is in no shape to suggest she do so. Both of them need and welcome the company of the other. Theirs is a strong case of familial bonding that started near a Texas border town decades ago, in a white stucco mission with a red-tiled roof.

Good-time music pulsating from the big old house on the ridge above Father Sam's back yard. The place some call the House of Wonder and others call the House of a Damn Shame, gets Sister Marietta to thinking. She has heard stories of the goings-on behind its dingy walls, but she's learned to look at things from the high road when it comes to the locals. That commiserating point of view sets her to thinking about the musical leanings of the men and women who hang out there. She thinks about establishing better communication between them and the Cherokee community. Communication requires a common language. Music is a common language.

After she makes the Cherokee moms comfortable in their usual wool-cutting endeavor at Father Sam's, she walks to Mabelline's Café to check up on his English class.

She peeks through the window of the back door of Mabelline's and sees Father Sam ready to nod off near the chalkboard. Molly dozes at his feet. Although there's a flatness in his everyday mood, he still has love in his eyes—when they're open.

Sister Marietta rethinks what he hinted at years ago when he returned to the fold: the cleansing of his soul is somehow associated with his brain tumor, which is somehow associated with his mystical journey, which is somehow associated with his auditory hallucinations, and it's all unseen. It's his unique experience with God. To everyone around him, it appears that he now leads a sedentary life, as the doctor ordered him to do.

She notes, Dr. Blackfox at a table in the far corner, studying the Cherokee book written by Father Sam's grandmother.

Instead of going inside right then, Sister Marietta trots around to the woodshed and picks up a couple pieces of cured hardwood for the stove. When she enters, the kids surround her. She asks them, "What do I have here, my dears?"

A couple of the children answer, "Firewood to keep us warm, Auntie. Thank you." She's pleased that their English is prompt and well spoken.

"Let's fill up the firewood box for Father Sam. Each of you go out to the woodshed and bring in one piece of wood."

The children all run for the door. Molly wakes up and senses a chance to frolic in the frost with the kids, and chases after them as they scoot outdoors.

"And thank you, my dears," says Sister Marietta. "Shut the door behind you, please."

Dr. Blackfox pulls himself away from the book. "Your grandmother was an anointed soul, Father."

Sister Marietta watches Father Sam open his eyes and recognize Dr. Blackfox's excitement.

She picks up a piece of chalk and writes words on the blackboard that have something to do with mountain music—*dulcimer, hogfiddle, pennywhistle, tin whistle, banjo.*

Father Sam watches Sister Marietta bustle about with

her never-ending energy. "Are you hijacking my English class, dear lady?" He hopes she gives him an affirmative nod. She leaves the blackboard, fills two mugs with hot coffee and delivers them to him and Dr. Blackfox.

She says, "I'm an old restless thief in the night, Sam. Forgive me."

"You are a restless angel is what your are," responds Father Sam.

Dr. Blackfox raises his mug of coffee. "Thank you, Sister. Father, I would like to share this book with my professor. He is also Cherokee and the head of the Sequoia Institute, where I work."

"I'm surrounded by restless angels. Of course, be my guest," says Father Sam.

From outside the entry door the kids try to turn the doorknob without dropping their firewood.

Sister Marietta opens the door. "Come in, my dears. How would you like to hear musicians of the Cherokee nation and musicians of your Appalachian neighbors, all playing their instruments together."

The kids cheer as they fill up the storage box with firewood.

"Very good. You will learn the names of their instruments before you hear them play music." She goes on, "What do you think, Sam?"

"Tell us more," responds Father Sam.

Sister Marietta nods excitedly in response to Father Sam's retort, "I will, once I know what I'm talking about."

She helps the children button up their coats. She borrows a long scarf from one of them. "Look, let's tie our scarves the French way." She measures the two ends together, then loops the scarf around her neck and pulls it tight.

The kids give it a try.

Sister Marietta asks, "Can someone say, it's very cold today?"

One of the boys says, "It's very cold today."

Dr. Blackfox closes the medicine book and rises from his chair. "I must introduce your grandmother to Professor Redhawk."

Father Sam acknowledges Dr. Blackfox with a smile. As the children strut about, showing off their French-tied scarves, Father Sam gets up and slowly walks to the blackboard. He studies the list of musical instruments, then turns to Sister Marietta and says, "I know a couple of those. When do we start?"

Sister Marietta ties a scarf around Father Sam's neck, French style, as the kids gather around to watch. "Don't bother yourself with 'when do we start.' I'm in the planning stage."

One of the kids brings Father Sam's winter coat to Sister Marietta.

Sister Marietta asks the children, "Would you like to walk Father Sam to his log house to meet your moms?"

Dr. Blackfox puts on his coat and hat, tucks the Cherokee medicine book into his leather satchel, and walks out the door with the kids and Father Sam.

There's a little bit of sweeping and straightening up to do, so Sister Marietta stays behind and gets busy with it. As she works, she wonders how to infiltrate the musical community embedded in the House of Wonder. Then she remembers that Sheriff Marcus will drop by later. They'll have a cigarette while he walks her home—she'll pick his brain.

CHAPTER 46

A Few Weeks Later

D r. Blackfox's Cessna 340 begins its descent. He lifts the handheld mic.

Professor Redhawk is sitting next to him reading. A snake light extends from the center console and illuminates the pages of the old deerskin-covered medicine book.

"Mustang One, requesting permission to land. Over."

Dr. Blackfox listens for a response from the control tower.

Permission granted. Runway two. Over.

The landing is smooth and once the airplane is secured in the hangar, they get in Dr. Blackfox's car and head for Mabelline's Café. They arrive in time for an early taste of bean bread, fried hominy, and eggs, all set up in serving trays, and a long cup of coffee before the party begins.

After the appetizer, Dr. Blackfox and Professor Redhawk review notes they'd like to share about Father Sam's book—critical insights.

Soon, Father Sam and Sister Marietta arrive.

Dr. Blackfox leaps to his feet and introduces his elder, Professor Redhawk.

All four of them exchange courtesies. As Father Sam, Sister Marietta, and Dr. Blackfox chat about the flight over, about the weather, and about the heaps of food anticipated for the occasion, Professor Redhawk remains silent and observant.

The chatting amongst the three friends comes to a polite interlude when Professor Redhawk reaches toward the table where he and Dr. Blackfox had been sitting. Not good at party chatter, he picks up the book reverently and holds it as if it were a gift from Alfred Nobel himself. Then he speaks to the curious faces watching him. "The language is Cherokee. The content is beyond our tradition. Your grandmother's vision has no cultural roots, sir. The gift-wrap is Cherokee language, but the gift—the gift is not of our culture. Future wisemen may better inform us of knowledge that originates outside the observable universe, because that is where the power of these writings originates, in my humble opinion."

The heavy silence continues to hold the room until Father Sam breaks it. "Grandmother was half-Cherokee, half-Scottish. She lived here, served the people. To them she was a medicine woman. Legendary."

"Her ethnic group is …" Professor Redhawk searches for the right word.

Dr. Blackfox helps. "Inconsequential, Father, which makes this book profound."

The infectious disclosure of the two scientists infatuates Sister Marietta. "Good heavens. So, she was not a medicine woman?"

Professor Redhawk elaborates, "We must assume she identified as a medicine woman. So, in that sense she was. But her writings speak to other persuasions. Beyond dogma, beyond denomination, beyond religiosity. And, at times, beyond her control."

Dr. Blackfox jumps in. "There are anecdotal testimonials. Many. Reports of readings your grandmother gave to locals. Many. She was able to diagnose and recommend exact personalized treatments for individual patients, using nature's pathway to a cure—certain food combinations, herbs and roots and tea. In one instance, for example, she sent a grieving mother to a local river to pick certain plants, but only the plants that grew on the north bank of the river, instructing the woman that the same plants on the south bank would hurt her child. These kinds of suggestions came only after she immersed herself into a state of unconsciousness. When she awoke, her guidance resulted in real healing." He points at the book. "It's all in there."

Professor Redhawk voices a possibility. "The cases she logged are dated. If the dates are correct, it puts her age at fifteen and on."

After a moment of thought, Father Sam raises a point, "Grandmother has come to my dreams. Perhaps she has brought us all together."

He glances at Sister Marietta with a look she instantly reads. He says, "I'm sorry. Do you mind if I sit?" Sister Marietta leads him to a comfortable chair. "Please come, and tell me more," says Father Sam.

The group ambles along with him as Professor Redhawk speaks, "As much as we are Native American, we are also Western-educated research scientists. The second half of her book is a different story, written later in her life on the subject of aging. She seems to ask, why are life and death separate experiences?"

"I would be pleased if you continue your study," Father Sam offers from his chair. "Forgive me, friends, I am tired." He drops his head and closes his eyes. Short notice is never a surprise when it comes to Father Sam's therapeutic naps.

Sister Marietta finds a blanket and drapes it across his lap.

Just then, a glowingly pregnant Wilma Blackfox arrives with her special dish of down-to-earth bread pudding made with fresh-from-the-tree maple syrup. She is leading the way for the Cherokee musicians and their wives who bring in warm dishes of home-cooked entrées to add to what is being prepared in the kitchen.

Sister Marietta instantly welcomes them with a big smile.

Dr. Blackfox and Wilma mingle with their tribal brothers and sisters. Time goes by and there is no sign of Sheriff Marcus and his badass posse.

Father Sam is rested and can plainly see everyone is gravitating toward the smell of the freshly laid out banquet. "I don't know what happened to Marcus and his crew. Do you mind asking the musicians to play something soft? I'll open things up with a reading from the Bible."

As the music of the Cherokee's and the intoning of Father Sam blend, a racket comes from the café area. Sheriff Marcus and the musicians and ladies of the House of Wonder bump up against the swinging door and push it open. When he realizes there is a meditative atmosphere, Sheriff Marcus stops and holds up his hand, halting his late-to-the-party merrymakers.

Father Sam remains immersed in the soft music and his biblical offering. "... and the Holy Spirit feast your saints with the vision of yourself, who are true light, the fulfillment of all desires, the joy that knows no ending, gladness unalloyed, and perfect bliss: through the same Christ, our Lord."

A pause suggests the prayer has ended. Sheriff Marcus takes a guess that it has. "Amen, and sorry we're late."

"You're just in time," says Sister Marietta.

Sheriff Marcus's gang rolls in, parks their musical instruments, and head for the food as he informs Father Sam, "We got ourselves a pack of hungry sinners here."

Father Sam pours himself a mug of pick-me-up coffee and assures Sheriff Marcus, "I'm glad they made it. Go, my friend, serve yourself now." He's getting tired again and looks around for the nearest place to sit with his coffee.

Sister Marietta sees the weariness in him. She holds his hot cup of coffee and leads him by the arm to an overstuffed chair.

The Cherokees and Appalachians eat up and play good-time music for several hours. Café patrons and other townsfolk and their children eventually fill the room. It is positively evangelical, observes Sister Marietta, who can't stop smiling.

In the corner, Dr. Blackfox and Professor Redhawk pore over the medicine book.

Father Sam makes good use of the overstuffed chair, sleeping soundly next to his coffee gone cold.

CHAPTER 47

The Party Is Definitely Over

The musical potluck settles down, and everyone heads for home except Sheriff Marcus, Sister Marietta, Deputy Sydney, a few old folks, who get busy setting up for the next day's consignment sale, and Father Sam, who awakens from his deep snooze in the overstuffed chair. His eyes open quickly as if a sound frightened him, but his body takes a little time to wake up. He's not quite ready to get to his feet.

Sister Marietta washes pots and pans in Mabelline's kitchen while Deputy Sydney and Sheriff Marcus help the old folks arrange tables and chairs and fix up a gated area with floor mats and toys for the toddlers. They will need somewhere safe to play in the morning while grown-ups sell pajama bags, potholders, plants, canned fruit, Grandpa's wood shop creations, and other mountain-life essential goods and services.

Sheriff Marcus studies Father Sam for a moment. "Father, you ready to go on home now? Maybe too much rock'n'roll for ya tonight."

"I'll wait for Sister," Father Sam replies.

"Sydney or I can see she makes it home. She might be in Mabelline's kitchen another hour, anyway."

Father Sam doesn't mind being talked into going home.

He feels a migraine coming. That dreaded feeling is what snapped open his eyes from a dead sleep a few minutes ago. Thankfully, his evening dosage of pills is waiting on the windowsill in his kitchen. "I'll go if you let me navigate myself back home, Marcus. You stay and make sure Sister Marietta is escorted later."

Trudging down Main Street, Father Sam hears a horse nicker behind him. He stops, clinches his jaw, and braces for the worst. But it's only Clayton, the town drunk, guiding Mabel, his old mare, coming up behind him. A violin case is looped around Mabel's saddle horn. "I'm a little drunk, Father. Don't mind me and Mabel here. That nun lady asked me to see ya to your door."

Father Sam is startled but relieved that it's just a friendly sinner and his horse.

"Glad you're not drinking and driving, Clayton." He's grateful that he has the mind to make a little joke after realizing the Appaloosa isn't behind him. "Thanks for fiddlin' tonight." Father Sam trips and falls onto the grass at the edge of the road.

Clayton helps him to his feet and swats dirt and grass from his pants legs.

Father Sam makes another joke. "Doggone it, I have trouble walking and talking at the same time anymore."

Clayton responds, "Well, you know I'm that way most of the time myself, Father. Why don't ya lean on the saddle there? Me and Mable are walkin' purty slow. It oughta do ya."

Father Sam hangs on till they arrive at his front porch. Clayton watches as he manages his way to the door. "Be seeing ya, Father."

Father Sam turns and gives Clayton and Mabel a weak wave bye-bye.

The migraine is now pulsating against Father Sam's temples as he lets himself in and heads for the kitchen. He sits down with a glass of water and a couple pills. A mighty throb hits his forehead, and the water glass jolts from his grip and shatters on the floor. The pills land in the puddle.

Then a loud whinny. It's not Clayton's mare.

Father Sam closes his eyes, leans back, and grimaces from a wave of pain. The pain increases. He voices his buried anguish to God, "I did everything I could … What else can I do?" His eyes shut, and he passes out. Unconsciousness is the only place he can go to escape the pain— physical and spiritual.

About an hour later, Sister Marietta lets herself in and observes the out-cold Father Sam and the mess on the floor. She steps around the broken glass and water puddle and traipses to the kitchen. She dampens a clean towel, grabs a mop, a broom, and a dustpan, places the towel on the forehead of her old friend, and keeps an eye on him as she cleans up the floor.

After the cleanup, she sits with Father Sam, dabbing his forehead with the wet towel till he opens his eyes. He looks around, and then looks up at Sister Marietta. "What happened?"

"You tell me, Sam."

He's thankful the pain has subsided and gives the moment a little tickle. "I've slowed down lately, haven't I, Sister? Did I ever tell you about my Haight-Ashbury days?" He rises from his chair and begins gathering items for the consignment sale in the morning. "Just a little bit to do here …" He wobbles as his equilibrium fails him.

Sister Marietta stabilizes him. "Well, you're not a flow-erchild anymore, Sam. I can do this." She takes him by the arm and walks him to his bedroom door. He takes her hand

and squeezes it softly, and with a little nod of gratitude, retires to his room.

Sister Marietta goes to the pantry and finds a dozen jars of Father Sam's homemade apple butter and a pile of his hand-made braided door mats from the library. She places them in Father Sam's handwoven Cherokee river-basket with the carrying handle.

Moving slowly in his room, Father Sam reaches up to pull his bedroom curtains shut. The reflection in the window, it's not him—it's nine-year-old Johnny Spinks. Father Sam closes his eyes and grasps the windowsill with both hands. Then he opens his eyes. Gladys Spinks appears, beautiful as ever. He holds off on closing the curtains, dazzled by her image, then slowly pulls them shut.

He changes to his pajamas, turns off the light and sits down on the edge of his bed. Hunched over with his elbows braced on his knees, he buries his head in his hands and thinks for a long minute about the last six months. How shallow his life has become. How emotionless his character has become. How real his hallucinations have become.

How heavy his eyelids. He falls back on his bed, halfway to a sleep state. In seconds, a lightbulb appears within his mental sanctum. It brightens fast and explodes. He bolts up to a sitting position, wide awake, and stares into the darkness.

He reaches for his Bible and holds it close to his heart. Tranquility fills Father Sam's room. It comes to him that tomorrow morning he must talk to Dr. Blackfox about hitching a flight to the big city.

He doesn't know how he knows, but he knows it's time to help John Spinks out of the mess he's in. If he has to die trying, why not? He's dying, anyway. Father Sam feels more at peace than he has for six months.

CHAPTER 48

The Sentence Is Death

I nside The Sequoia Institute, Dr. Blackfox and Professor Redhawk are horror-struck by what they are watching on a local news channel.

The two Cherokee scientists see bundled-up DA Fenton Jones on screen pontificating at a campaign rally of bussed-in shills. It's close to zero degrees outside as he flails his puffy, mitted hands to punctuate a contorted sermon in front of the city jail. Enticed devotees have gathered to show their allegiance to the second coming of Jim Crow.

DA Fenton Jones soldiers on. "I will take a stand against rainbow radicals, inner-city baggy-pantsed gangbangers, social deviants of all colors, and as you know, murderers who provoke violent, perverted crime in our fair state. I believe your Attorney General must know the streets, and I have come from the mean streets, my friends. My American citizenship was hard-earned by my immigrant parents who hailed from an island nation, and I know that every citizen watching their television at this moment feels as this proud American citizen feels. Don't let my natural tan fool ya, my friends. Inside me, I'm the same as y'all are."

The camera's lens pans away from DA Fenton Jones and cuts to the crowd of stern-faced, pious folk. One of those stern faces is out of place.

Dr. Blackfox points to the screen. "There he is."

On camera, Father Sam, wearing a heavy black scarf and a grey wool fedora, is almost hidden behind the exhale of his misty breath as he turns and walks away from the mob of winterized fanatics who are lapping up DA Fenton Jones's promise of a freewheeling vendetta against the "scum of the earth."

Father Sam heads for the city jail with his bag of weapons. As he rounds the corner to the visitor's entrance of the city jail, he walks by an idling school bus that's been converted into a yellow billboard on wheels. Bold, black words HOLY TRINITY OF THE RIGHTEOUS are garnished across both sides. Only two people with enough sense to keep warm are seated inside the parked bus, the driver and Miss Matilda.

DA Fenton Jones's spiel grows fainter. "Every rapist and killer who feeds upon the innocence of our citizens, and our citizens' sons and daughters, and denies accountability for their heinous encroachment on our human rights …"

On a steel-bolted mount fastened to a concrete wall, a small-screen television is visible through the bars of John Spinks's temporary holding cell. He watches DA Fenton Jones's finale on the black and white screen. *I heard the good citizens of my state demand accountability, and I acted on that demand. John Arthur Spinks was found guilty months ago but today his sentencing finally sends him to death row. Only God can help him now!*

Father Sam enters the visitor's entrance of the jail house. Security stops him before he makes it to the walk-through metal detector. "Place the bag in the holding area and remove the contents."

Father Sam places his heavy satchel in the holding area as instructed. He releases the clasp that secures the leather cover. He pulls open the satchel, reaches inside and removes an assortment of munitions meant to liberate the mind.

The guard flips through each book. "We'll take these inside for ya, Father. Come on through and stand in front of the door ahead of you."

Father Sam walks through the metal detector and positions himself in front of the door. The door lock releases. He pulls it open and enters. An armed guard follows, carrying the books.

John Bagley is sitting alone, numbed by what he watched on the television screen. He's not expecting a visitor, much less this one.

Father Sam receives the pile of books from the guard and crosses to the bench on the outside of the visitors section separated by steel bars. He waits for John to get used to him and the stack of books on the bench beside him.

John stares at him for a long minute. "I just saw you on television, listening to that liar?"

"I was on my way to visit you," answers Father Sam.

"I heard you were in a nuthouse."

"Not yet, son."

"That DA ought to be in one," offers John.

"Who told you I was in a nuthouse?"

"Sydney told me you was talkin' to imaginary people. He said he watched you get taken away. He didn't say where they took ya."

"Nuthouse would be a fair guess," says Father Sam.

"What happened? He said you were near dead."

"I had a breakdown. Collapsed. Old war wounds."

"Which war?"

Father Sam gives it some thought. "The war within."

"The war within?" John lies down on his bunk and stares at the ceiling. "Who's winning?"

"Some days I win, some days I lose," says Father Sam.

John continues to stare at the ceiling. "Sydney said you was fighting for me. I guess you lost that war."

"As they say, the battle, but not the war, son."

John withdraws from the conversation and goes back to staring at the ceiling.

Father Sam doesn't push. A few beats of awkward silence passes. "What are you thinking about, son?"

"Tortillas?"

Father Sam plays along. "Corn or flour?"

Slightly upbeat, John snickers. "Flour. Warm. Fresh from Anita's griddle."

Father Sam nurses the friendly dialogue. "Oh yeah. When I was a young seminarian, I lived close to the Mexican border in …" He stops. He almost said too much. "Close to the Mexican border—tortillas were real tasty around there."

"Yeah? When I was a boy, I lived close to the border, too. I've been remembering things about my childhood back then. Don't know where it was. But the border wasn't far. Me and my real mom and step-dad were poor and drunk most of the time."

Father Sam's thoughts start to take him back to events he has tried to forget.

Real mom. That would be Gladys.

He guides the conversation away from the subject of his seminarian days. "Tortillas. Melted butter. Refried beans. Can't get them at Mabelline's Café.

John asks, "Where's that?"

"Mabelline's. She made all your meals while you were visiting us."

"Oh. I oughta be eatin' my meals with my family. But you can thank that Mabelline for me, anyway."

"Will you tell me about your family, son?"

"Sure, Anita's mamma raised me. Anita's brother, Ramon—me and him we're like brothers. He's older. He taught me flyin'."

"Flying?"

"On a trapeze. I did bicycle tricks when I was a boy. Jumpin' hoops, parrots on the handlebars. But I got older. Ramon—he gave me wings, man. They called me el pelirrojo águila."

"Why'd you leave it?"

"Everything ended bad. Ramon was my catcher. He was climbing up to me. The ladder broke. We weren't a five-star operation. But we were happy."

"I'm sorry," says Father Sam.

"They were all circus. When Ramon went down, there was no money. They started farmin'. I heard oil fields were hirin' in Texas. So, I headed for the US border. Was gonna bring home US dollars."

Father Sam hopes he can bring up the subject of reading.

John brings it up instead. He gets up and walks to the bars. He gestures toward the books. "What are those for?"

"For you." Father Sam looks around to the guard at the end of the cell block. He signals a request to hand the books through the bars. The guard responds affirmatively.

"If you want them," says Father Sam as he gives the books to John.

"What are they about?"

"Spiritual stuff."

Steven Boergadine

"Right, you're a preacher."

"Yes, that is true." He jokes, "On the occasion that I'm allowed out of the nuthouse."

John grins and picks up the book on top of the pile. "What's this one about?"

"Meditation."

"Is that how you fight your war?"

"One of the ways, yes."

"Can I learn to do that?"

"It takes time, but …"

"I got time."

CHAPTER 49

Mayor Swenson's Comeuppance

Sheriff Marcus is glad Father Sam is out of town because he wouldn't want to look him in the eye this evening. Sitting in the jailhouse, he gets up, and looks at the firearms slotted in his gun rack, picks out the Remington Model 8, and heads for the door.

On the edge of town, getting situated at the airstrip, Bouncer Bill flips on the recently repaired runway lights. Mayor Swenson stands by. "Bounce, you keep your rifle handy. I don't know much about this new client of ours."

Bouncer Bill pats a rifle that lies ready on the console.

A small aircraft begins its descent.

"I'll go meet and greet. Keep him in your peep sight." Mayor Swenson swaggers to where the aircraft will end up and waits. The plane lands and rolls to a stop near Mayor Swenson's position. The pilot sits tight in the cockpit, lights a cigarette and doesn't remove his goggles and headgear.

Mayor Swenson strains his eyes to see the pilot. Then he turns his head toward Bouncer Bill and gives him a look that conveys a warning of high alert. He turns his face back to the mystery pilot and mumbles to himself, "C'mon out now. Business is waitin.'"

The sound of an owl breaks the silence of the night. But it's not an owl. It's the young Cherokee trapper in a tree, signaling ten shooters with hunting rifles to take aim from the shadows of the woods' edge.

Finally, Mayor Swenson expresses some impatience with the pilot. "You gonna get on out of that airplane or what?"

The pilot continues to smoke.

Mayor Swenson turns to walk. "I don't have time for this."

The pilot climbs out of his cockpit. Mayor Swenson turns around to greet him.

"I like a man that takes his time. But doggone it, me standing like a beggar in front of your damn airplane ain't no way to get things goin'."

The pilot removes his goggles and hat—it's Paparazzi Mickey's pa. He hasn't finished his cigarette.

Mayor Swenson has never met Mickey's pa. But there's something foreboding in the manner of the man in front of him.

"Bounce, might gonna need ya here." Mayor Swenson looks over at Bouncer Bill's console. He's gone. Mayor Swenson tries to sound calm. "What'cha got in mind, Mister?"

Mickey's pa has two words for Mayor Swenson. "You. Dead."

Mayor Swenson turns to walk away. He's in a hurry now.

Mickey's pa flicks his cigarette to the hard-grass runway—that's the signal.

Ten rifles fire—nine bullets hit their mark.

CHAPTER 50

Two Years Later

Aloneness is the battlefield where the *war within* can be won or lost. A man can be no more alone than when sitting on death row.

It's a scorcher today. The temperature is over a hundred degrees. Sgt. Karol walks by Eugene's cell. "How ya doin', Eugene?"

Eugene isn't winning the *war within*. He yells at Sgt. Karol, "Man, can't you get me a fan in this motherfucker?"

"Look at me, Eugene. I'm sweating. We're all sweating." Sgt. Karol moves on to Purdue's cell.

Purdue is dipping a hand towel in the toilet bowl and swabbing his face. "A swamp cooler. That'd do it, Sarge. Blow us a big wind right through this avenue of hell."

Sgt Karol stops and thinks outloud, "The avenue of hell? There's your next poem, Purdue."

Purdue spouts off, "For why? Oh my. Why should I try? Get a swamp cooler so I don't die. Else Old Sparky won't have me to fry."

Sgt. Karol moves on. "Well, it rhymes, Purdue."

He approaches Woody's cell. Woody isn't wearing a stitch. Sweat is draining off him. "Take my appeal away. I don't want it. Mr. Sparky, deliver me."

Sgt. Karol moves on. "Be careful what you wish for, Woody."

Halting at John's cell, Sgt. Karol watches him meditate. John has no sweat on him, no sign of discomfort, no agony written on his face. On a shelf, books are crammed together. "Hey! Spinks!"

No answer.

He tries again. "Hey, Spinks!"

John opens his eyes.

"Don't you ever sweat, man?" Sgt. Karol pulls a hankie from his pocket and swabs his own face. "You got a visitor—your priest. Come on."

John stands and backs up till his two arms extend through the meal tray slot. Sgt. Karol cuffs him and then opens the cell door.

Father Sam enters the small, gray visiting room, carrying books and a small box of red licorice. Contact visits are allowed here for death row prisoners when the visitor is your lawyer or your clergyman. Father Sam lays out the books and red licorice.

John picks up the licorice. "How'd ya know I like this stuff?" Father Sam tells the ironic truth. "An angel told me."

John looks at the book titles. "Kierkegaard, Hesse, Emerson, and Freud?" He pulls a stick of licorice from the box and jokes. "Where's your Matthew, Mark, Luke and John?"

"I think I can fix you up."

"Nah, everybody gets a Bible in here," John says.

"I hear they make terrible pillows," says Father Sam.

It appears something is bothering John.

"What's on your mind, son?"

"I read that I could bring myself to account to God. What would that do?"

"Well, it'd show God you want to improve your spiritual identity. We need to show Him every day. I think you do that. How is your meditation going?"

John gives a reflective answer, "That's the thing. Memories been comin' back to me since I been meditating."

Father Sam has some general wisdom on the subject. "Sometimes we suppress …"

But John needs to get specific. "About my mama."

Not a subject Father Sam was expecting. "Uhh …"

John unburdens his heart. "My real biology-mama. I even remembered her name—Gladys. My upbringing memories are full of Mexico, my Mexican schoolin', my Mexican family … my little one, Sarita … she would squeeze my cheeks with her little hands." He holds his own cheeks between his thumb and index finger and squeezes—emulating Sarita's childish manner.

"Don't forget Anita's tortillas fresh off the griddle." Father Sam smiles at his own one-liner.

John acknowledges Father Sam's charm as he holds a stick of red licorice under his nose and inhales memories. "It takes me back. You want one?"

"No, thank you." Father Sam doesn't want to inhale memories.

"I'm thinking, I wanna do that thing. Account myself for God. Is that like a confession?"

"No."

"How can I confess?"

"We would need complete privacy. Sacramental seal. Not possible here." Father Sam looks toward the guard. "But I have personal experience. Confessions come in all shapes and sizes. You can be accountable to God without the formality of confession. Go ahead and talk to God, and I'll eavesdrop. That'll probably do for now."

"I left my ma." John looks for a response.

Father Sam feels the expectation. "Oh? We all leave our mothers, sooner or later. It's not a sin."

"She needed me. She was messed up. My step-dad was dead. I was messed up. I turned my back on her and everything. Erased it all. Nobody asked questions. I fell asleep and ended up in Mexico. I don't know where my ma is today."

Pretending to not know, Father Sam asks, "You were a boy. How old were you when that happened?"

"I turned nine years old on the day I ran away, Father."

"Tell me about it, son." Father Sam has never known what happened the day he drove away from Gladys in his pickup and lost his mind. He closes his eyes. Best to try to convey a state of beatitude. It'll give John the freedom to pour himself dry. Father Sam also doesn't want John to see his eyes lie as he pretends to hear about Gladys and nine-year old Johnny Spinks for the first time.

CHAPTER 51

Nine Years Old And Drunk

It's Johnny Spinks's birthday. Nine years old and drunk.
Johnny races home on his old bicycle. Playing cards
clamped onto the frame hit the spokes when he rides.
Aces, kings, queens. They make a fun motorcycle sound
that nine-year-olds like to make.

Not paying mind to the pickup parked in the front of
his house, he drops his bike by the porch and walks in the
front door. He's got a pocketful of shoplifted batteries for
his stepfather's camera. It's set up in the basement for his
dirty business, and it's not the dirty booze business.

The first thing Johnny sees when he opens the front door
are groceries scattered on the kitchen table. He remembers
that today his mama went to the federal food center next to
the religious mission on Gowdyville Road. There has to be
a package of red licorice somewhere on that table. He spots
it underneath a box of devil's food cake mix and crams it
into his back pocket. He knows it's for him. Mama always
remembers his red licorice.

He hears someone let out a yelp and looks in the direction of the bedroom, where he sees a pair of spooky eyes
staring at him through a thin opening of the door.

Johnny runs to the end of the kitchen, where he exits
to the wood stairs that go to the basement. He'll be pro-

tected there. Down the stairs fast, and then he stops, almost stepping in a big puddle of sloe gin and broken glass. His stepdad is sitting on the concrete floor with his back against the basement wall, an open bottle of Benzedrine in his hand—its contents scattered and soaking in the ruby red puddle. "Hey, Jim. I'm back." He pulls out the packet of batteries and tosses them next to a 35mm camera attached to a tripod. "Someone is upstairs, Jim. Can you go look?"

Jim Spinks doesn't answer. He can't. Booze, pills, and debauchery have caught up with him.

Johnny realizes the fixed eyes and stone-cold touch mean his stepdad died of something. He's afraid the spooky person upstairs might have murdered him.

Jim Spinks had been admiring his latest handiwork when he stroked out. In his left-hand, photos of *Cute American Boy Jesus* are spilling out of a manilla envelope. In his right hand is a price tag that he was about to tape on that manilla envelope—$50 US.

Johnny double-checks the corpse, "Jim? You fakin', Jim?" He hears his mama yell at somebody upstairs. A bottle crashes against the kitchen wall.

The kitchen door opens at the top of the stairs. Johnny moves out of the throw of light that shoots down to where he is standing.

Gladys starts down the stairway in an icy daze. "Johnny?"

Johnny darts behind the wood stairs. Maybe the murderer is poking his mama with a gun barrel. She's not allowed to come down to the basement.

She hangs on to the banister with two hands as she slowly makes her way sideways down the wood stairs. "Jim? Johnny?"

Johnny watches through the stairway as his ma's bare feet come into view, then the back of her legs, then she steps into the puddle of sloe gin and glass. There's no murderer poking her with a gun barrel.

She hasn't yet realized Jim Spinks is dead. "I know you told me not to come down here. Jim? Jim?" Then she touches him. "Oh God, you're dead and gone, aren't ya?" She touches him again to be sure and shrieks desperate, primal demands at his lifeless form. "What the fuck am I gonna do now, Jim? What about the rent? What about Johnny?"

Johnny bends down to a crouch and covers his face with his hands, peeking through his fingers at the madness.

Gladys moves through the gouging glass and sticky gin. Not feeling the skin of her bare feet puncturing and bleeding, she pulls out the circus tickets and waves them with a shaking fist at her dead tormentor as if finally liberated, spouting unsuppressed defiance. "A sweet man came by. He laid himself on me. He brought something for Johnny. See these circus passes, Jim Spinks? And he said, 'forgive me.' A sweet, holy man. Not like you … not like you." She slips in the gin but steadies herself. "What is that?" She spots the $50 US price tag and the manilla envelope. "What is this?" She grabs the envelope and hopes for money. It takes a few seconds to sink in that there's only pictures. Pictures not meant for a mother's eyes. "What? You son of a bitch! This is Johnny! This is Johnny! Oh my God, Jim Spinks, you fucking monster! You monster!" Crazed, she beats and kicks his corpse as the photos and circus tickets sail from her hand.

One circus ticket flutters through the air and lands on the stairstep near Johnny's face. He can make out its printed instructions—the circus is happening now.

Her maternal rage out of control, Gladys picks up a large piece of the broken gin bottle and slashes the neck and body of Jim Spinks.

Splattered with blood from the corpse of her pedophiliac husband, she stumbles to the manger and smashes the photo gear to pieces, then falls to her knees in the straw, inconsolably weeping in the manger where *Cute American Boy Jesus* has been photographed numerous times.

Johnny plucks the ticket from the wooden step in front of his face and sneaks up the stairs. He breaks for outdoors, mounts his bike, and peddles furiously. The cards clattering against his spokes don't sound fun anymore.

His skinny legs tire of peddling full speed so he pulls to the side of the road and parks behind a pile of railroad ties and heaves his guts out. His nine-year-old body hasn't gotten used to the life it has been leading.

Several black Dodge Coronets whiz by. He doesn't know the FBI is headed for his house.

Johnny pulls the cards off his spokes and peddles on. He sees the bigtop down the road.

He comes up behind eleven-year-old Butch and thirteen-year-old Shorty who are riding double on their crumby old bike. Johnny knows them as brothers from a family worse off than his. They don't like that he has his own bike and can pass them.

Butch yells at Johnny from behind, "Fuckhead."

Johnny flips up his middle-finger without looking back.

Butch responds, "Hey, Spinks! Your mother stinks!"

Johnny flips up both middle fingers as he peddles ahead hands-free.

He arrives at the circus gate, jumps off his bike, and flashes his ticket. He figures Butch and Shorty will steal his bike but he doesn't care. He'll steal someone else's when he leaves the circus.

Security stops Butch and Shorty at the gate.

Johnny sees the last of the trapeze act. Its awesomeness lights up his nine-year-old eyes. The fantasy that fills the bigtop fills his troubled mind.

The ring announcer's basso voice comes over the big speakers. "Ladies and gentlemen, boys and girls, El Circo Familia pequeño del Cuernavaca will be back next year."

The high-wire flyer poses on the trapeze. The crowd roars.

Johnny sees Butch and Shorty sneak in. He runs under a bleacher and encounters a little clown smoking a cigarette. Butch and Shorty spot Johnny and come for him.

The little clown sees that Johnny is afraid. She stomps her cigarette and leads him to a travel trailer. They hide inside.

The little clown removes her mask. Her name is Anita Vallejo.

Johnny shares a red licorice with her. She's nine-years-old, too.

Just then, Mama Vallejo calls for Anita from outside the trailer. "Anita, dear, are you in there?"

"Yes, Mama." She whispers to Johnny, "Get under there."

Johnny scoots under the bed and hopes he never has to come out.

Mama Vallejo pops her head inside. "We must go, sweetheart."

"Yes, Mama."

"We are returning to Cuernavaca."

Anita is happy they are going home. "Yay!"

Johnny's eyes get heavy. His mama's grown-up lamentation reverberates within.

What the fuck am I gonna do now, Jim? What about the rent? What about Johnny?

"Don't worry, Mama, I found a friend. She likes red licorice, too," whispers Johnny as the Sandman takes him away.

The heavy, steel sound of a big key unlocks the steel door, and the intrusive manner of the guard entering the small, gray visiting room of death row cues John Spinks to conclude his remembrances.

"I left her there, Father. I left Ma there with nothing but a dead husband. She was crying for me. She had nobody. That's my confession, Father. Can you talk to God for me?"

Father Sam is barely able to talk, let alone talk to God.

The guard accompanies John back to his cell on death row.

Father Sam sits, staring at the floor, emotionally done in. He mutters, "She didn't kill him. The son of a bitch was already dead." He stares at the floor another five minutes till a guard taps his shoulder.

CHAPTER 52

Four Years Later

On the television screen at the Sequoia Institute, Dr. Blackfox and Professor Redhawk watch a local anchorman reporting the news of the hour. "Our top story: a Catholic priest's personal intervention for a convicted murderer has failed. John Spinks has lost his final appeal and has only days to live. Spinks, who murdered his gay lover in an Appalachian brothel six years ago, is scheduled to die in the electric chair on …"

Dr. Blackfox snaps off the TV and turns to Professor Redhawk. No words. They go back to work. The work they are doing based on Father Sam's Cherokee medicine book has rendered unusual results.

In the lab, Dr. Blackfox holds a rabbit while Professor Redhawk injects it. The rabbit's motor skills diminish slowly. "Father Sam should be here soon," says Dr. Blackfox." Professor Redhawk takes the rabbit's body from Dr. Blackfox and gently places it in a cage.

A taxi drops Father Sam off at the front entrance of the Sequoia Institute, where he presses the entry button.

Dr. Blackfox opens the door to meet and embrace him.

They go inside the lab and find Professor Redhawk placing food and water inside the dead rabbit's cage.

"Father Sam is here." Dr. Blackfox gets Professor

Redhawk's attention.

The rabbit cage door is still open as Professor Redhawk finishes preparing the food and water. "Greetings, Father."

Father Sam notes the rabbit appears to be dead and gestures towards it. "Is that rabbit dead?"

Professor Redhawk taps the stiff corpse.

Father Sam thinks it's strange to prepare food and water for a dead rabbit, but he doesn't say anything. Maybe they pay tribute to the departure of the animal spirit this way.

"You must have heard the news," says Father Sam.

The scientists' solemn expressions tell Father Sam that they know John's execution is only days away.

"Let us sit and chat over a quiet dinner. You did your best, my friend." Dr. Blackfox leads the way toward the door of the Sequoia Institute, flipping the main light switches and locking up. They walk around the corner to share a bite to eat.

The lab is quiet. Only the work light glows. Nothing stirs in the dimly lit interior for the next hour—until the rabbit cage jiggles slightly. The cold, stiff, *dead* rabbit quivers. Moves its ears. Twitches its nose. Opens its eyes. Walks. And eats.

After a quiet dinner conversation in a private room, the three friends return to the lab. Inside, Dr. Blackfox flips on the lights, and they walk straight to the lab.

The food is gone from the cage, and the dead rabbit is as alive as they are. Father Sam is speechless.

Professor Redhawk pats the Cherokee medicine book they have been studying for years.

They sit down in the small conference room, where the scientists spell out the theoretical advantages of the "like-death" serum.

CHAPTER 53

Innoculation Inspiration

Flying back home with Dr. Blackfox, Father Sam has a lot on his mind and remains wide awake during the flight, not reading, not chatting, just thinking about the rabbit experiment he saw in the lab and the insightful conversation with the two scientists afterward. By the time they enter Appalachian air space, he has a plan. It's a longshot but he's going to take chances that could get him killed or put in prison.

They land and Father Sam reads the old thermometer outside the hangar door. It's darned cold, and it's flu season. As Dr. Blackfox drives Father Sam to his log house, he asks Father Sam how he's feeling and what his plans are for tomorrow.

Father Sam replies, "I'm going to Doc Willard's tomorrow. Flu season means flu shots. How about you, Joe?"

DOC WILLARD REMINDS FATHER SAM EVERY YEAR AT FLU season to come into the office for his free flu shot. In fact, he extends the offer to all of his friends. So, the next day, Father Sam, Sister Marietta, and Dr. Blackfox show up at his office. Sheriff Marcus has already had his.

Father Sam is the first one to be vaccinated. Doc Willard reaches into his cabinet for syringes, fills one with vaccine, and plunges a needle into Father Sam's shoulder. Sister Marietta and Dr. Blackfox sit in the waiting room.

"I am relieved you have all consented to get your flu shots. We're not getting any younger," exclaims Doc Willard.

Father Sam replies, "I, for one, am feeling it this year, Doc."

"Well, I think your grandmother would approve. It is the twentieth century, you know."

Father Sam watches Doc Willard discard the syringe into a small waste can. "Throwaways, huh?"

"Yep, plastic. One time only."

"Funny how much plastic has come into our everyday lives, huh?"

"I s'pose, yes," agrees Doc Willard.

"No metal at all in those, huh?" asks Father Sam.

"Just the part I stick you with. Okay, you can put your shirt on."

Father Sam takes his time putting his shirt on as Doc Willard exits to the waiting room to bring in the next patient. Father Sam quickly reaches for the discarded syringe and pockets it. Then as he buttons up his shirt, he follows Doc Willard to the waiting room where he tells his friends he has an errand to run and will meet them later at Mabelline's for the lunch special. "I hope you can join us, Doc," he says as he departs to the jailhouse.

He asks Sheriff Marcus to drive him north of town to *Harmon's Survivalist Store*. They drive the short distance to Harmon's and park. Mr. Harmon greets them. "Good day, gentlemen, you lookin' for anything special today?"

Father Sam gets right to the point. "Shoes, Mr. Harmon. Good shoes for protecting my poor old feet. Drop an axe or a wedge or a darn piece of wood on my cold feet, and I tell ya, my toes aren't happy about it."

Mr. Harmon leads Father Sam down an aisle of footwear and picks up a black oxford. "You about a size ten? These here are double-lined. Real warm for ya, and look at this." He taps on the toe.

Father Sam taps the toe of the oxford, too. "Is that metal?"

Mr. Harmon points at a label on the shoebox. *Steel Toes, Black Lowtop.*

THE NEXT DAY, FATHER SAM AND SISTER MARIETTA ARE sitting by the fireplace. She watches him pry the heel off one of his new steel-toed oxfords and carve a crevice in the underside of the heel. She hands him the sterilized metal syringe needle. He fits the needle into the crevice and reattaches the heel and hands it to Sister Marietta and asks, "What do you think?"

Sister Marietta picks up the modified shoe and studies it. "What do I think? I think we're both going straight to hell." She gives Father Sam a supportive and submissive smile. "But you know me, Sam. Always up for an adventure."

CHAPTER 54

All Or Nothing

Father Sam passes by the huddles of capital punishment opponents, proponents, photographers and reporters staked out across the road from the prison execution unit.

Inside the death house, Sgt. McDougal addresses John Spinks at his holding cell. "Your clergyman will be here momentarily."

In a caged office, Sam shows his documents to a clerk. "My ordination papers, my birth certificate." He is cleared by the clerk and proceeds to a metal detector.

Sgt. McDougal waits on the other side. "Good evening, Father. Empty your pockets, if you will." Father Sam removes keys, wallet, coins, glasses, and a prescription bottle of meds.

"Can't allow these inside, Father. You should know better than that." Sgt. McDougal dumps the meds and sets the empty bottle with his other articles in front of an inspector.

"You can keep the prescription bottle. The content has to be tested as contraband. You'll hear from us if there's a problem," says Sgt. McDougal.

"Yes, Sergeant, I'm terribly sorry. I have a condition. I wouldn't bring …"

"Doesn't matter. I trust ya. It's the system. Proceed now."

Father Sam keeps his cool and walks through the metal detector. It buzzes.

"Hold it. Step back if you will."

Father Sam pretends to be surprised that the metal detector sounded off. "Oh, my. It's not my day, is it?" He steps back to comply with Sgt. McDougal's command.

"One more time now. Step on through."

Father Sam passes through again. It buzzes.

Sgt. McDougal is patient with the good Father. "Step back, Father. It happens. Let's try 'er again there."

"Ahh. Wait a minute, Sergeant. By golly. I think it's my shoes."

"No, sir, the machine is calibrated to overlook iron shoe tacks and …"

Father Sam cuts him off politely. "Well, Sarge, maybe these are different." As he bends over to remove one of his oxfords, he keeps up the banter. "A man of the cloth who chops his own firewood. Can you imagine? I dropped a chunk of madrone on my foot recently. Learned my lesson." He lifts up the shoe and taps on the steel toe. "There's your metal, right there."

"All right, Father." Sgt. McDougal lightens up. "How's the fishin' up there in your parts?" He taps on the oxford's toe.

Father Sam keeps the small talk going. "Our fly fishing in late November? For browns and rainbows, best streams in the world."

Sgt. McDougal points to the other shoe. "You don't say. Give me the other one there, Father."

Father Sam hands over his other shoe. "And we sure welcome our friends."

Sgt. McDougal gestures for Father Sam to walk through, socks only. No buzz.

"Go ahead and put your shoes on now."

Father Sam slips into his steel-toed oxfords and scrapes up his glasses, wallet, change, keys, and the empty prescription bottle.

"Let's be going now, Father. We need to stay timely."

López, a South American trustee, is mopping the hallway floor as Sgt. McDougal and Father Sam stride by him. López doesn't speak English but gives them a friendly warning in Spanish. "Be careful, my friends. Don't slip. The floor is wet."

"We don't speak Mexican, López. Mind your job," says Sgt. McDougal.

Father Sam sees the steel death-chamber door fifty yards ahead.

They make an immediate right and walk another fifty yards to John's cell where Sgt. McDougal relieves the on-duty guard. "You best get on with it, Father." He turns his back, finds a nearby chair, and plops down.

Father Sam asks, "How much time do we have?"

Sgt. McDougal points to a wall clock. "We start the walk in twenty-one minutes." He picks up a magazine.

A fog of incurable injustice hangs over Father Sam and John as they look through the bars at each other. John speaks with resignation. "I guess this is it, huh, Father?"

Father Sam glances at the clock. He has made it this far, but holding on to his plan is taking its toll on his frame of mind. "Twenty minutes," he mumbles to himself. Then he pipes up louder than necessary to make certain that Sgt. McDougal perceives this as strict clerical ritual. "Admit sorrow and remorse for any wrong you have done."

John is puzzled at the distant manner of Father Sam. "I didn't do no wrong. What are you talking about?"

Father Sam lowers his voice. "Don't argue. Just hear me."

"I'm ready to go," insists John.

"No. You are not." Father Sam opens his Bible, raises his voice again, and chants, "May the Lord who frees you from sin save you, my son."

Sgt. McDougal continues reading the magazine, unmindful of the drama a few yards away. He's seen and heard these spiritual epilogues too many times.

John listens patiently as Father Sam's intonation turns to the Spanish tongue. Father Sam is gambling that Sgt. McDougal will think the Spanish is the Latin prayer of commendation for one near death. Father Sam intones directions to John in Spanish, "The guard does not understand. Do as I say."

John spits out a response in English, "What? Why are you speaking Spanish?"

Sgt. McDougal looks up. John quiets down.

Father Sam noticed that Sgt. McDougal was alerted by John's heated response, so he raises his voice and answers John in a pastoral tone again—in English. "Sacrament of reconciliation, John Spinks."

John doesn't get it.

Father Sam asks in conversational Spanish, "Is he looking at us? Does he look suspicious? Just say, Yes, Father, or no, Father."

John's willingness to meet his maker is diminishing. Confused, he looks at Sgt. McDougal, then back to the pleading face of his friend.

Father Sam continues in Spanish, "I will fall to the floor. Be ready to do exactly as I say. Yes, Father or no, Father. Tell me you understand. Yes, Father or no, Father!"

"Don't fuck with me, Father. I'm ready."

Father Sam keeps at John, speaking to him in calm Spanish, "We've got to do this. Be ready to do exactly as I say, I beg of you. I am going to try to save your life. I will have an attack, an epileptic seizure. The guard will leave us to find a doctor. You need to cooperate with me and do exactly as I say once we are alone. In Spanish. Tell me you understand. Tell me you will do as I say."

John has had it. He blurts out in Spanish, "I don't know what the fuck you are talking about!"

Father Sam gasps for breath. He clutches his chest and falls to the concrete floor.

Sgt. McDougal jumps up and runs to the cell, yelling at John and slamming a baton against the bars. "Get back! Now!"

John moves back as Father Sam acts out a violent seizure.

Sgt. McDougal kneels to help Father Sam. "God almighty, what is it, Father?"

"Help me. My pills. He wheezes for air.

"Your pills? My Jesus, I'm sorry. A doctor. I'll get a …" In a panic, Sergeant McDougal runs off, yelling commands, and disappears down an empty hallway. His call for medical assistance reverberates back to Father Sam and John. "Where the hell is the coroner? The priest is having an attack."

Father Sam moves quickly to remove his shoe. He tugs at the heel. It's the wrong shoe. He realizes his mistake. Panic. "Oh God, help me." He yanks and twists the heel of the other shoe till it loosens, then pulls it off. Crazy nerves. There's the needle. "C'mon, c'mon." He exhorts himself as he reaches down the backside of his trousers far enough to grab the plastic syringe and pulls it out. He removes the cotton plug from the opening of the syringe and attaches the needle.

The sound of men running in the corridor gets louder. They haven't turned the corner yet. When they do, it'll be fifty yards for them before they get to John and Father Sam.

Father Sam waves the loaded syringe toward John. "Come here! Take this. Inject yourself."

John is dumbstruck.

"We have no time, son. Please. They're coming fast."

John backs away. "I am ready to go, Father."

"No, you're not. You're not going. Come here."

Labored breathing and running sounds get closer.

Father Sam pleads, "They are coming."

John steps forward, grabs the bars with both hands, and nose to nose with Father Sam, yells, "You're crazy!"

"I'm not crazy." Father Sam reaches through the bars, grabs John's arm, and plunges the needle into his shoulder. Then he shoves the empty syringe into his coat pocket, hits the floor, and slams on his shoes.

When Sgt. McDougal and the coroner arrive, he is struggling to sit up. The coroner worries over him. "What is it, Father? No, no, don't get up." He barks at Sergeant McDougal, "Get that chair over here."

The coroner helps his patient to sit down. Father Sam assures him, "I'm epileptic. It was a seizure. Thankfully, a mild seizure."

The coroner is relieved. "Stress doesn't help, does it?"

"No, it doesn't. And thank you. I'm better."

"All right, Father. Please excuse me. I must attend to the preparations." The coroner walks away. Sgt. McDougal retrieves his chair and leaves Father Sam and John to themselves.

John is still confused. "I was ready, goddammit." Sgt. McDougal hears John curse. "Watch your mouth, Mr. Spinks."

Father Sam gestures to Sgt. McDougal that all is well. Then he turns to John. "What do you feel? You should feel, I don't know, drowsy."

"Nothing. I feel nothing."

CHAPTER 55

Tough Love

I t seems more like twenty-one seconds for twenty-one minutes to tick off the clock on the wall next to John's holding cell. Time flies when dying as an innocent man is on your daily planner.

John isn't showing any sign of slipping into a near-death state.

Sgt. McDougal lumbers out of his chair to receive the warden and the strap-down team—a foreboding foursome. They could be loaners from an NFL front line. "Father, I'll ask you to move away from the cell now, sir."

The warden unfolds an official document.

Father Sam glances at the clock. *Buy some time.* His thoughts spin. *Must give it time to work.*

"Father, I will now read the death warrant to Mr. Spinks," says the warden. "State regulation."

"Afterward, I'll walk with the prisoner, if you don't mind. State regulation," says Father Sam.

The warden agrees. "Of course."

Father Sam is hoping the warden is a slow reader.

The warden looks at Father Sam's feet. "Your shoes are untied, Father."

Father Sam looks at his feet and makes something up. "Yes, that they are. Thank you. I, uh, I don't know what's worse, the seizures or the peripheral neuropathy that follows the convulsions." Father Sam takes his time as he bends over to tie his shoes.

The warden patiently waits. "Yes, I understand you had a health crisis."

Fidgety Sergeant McDougal nudges the warden. "It's time."

Politely, the warden hints. "Father?"

Father Sam ends the shoe diversion.

The warden holds open the document and reads. "Case number 8203305. The Court orders John Arthur Spinks to be executed by the Department of Corrections according to the law of the land on this date at the time of twelve o'clock midnight."

While the warden finishes the formalities, the strap-down officers move into position as Sgt. McDougal unlocks John's cell. They shackle John and direct him out of the cell toward the corridor that leads to the execution chamber. A one-hundred-yard walk.

Father Sam must find a way to stall for time.

John tries to regain the calm he lost when his lunatic friend attacked him with a syringe, but it isn't coming to him.

Father Sam walks close beside John as the warden and the strap-down team follow ten feet behind.

They turn the corner onto the corridor in view of the steel door to the execution chamber. Fifty yards to go. Father Sam must buy time, somehow, to allow the death serum to activate in John—if only it will.

Father Sam asks, "What do you feel, son?"

It's no time for niceties. John answers curtly, "What the fuck do you mean, how do I feel?"

"I said, *what* do you feel?"

John doesn't answer.

The execution chamber is forty yards further.

"There it is. Don't let them."

"What?"

"It's now or never, my son."

John stops and turns to Father Sam. "Why are you doing this?"

"Move it along, Mr. Spinks," commands Sgt. McDougal.

John looks deep into Father Sam's soul. His eyes beg for the spiritual sustenance that had replenished him so often through the years.

Father Sam can't give it to him now. He realizes he must do the unthinkable—it's the only plan he can come up with.

"Move it," repeats, Sgt. McDougal.

They continue the walk.

Father Sam reaches the end of his rational mind. *Let my life end here with John's if this doesn't work.*

John quietly appeals to Father Sam, "I am out of time, Father. Recite something from the Bible?"

"The Good Book, John?"

"Yeah."

"I have a better idea. May I share?"

"Share."

"How about I tell you a true story, John?"

"Yeah, anything."

"It's all been bullshit, John. I've been trying to save my own pitiful soul for laying with your white trash mother. I've used you to work off my own guilt."

John tries to fathom what he is hearing. "What?"

"You were a nine-year-old brat in a Texas border town. That day, you came home, and someone was in the bedroom with your mother. I was that sweet Catholic boy. You looked in my eyes, John."

John is cracking. "I told you that story."

"The red licorice I brought to your cell, John. How'd I know? Your bike had cards in the spokes. We heard you pull up to the front door, and I watched you pick through the groceries on the table. You found the package of red licorice and put it into your back pocket. My pickup was parked outside of your house. The circus ticket? I brought it—them. There were two tickets. Your mother seduced me. And I wanted her, John."

John is seeing it.

"I worked at the mission. I didn't wear a white collar. Sometimes, you came in with your mother. There were day-old donuts in a pink box—always. In the sitting room, there's a painting of Chief Joseph. It was always tilted. I was a young man, full of lust, and your mom was my fantasy—and I was hers. You were nothing—a worthless kid who came home too early that day."

John's resignation, reduced to its last thread, snaps. He screams at Father Sam and knocks him to the ground. The strap-down officers pull Father Sam aside and beat John mercilessly.

Father Sam scoots away, gets up, prays for the magic to happen, and weeps for the loss that he will never get back.

John rages against the officers. He hasn't a chance. They continue to beat him. John fights back and bleeds badly for his trouble.

Then suddenly, John's light goes out. Subdued. Limp. Lifeless. The batons continue to crash down on his body and face.

Sgt. McDougal bellows, "Stop it, stop it now!"

One officer keeps hitting John until Sgt. McDougal pulls him off.

Father Sam's prayers and tears are fervent. He backs away from the action to pull himself together.

John's body is motionless.

The wide-eyed warden takes over. "My God, look at him. Stand back, stand back. Where's the doctor?"

"Right here, warden." The coroner points to the offending officer. "I want his name and badge number." Then the coroner checks John's vital signs. He looks puzzled. He checks again.

The warden is thinking of the worst. "What can you do about his face? The witnesses. Oh God."

"His face is the least of your worries, warden. This man has no vitals."

"My God." The warden is about to ask, but the coroner answers his question before it's asked.

"This man is dead," proclaims the coroner.

"Are you absolutely certain?"

"It is what I do here, Warden. I pronounce death. He's dead."

"Oh God, the press is outside. The state's witnesses waiting in there to see him die. What do I tell them?"

"How about telling them he died? I will order an autopsy."

"Wait, Doctor, wait. What's your best guess? The cause of death, I mean?"

"My best guess? Head trauma. Look at him."

"They'll cry police brutality."

"Unfortunately, Warden, that's what I witnessed."

"I can't have this. What'll we do? What time is it?"

At the back of the group, Father Sam has pulled himself together, but he hasn't stopped praying. A door opens in his mind and light floods in. He knows what he needs to do. He needs to lie. Father Sam raises his voice. "John had a very weak heart."

A sudden quiet fills the corridor as they all wait for someone to take the bait.

The coroner speaks up. "Oh. Did he?"

The warden catches on quickly and invents a scenario, "His medical records show that much! Don't they, Doctor?"

"Yes, I'm sure they do, if the good father says so." The coroner observes Father Sam's unwavering countenance.

The coroner draws the warden, Sgt. McDougal, and Father Sam into a private huddle and lowers his voice. "Look, let's make this easy on everyone. He was, after all, going to be dead by now anyway."

Father Sam lays down a bargaining chip. "His body must be transported to his family in Mexico."

"Yes, of course. Out of the country, very good," says the warden. "I've made arrangements for the body," adds Father Sam.

"Good enough. Very good. Yes, good, good. A heart attack. Excellent. Sergeant McDougal you go speak to the witnesses, and I will go face the press."

AT THE LOADING DOCK, FATHER SAM INTERCEPTS A prison nurse who is there to clean up John's face. "Allow me."

The nurse yields the basin of warm water, soap, and towels and exits.

Alone now, Father Sam doesn't have to resist the fear any longer—the fear of being discovered as a lunatic priest gone rogue. His adrenalized composure crashes hard. His brain tumor wants its way.

On the prison steps, the warden makes his official statement to the activists and press members. "Ladies and gentlemen, John Arthur Spinks was pronounced dead at five minutes after midnight by the state coroner's office."

Steven Boergadine

CHAPTER 56

Go Home Now

Sister Marietta doesn't know what happened inside the prison execution unit. If Father Sam is wearing handcuffs the next time she sees him, she'll know the worst happened. It will mean John is dead and Father Sam isn't far from it. Backing the hearse up to the loading dock, she thinks about offering a Hail Mary but she's not sure she's on the right side of God just now.

The steel door activates and slowly rolls open. When she spots Father Sam in her side-view mirror standing, hollow-eyed, beside a plain wooden casket, not wearing handcuffs, she says the Hail Mary anyway.

Two minimum-custody inmates roll the casket into the hearse.

Father Sam climbs off the loading dock, and slides into the hearse's passenger seat—sapped and quiet.

Sister Marietta can't get out of there fast enough. A sidelong glance at Father Sam makes her heart sink. His face is fallen, morbid and aged.

He exhales a thank you. There's no eye-to-eye communication.

Sister Marietta shouldn't ask right now, but does anyway, "Did you do it? The injection?" She looks again for an answer. He has passed out. "Get better, dear." She heads for the I-35 South. It'll be an all-nighter.

The next day, Father Sam awakens in the hearse. It's parked along side a country road somewhere in Mexico. He sees Sister Marietta napping behind the wheel. The worst headache he's ever experienced greets him.

He reaches for the prescription bottle. *I'll swallow all of them. If God won't deliver me, I'll leave on my own.* It's empty. He doesn't remember the pills were confiscated. He doesn't remember much, only telling John of the tryst with his mother—and the beating. He felt every blow of those officers' batons along with John.

Suicidal angst yields to sleep's whisper. *I form light and create darkness, I make well-being and create calamity, I am the Lord, who does all these things.*

Sister Marietta awakens and sees the empty prescription bottle in Father Sam's open palm. She stops at a roadside Farmacia. She shows the empty prescription bottle to an apologetic clerk who shrugs negative.

As they head down the highway, Sister Marietta hopes Father Sam will keep sleeping for his own good.

But a few hours later Father Sam's eyes flutter open. He moans, "Stop soon, please." She pulls the hearse into a petrol station.

Father Sam finds a door marked Caballeros, and enters. He turns on the faucet and throws water on his face. He looks at the mirror and sees the tilted painting of Chief Joseph on the wall behind him. He turns around. No painting. He turns back around to the mirror and sees Gladys— she speaks to his heart.

Johnny needs some influence on his soul. Can you be that influence now and then, Sam?

Seeing her face, hearing her voice, overwhelms Father

Sam's fragile mind. He whispers, "Yes, yes, yes. I tried, Gladys. I tried." Tears flush out of his bloodshot eyes. He doesn't know that the cerebral tumor metastasized some time back. It's on a progressive tear. His body and brain surrender, and he slumps to the floor.

Ten minutes later, Sister Marietta knocks on the door marked Caballeros. "Sam?" She forces the door open and takes in the scene. On her knees beside him, she shakes him till he comes to.

An attendant and Sister Marietta help Father Sam to the hearse.

CHAPTER 57

The Olive Tree

H ours pass as Sister Marietta continues driving across the Mexican flatland. She listens to Father Sam mumble in Cherokee and prays quietly for him to survive the war within.

He stirs awake, turns his head, and watches her as she drives. He blinks to clear his eyes and sees his Cherokee grandmother at the wheel. At that moment, Sister Marietta slows it down. They are somewhere in the Mexican desert on a quiet highway. Father Sam speaks to his grandmother in Cherokee. "Grandmother?"

Sister Marietta looks at Father Sam as he mumbles. She sees he's having trouble sleeping. "We'll be there soon, dear. You're going to be fine."

Father Sam is warmed by his grandmother's promise. He closes his eyes.

The hearse comes to a stop. Grandmother speaks to Father Sam in Cherokee. *It is time.*

Through the windshield, he sees a magnificent Appaloosa stallion standing in front of the hearse.

Grandmother presses the palm of her hand on Father Sam's cheek and tells him, *We have brought you to the white light. No longer must you walk the groaning earth. We are proud of you. And we are ready for you. Come to us now.*

Father Sam opens the hearse door, gets out, and walks to the Appaloosa. With a spry stride, Sam, the young seminarian, wearing his Tony Lamas, blue jeans, and denim shirt, suntanned, and handsome, swings his leg over the Appaloosa stallion and gallops into the warm, inviting desert.

The hours pass by as Sister Marietta drives. She realizes her best friend is no longer restless. She snaps on the dome light to get a better look. She knows even before she touches his face that everlasting peace is finally upon him. She reaches to his eyes and shuts them. And keeps driving. She blinks away tears as memories of their years together keep her company.

Entering the Cuernavaca countryside, Sister Marietta recalls the landmarks that will tell her the farmhouse is just ahead. She slows the hearse.

At the end of a long, hard-dirt driveway a welcome party is busy preparing for the arrival of Father Sam, Sister Marietta and John Spinks. Ramon, John's brother-in-law, is sunning himself in a wheelchair on the front porch. Gathered near Ramon, several women chatter happily as they wrap tamales. Out in the field, jubilant men are clearing and leveling a long, narrow strip of ground.

There aren't many hearses driving along the back country roads of Cuernavaca, so the family and friends easily spot the one slowing down on the distant road. Everyone waves.

John's wife, Anita, stops pushing their daughter, little Sarita, in a tire swing. The two of them go to Ramon's wheelchair to push him to where the small festive crowd is converging.

Sister Marietta navigates the hearse over the long, bumpy entry drive that leads to the cheering, welcoming Mexican family.

Everyone greets Sister Marietta with an air of expectation that deflates as they view Father Sam's lifeless body.

One of the men takes over the wheel and backs the hearse into a barn.

Several men carry Sam's body and gently place him onto a square of hay bales. They roll out the casket and lift out John's body.

Sister Marietta replaces the lining of the casket with new white linen. She washes Father Sam's face and hands and combs his hair. The men lift his body and place it into the coffin.

Sister Marietta stays with Father Sam as the family leaves them alone. She touches his lips with her fingers. Then she goes to the foot of the casket and removes the shoe that held the metal needle, pulls the heel off and sees the empty crevice. With a slight smile, she replaces his shoe. She checks his pockets for personal belongings. There it is—in his jacket pocket—the syringe. She holds it up to the light and sees the chamber is emptied of the serum. Overcome with emotions, the kind she might feel if ever a vision of a saint or angel appeared before her, she sits on the barn floor and weeps. There was always something about him that from her cloistered, protected perch she could not relate to. She could be amused and often envious of the passion of his wild, searching heart but the seeming mismanagement of his Catholic priorities always frightened her for him. But not now. The end came for him exactly as it should have—it came heroically. And if God is the all knowing, all perceiving, all gracious, ever forgiving, loving Creator, then Sam is walking on streets of gold.

She opens the palm of her hand and stares at the syringe. "Oh Sam, you did do it, didn't you? I wish I could have seen you in action. Perhaps John can tell us about it someday. I loved you, my friend, so very much. You were always what God wanted you to be."

The distant hum of a small aircraft gets louder. It's Dr. Blackfox's Cessna approaching the landing strip that the men have prepared. The solemn group walks to the airplane to welcome Dr. Blackfox, Professor Redhawk, Sheriff Marcus, and Doc Willard.

Once the guests are taken to the farmhouse, several of the menfolk pick up shovels and head up to a lone olive tree standing on a knoll overlooking the family home.

Early the next morning, the casket sits on a wagon drawn by two horses.

Father Sam's friends and the Mexican family follow slowly behind the wagon as it rolls to a fresh grave site next to the olive tree, where his body will rest in Mother Earth's embrace.

Later in the day, while everyone is eating a tamale lunch, Sister Marietta asks Dr. Blackfox, "How much longer?"

Dr. Blackfox shrugs. "It's a gamble. No aspect of the scientific process was applied to a human subject. John was the first. And let's be frank, we don't know for certain that Father Sam injected John."

Sister Marietta says, "He did. I know."

Doc Willard says, "Well, if that's so, it's only been a little more than twenty-four hours since the inoculation. It could take three days or so before physical signs of decomposition set in."

Sister Marietta adds biblical context. "Elijah brought a mother's son back to life, you know. The mother was certain that her dark past was the reason for her son's death."

Sheriff Marcus recalls the jailhouse confessions by Father Sam, how he thought that his dark past contributed to John

Spinks's bad luck. "I believe I'll step out and think about those words, Sister." He excuses himself and leaves the table.

Outside, Sister Marietta catches up with Sheriff Marcus, and they continue up the path to the lone olive tree. He lights up a cigarette and shares it with her. Nothing much *they* can do for John Spinks. If there's anything that can be done from the other side, they both are pretty sure Father Sam is doing it.

Late night comes, and everyone is asleep except Anita and little Sarita, who walk up the stairs quietly to look in on John and go to his bedside. Sarita holds her daddy's lifeless hand.

Anita speaks to little Sarita, "Say good night to your papa, sweetheart." Sarita doesn't say good night to her papa. She likes holding his hand.

Anita repeats, "Time for you to sleep, sweetheart." She's about to flick off the light switch.

Sarita holds her father's hand and says, "I have to go sleep now, Papa." Her hand doesn't move from John's. It can't. He won't let it.

John's eyes open. He stares at Sarita. Not a blink. Transfixed.

He never imagined that heaven would be—like this. That there would be an angel there to welcome him—like this.

"Papa?" Sarita squeezes her father's cheeks. "Papa."

On the knoll, a gentle funnel of wind dances around the moonlit olive tree as the windows of the farmhouse below it illuminate one by one.

Milton Keynes UK
Ingram Content Group UK Ltd.
UKHW012119271123
433389UK00010B/382/J